Bound by Angels, Captured by Demons

"The angel that arrived with me has been the source of untold trouble for me," Vhok said. "I want revenge. I will sell the information I have gleaned at the angel's expense to the highest bidder."

"No one will listen to you," Vhissilka scoffed. "You will be slain and cast into a pit the moment you set foot within an archdemon's territory."

"Not if I am your ally," Vhok replied. "Not if I allow you to claim much of the credit for the knowledge. It's the end result that matters to me. I want a chance to make all the creatures of the House of the Triad regret they ever crossed me. You help me make that happen."

Sustained by One Thought: Revenge

FORGOTTEN REALMS

THOMAS M. REID

The Empyrean Odyssey

Also by Thomas M. Reid

The Scions of Arrabar Trilogy

R.A. Salvatore's
War of the Spider Queen

FORGOTTEN REALMS

THE
CRYSTAL
MOUNTAIN

THE
EMPYREAN ODYSSEY
Book III

THOMAS M. REID

Wizards
OF THE COAST

The Empyrean Odyssey, Book III
THE CRYSTAL MOUNTAIN

©2009 Wizards of the Coast LLC

Cover art by Jeff Nentrup
First Printing: July 2009

9 8 7 6 5 4 3 2 1

ISBN: 978-0-7869-5235-9
620-24197000-001-EN

U.S., CANADA,
ASIA, PACIFIC, & LATIN AMERICA
Wizards of the Coast LLC
P.O. Box 707
Renton, WA 98057-0707
+1-800-324-6496

EUROPEAN HEADQUARTERS
Hasbro UK Ltd
Caswell Way
Newport, Gwent NP9 0YH
GREAT BRITAIN
Save this address for your records.

Visit our web site at www.wizards.com

DEDICATION

To Realms fans everywhere, for keeping me on my toes
and making Faerûn such a fun place to play.

CHAPTER ONE

Black unconsciousness became . . . buzzing.

Joints ached. Muscles quivered. A body convulsed with pain.

It lay upon hard, frigid stone that quaked one moment and rippled and melted the next, blistering skin with intense heat.

The stone vanished, and the body floated without any bearings at all.

A voice groaned, sounding odd. Distant.

An intense crackling filled the air, and the tingle of electricity raced across the body's skin. Loud, staccato pops, roars of wind, and high-pitched whines interspersed themselves amidst the charged crepitation.

A head throbbed, threatening to split open.

A whiff of sulfur, mingled with something charred, wafted past. In rapid succession came the scent of flowers, blood, sewage, and old ice.

A thought formed.

Aliisza.

I am Aliisza.

She realized she was not breathing. Her lungs ached. She drew a deep, ragged breath and exhaled in relief. She dared to open her eyes.

Color flashed in the half-demon's vision. Not merely light from somewhere else, not some rainbow effect reflecting off walls or furniture or landscapes. A million hues filled the veil of her sight.

Nothing *but* color.

Washes of it swirled and fractured, split by the void of blackness. They reformed, became a haze, then a swarm of light points, then an undulating sea. All of it assaulted the alu, crashed against her, made the pounding ache behind her eyeballs grow.

With a gasp, she clenched her eyes shut again and retched.

For long moments that stretched on and on, the half-fiend squirmed and whimpered as the cacophony of sounds, textures, and scents pummeled her. She feared it would last forever.

The world has gone mad, she thought. Or perhaps it has ended, and I just don't know I'm dead.

Sometime later—she was not sure how long—the universe popped around Aliisza. She felt her body react, as though an immense pressure had been released. The torrential storm abated. The snaps and roars faded. Everything returned to normal.

The pain coursing through the alu's body diminished, and she felt solid, unyielding stone beneath her. The scents had nearly vanished, though she could still detect the faint odor of something foul, a mixture of stale sweat and singed flesh.

She realized she could sense light through her closed eyelids. Not the crazy multi-hued swirl from before, but a persistent, stable glow. Though her mind told her it was safe, she was afraid to open her eyes again, afraid of becoming inundated by the insane sea of color.

Taking a deep, slow breath to calm herself, Aliisza let her eyelids flutter the slightest bit, ready to clamp them shut again if the color-storm bombarded her. When it did not, she opened them wider and took in her surroundings.

The half-fiend lay on her back, sprawled upon cool paving stones, staring into the face of a handsome man with long, flowing black hair and a matching mustache. The thick, dark locks fell in a disheveled mess about his neck and shoulders. The glow that had penetrated the alu's tightly clenched eyelids emanated from him like the dim, flickering gleam of a firefly. Dressed in robes of black and gold, he struggled to remain upright on unsteady hands and knees.

"Well met," the man said, smiling warmly. "Are you all right?"

Fear and hatred slammed into Aliisza. "Bastard," she snarled before she even realized the word was out of her mouth. "You should be dead!" She couldn't remember why she thought that, but it didn't matter.

She reached for the man's throat to strangle him.

Her hands scrabbled at his neck, at his silken tunic, but her limbs had no strength and could not gain a firm grip.

A name blossomed in her mind.

Zasian Menz, priest of Cyric.

She wanted to claw his eyes out, but her weak limbs groped fruitlessly.

Aliisza sobbed and let her arms drop to her sides in

exhaustion. "Bastard," she cried again. Do it, she thought. Just kill me. Finish it!

But Zasian did not. At her vehemence, his eyes grew wide and he retreated from her, staggering a bit and falling on his side. "I . . . I'm sorry," he said. "What did I do?" His gaze did not convey the cunning of the priest she remembered. A mixture of innocence and confusion filled his eyes.

Aliisza stared at the man. You take me for a fool? she thought. What did you do, indeed! But his troubled, blinking expression never changed, never gave any hint of duplicity. He seemed perfectly sincere.

She groaned and stared past the priest at the rest of her surroundings, trying to understand.

The only illumination came from Zasian. Darkness cloaked the rest of the chamber. Aliisza lay near the center of a circle of stone columns rising toward a domed ceiling engulfed in shadows. Deeper gloom filled the spaces between those marble sentinels, hinting at vastness beyond the feeble light. The remains of her retching spattered the floor near her head, and Aliisza felt chastened for a moment, guilty at her own disheveled state in the austere chamber.

The alu turned her head to one side and spotted a body lying near her, a dark-clad figure in plate armor crumpled beneath one of the columns, facing away. The hilt of a slender blade jutted up from the figure's torso.

Dread filled the half-fiend anew as she remembered. The angel Micus had driven the blade—her blade—deep into the knight.

A knight of Torm.

Kael.

Her son!

No!

Aliisza struggled to get to her hands and knees, to crawl to Kael. She had no strength. She dragged herself across the paving stones toward him.

I didn't mean to. I was a fool!

Aliisza had almost reached her son when reality around her flickered, unstable, like some half-effective illusion. A wrinkle passed through the room, making the walls and columns of the rotunda ripple like a flag snapping in the breeze. Aliisza thought she would be sick again.

The ripple was gone.

The alu felt stronger, enough that she could finish the journey and reach her son's side. She pressed her hand on him and peered at the half-drow's face.

He still breathed, but barely.

Aliisza crumpled against him, succumbing to her relief.

From behind her, in the direction of the unsteady light, a soft murmur reached Aliisza.

She gingerly rolled back over, her joints and muscles still aching.

Zasian loomed over a second figure sprawled near another column.

Tauran, the fallen angel of Tyr.

For a heartbeat, Aliisza thought the priest meant to do Tauran harm, but she realized Zasian was instead tending to him, being quite gentle. The priest's eyes were closed and he chanted softly. When he opened them again, Zasian saw her looking at him and said, "I've done what I can. I think he'll be all right, now."

Tauran's curly golden hair lay matted against his face, sweat-soaked and limp, and he was pale. His white feathered wings, torn and scorched, did not move. Numerous wounds covered his singed skin, but his bare chest rose and fell in slow, even breathing.

Aliisza recalled Tauran's look of pure anguish just before he fell, believing she had betrayed him. She remembered bringing Micus to the chamber to try to stop them from fighting with Zasian.

I *did* betray them, the alu thought. Misery washed over her.

And yet there the priest was, trying to save the angel's life. None of it made sense.

Zasian gasped. Aliisza looked up, but the priest peered with wide eyes somewhere beyond her.

Aliisza spun her own gaze around.

The sweat-soaked face of Micus the angel stared back at her. His eyebrows furrowed in confusion and his mouth parted as if to say something, but no words came. His close-cropped dark hair glistened in the eerie light, which gave his pale skin an unhealthy pallor. The deva stood upright, as though just emerging from the shadows beyond, but something was wrong.

A second set of arms, blue and scaly, protruded from beneath his own. Where his abdomen should have been, a second head jutted forward, all blue-tinged snout and gaping mouth.

Myshik of clan Morueme.

The half-dragon also stared at Aliisza. His beady eyes glittered in Zasian's strange light, and he licked his lips as though anticipating a meal.

Micus tried to take a step, but he couldn't quite make his legs work right, and the reason soon became clear to Aliisza.

The rest of the draconic hobgoblin's blue-tinged body, thick and stout, sprawled out behind the angel, fused with him.

It reminded Aliisza of some sort of twisted centaur, but with draconic, rather than equine, qualities.

The abomination that had been Micus and Myshik staggered forward another step, two human and two draconic legs struggling to work in concert. The thing spun in place as Micus stared down at himself, his mouth agape and his eyes haunted. Two sets of wings, one pair bluish and leathery, the other covered in pure white feathers, fluttered against his flanks. One moment they folded tightly against the horror's body, the next they fanned out like a butterfly's.

Oh gods! Aliisza thought and doubled over. That time, she *was* sick again.

"What happened?" Micus asked, his words faint, almost strangled.

"I don't know," Aliisza admitted in a near sob after she had recovered. She stared at the stones in front of her face, afraid to look upon the grotesque thing the two creatures had become.

When Micus growled at her answer, she scrambled backward, retreating toward Zasian, who stared at the abomination with horror. Despite her fears she, too, peered up at the stricken angel once more.

Micus glared at the two of them where they flanked Tauran. Then his feverish eyes widened in recognition. "Traitors!" he roared. "You tricked me, led me into a trap! You have damned me!"

"No!" Aliisza shouted. She shook her head. "It was Shar! She was going to kill Mystra." Her voice trailed off. I tried to stop you, she thought. I tried to stop all of you!

A wail burst from the angel, a haunted, hopeless sound that tore through Aliisza and made her cringe and clamp her hands over her ears. Micus, his expression crazed, drew a deep, ragged breath before screaming again, louder than before. His arms, all four of them, alternated between flailing and grasping Myshik's war axe. It appeared the transformed angel could not decide which limbs to use.

The abomination reared up on his hind legs and raised the war axe high. Micus gave one final shout, a screech of fury and despair. At the same time, Myshik's head growled in delight. Then they lunged at Aliisza as one body.

The alu struggled to get her wobbly legs beneath her. With what little strength had returned to her, she frantically kicked herself to one side. Zasian lunged in the opposite direction.

The war axe slammed down, striking the paving stones with a shrill clang where she had been. On her hands and knees Aliisza scrambled away toward a column. She could hear Micus follow.

"I will send you back to the fires of the Hells, she-demon!" the warped angel screamed behind her. "I will rend you into a thousand thousand pieces!"

Aliisza reached the column and spun, putting her back against it. The abomination that had been Micus and Myshik stalked her. The hobgoblin's eyes glittered in feral hunger and its mouth drooled and snapped, but the draconic head said nothing. Only Micus appeared to retain his sentience. He stared at her with baleful hatred and raised the war axe again. With each unsteady step, he gained better control over his twisted form.

Beyond the wretched creature, Zasian crouched behind

another column, peering around it, his own expression stricken with revulsion.

"Micus, wait!" Aliisza pleaded. "Stop this. Let me find a way to help you."

The twisted angel snarled and lunged at her again. He raked the war axe from one side in a great, sweeping arc, aiming to sever the alu's head from her body.

Aliisza cowered and ducked, feeling the wind of the blade's passing. She scrambled away, her boots slipping and sliding on the stones of the floor.

Micus followed her.

The alu moved to the back side of the marble pillar, struggling to flee the mad angel. She kept circumnavigating the column, trying to keep it as a barrier between herself and her foe. She managed to dodge to the right just as the war axe slammed hard into the stone edifice on her left. The force of the blow reverberated in the floor beneath the half-fiend.

She dodged right again, expecting Micus to continue chasing her in that direction, but the twisted angel had anticipated her maneuver and reversed course. One of his front legs kicked up at Aliisza's head and caught her squarely in the side of the jaw.

The alu grunted in pain as the powerful blow snapped her head to the side and slammed it against the column. Spots swam in her vision as she sprawled backward hard onto her rump.

Aliisza couldn't catch her breath. She lay gasping as Micus trotted around the column toward her.

He hoisted the war axe as high as he could, then slashed down.

❖ ❖ ❖ ❖ ❖ ❖ ❖ ❖ ❖

Eirwyn awoke in a panic. She flailed in the dimness, unsure of anything, before the sinister dream faded and memory returned.

Her cottage, perhaps just before dawn.

The angel blinked, sat up, and peered around. Everything appeared just as she expected it to—every item in place, nothing missing—but she did not feel right. She could feel tremors beneath her, rumbles in the ground.

That shouldn't be, she thought, alarmed. Not here.

The tremors subsided, and the angel was left sitting in the pre-dawn quiet of her bedchamber.

She closed her eyes and tried to remember what she had been dreaming. Nothing returned from the depths of her slumber, but her worry did not abate. It was the third time in as many nights that such night terrors had afflicted her, and she had yet to recall anything about them.

Eirwyn rose and dressed. She began to wonder if she had merely imagined the shaking of the ground. Either I'm getting old and infirm, or something truly dreadful is approaching, she decided. Not that knowing can do me any good.

The angel went through the motions of preparing a morning meal, though she no more needed it than she needed to sleep. Both were simply a means of passing the time. As she moved around the small kitchen within her quaint prison, she expected the nagging feeling of dread to pass, just as it had the previous two days, but it would not. As a result, she only picked at her food. Finally, Eirwyn gave up the pretense of eating and went outside.

The morning promised to be a fine one, as all such day-breaks were within the House of the Triad. The sun, on the verge of breaking past the clouds on the horizon, splashed them with pinks and oranges. The angel imagined soaring among them, gliding on her white, feathered wings without a care. She closed her eyes and could almost feel herself among the wispy things, but a fantasy was all it could be. She could no more fly at that moment than she could reverse the course of the sun.

Eirwyn opened her eyes and took in her place of exile.

The cottage, a simple whitewashed building of two rooms, sat nestled among a handful of trees along one side of a clearing. A small spring bubbled up from an outcropping of rock and spilled into a pool in the middle of the tiny glade. From there the cold water meandered away as a small stream into the thick brambles that made up the border of her domain. Though she could not see it, beyond those brambles lay the edge of her tiny world. The prison builders had placed the thick foliage there so as to maintain the illusion, but the angel knew otherwise.

Eirwyn recalled the day Tyr's archons brought her to the tiny island of rock, accompanied by Viryn, the solar charged by the High Council of the Court with delivering her to her own personal purgatory. Such was her punishment for defying the blind god—an eternity spent pretending to keep house far, far away from Celestia, the great mountains of the gods. She had been given a refuge and was left wanting for nothing. Her cupboards were never bare and the little garden that grew in the clearing just outside her front door offered a means of keeping busy. No, she had want of nothing—except for her freedom, of course.

It's not such a bad way to be put out to pasture, Eirwyn told herself for perhaps the thousandth time. There are certainly worse fates than this. And I did what was necessary.

The angel smiled softly as she thought of Tauran. A mixture of satisfaction and sadness washed through her as she wondered where her friend might be at that moment. She had done the right thing in protecting him. She knew that. She only hoped it had been enough.

Did they succeed? she wondered. Did they uncover the truth? Would anyone come to tell me if they had?

Stop feeling sorry for yourself, Eirwyn scolded. His sacrifice was as great as your own, if not worse. You lost Helm's patronage because he died, not because you were forced to turn from him. Tauran has willingly accepted the far more tragic fate.

If Eirwyn still had a god to pray to, she would have murmured a blessing for Tauran's safety and health. As it was, she could only send him good wishes in her thoughts.

The angel mourned Helm's death anew. The emptiness created by her deity's demise still filled her, still felt like a fresh wound that would never scar over. It was more than just the absence of his dedicated love, and more than the loss of her angelic powers. Eirwyn missed her sense of purpose, of responsibility. The joy of serving had gone from her life, and she was left with merely being.

Not a terribly promising existence for an immortal creature.

The sun broke through the clouds, a burst of morning brightness heralding the coming of another beautiful day. It was in many ways a false portent to Eirwyn, but it did remind her that life continued on despite her—or anyone else's—trials and tribulations.

Eirwyn was on the verge of returning indoors when a flash in the sky caught her eye. She turned fully toward it and watched, bringing her hand up to shield her vision from the brightening sun.

The second time it flashed, the angel got a better fix on the point and focused her gaze there, waiting.

Two figures grew from twin specks against the backdrop of the lightening sky. By the time they were distinguishable, Eirwyn could tell they were celestials, flying toward her on wings of white. When it became obvious that they were coming directly toward her, the angel's heart leaped in excitement, though a shadow of foreboding, a residual worry from her unremembered dream, also coursed through her.

Initially, she thought it was a solar and a planetar approaching, but as the pair got nearer, she realized that the green-skinned creature was, in fact, a trumpet archon. It had been the archon's long, silvery trumpet gleaming in the morning sun that had tipped Eirwyn to their presence.

The two celestials arrived and settled to the soft ground. Together, they bowed before Eirwyn, who returned the affectation with no small amount of curiosity. Despite her puzzlement, she was deeply grateful for the visitors. It had been quite some time since she had been given the chance to interact with anyone.

"We bid you good morning on this blessed day, Eirwyn," the solar said. She knew him. Viryn had commanded the escort that had brought her to her prison. "We hope this visit finds you in good health and spirits," the archon added, "and we trust that we are not interrupting anything of import?"

Eirwyn laughed. "I think you both know that I would welcome *any* interruption. Viryn, there's no need for formalities; I do not hold you in contempt. You were just doing your duty."

The other angel inclined his head slightly in thanks. "I am glad to see you taking this so well, Eirwyn. It gave me no joy to leave you here."

Eirwyn shrugged, then frowned. "If you've come to see if I will reconsider and testify before the High Council, I'm afraid you've made the journey for nothing. I still believe in the rightness of my actions, and of my freedom to make such a decision. I'm afraid I still share Tauran's sentiment that Tyr was not acting in his right faculties, and that will not change."

The two visitors looked at one another and frowned. "Of course, there's no way you might have known," Viryn said solemnly, "but I thought you might suspect . . ."

Eirwyn cocked her head to one side, puzzled. "Suspect what?" she asked. "What has happened?" Then her heart leaped in joy. "Tauran's returned! He's brought news of his success!"

Viryn's frown deepened.

"Alas, he has not," the other angel replied. He opened his mouth to add more, but the archon cut him off.

"Have you not heard the summons?" the trumpeter asked. "Have you not felt the Seer's connection, calling you?"

Eirwyn's eyes grew wide. "Erathaol has been trying to contact *me*?" she asked. The notion of the great archon who ruled Venya, the third layer of Mount Celestia, reaching out, stunned her. "Why?" Then she recalled the tremor that had awakened her.

And her dreams.

Eirwyn seized on the palpable worry radiating from the two creatures standing before her. They had come bearing profound news. "Tell me," she commanded them.

"For three days, portents have come to the Seer, announcing something profound and dire. He has been attempting to interpret these warnings, but the only insight he has gleaned thus far is your name. He's been trying to summon you to him, but to no avail. It was only this morning that he learned you had been banished. He sent me to intervene, and we rushed here at once, but now I fear we may be too late."

"Too late for what?" Eirwyn asked. How could I be a part of the Seer's visions? she wondered, feeling overwhelmed for the first time in eons.

"It seems you and Tauran were right," Viryn said. "Mystra has been slain. By Cyric."

Eirwyn gasped and sank to her knees. "No!" she breathed. "This cannot be!" Oh, Tauran, she thought. You saw it coming, didn't you? And no one believed you. She prayed that her friend still lived.

"Sadly, I am not finished with the dire news," Viryn continued. He placed a hand on Eirwyn's shoulder to offer her comfort. "Dweomerheart was destroyed in the process. Savras is dead, Azuth is missing. The World Tree is no more."

New sorrow welled in Eirwyn's heart. "So many lives lost," she murmured, trying to absorb what the deva was telling her. "So much death and destruction. What has Cyric wrought?"

"I do not know," Viryn answered. His voice sounded grave, frail. "Everyone is trying to determine how far the aftereffects reach." He took a deep breath. "But that's why we are here. You must return with us to the Court of Tyr at once. You have been pardoned. It appears that you have some role to play in all this, and the council wants to find out what."

CHAPTER TWO

Kaanyr Vhok's consciousness returned to the sound of forge hammers ringing on anvils. The loud, clanging blows of metal on metal reverberated through the cambion. Each concussive strike made his head pound, and he winced at the noise.

The dwarves of Sundabar are worthless wastes of life, he silently grumbled. They should all be impaled and quartered for making that racket.

The half-fiend groaned, grimaced, then tried to sit up. The pounding in his head made him dizzy, and he feared he would be ill.

What's the matter with me? he wondered. Am I injured?

Kaanyr couldn't remember what happened. He took a couple of deep breaths and tried to clear his head. He kept his face on the cool stones beneath him and waited until his equilibrium stopped spinning.

Stones, he thought. Did I fall?

He reached out with one hand and began to feel his own body, testing for broken bones. Everything was intact.

A familiar feminine voice cut through the fog of his wooziness. "Micus, wait!"

Aliisza.

"Stop this. Let me find a way to help you," the alu said. Her voice sounded desperate, frantic. It filled him with worry.

Micus! He knew that name!

Memories tumbled back into Vhok—

The rotunda . . .

A battle with Myshik . . .

The thrice-damned hobgoblin nearly cleaved me in twain, Kaanyr remembered. I should be dead. The cambion reached behind, feeling the place along his back where the half-dragon had struck.

He found no sign of any wound.

Fearful that he would suffer another attack from the cunning Myshik, Kaanyr forced himself to open his eyes and sit up.

He rested near the very periphery of the rotunda, deep in shadow. A single glow of light, oddly dim and unsteady, flickered from near the center of the chamber. He spotted no sign of the draconic hobgoblin, but there was movement to his left, among the columns holding the dome aloft, where Aliisza's voice had emanated.

As Kaanyr rose unsteadily onto one knee, he spied his blade, crackling with purplish black energy, near his foot. He reached down and took hold of the weapon, then heard the sound of flesh striking flesh, followed by a soft groan.

Aliisza!

Kaanyr forced himself to his feet and staggered toward the sound.

The cambion had to follow the curve of the columns to

reach the source, and when he stepped into view, he nearly stumbled to the floor in shock.

A dreadful creature nearly filled the space between the curved wall and the columns, a beast made by foul magic. Half man and half something else, it raised a massive axe high and reared like a horse on back legs. Aliisza slumped before it in a daze, unwilling or unable to retreat from the impending strike.

Kaanyr flipped his sword around, snatching the blade end out of the air. In the same smooth motion, he yanked his arm back and then snapped it forward, flinging the weapon at the abomination before him. The sword spun across the distance between Kaanyr and the monstrosity.

In his haste, Kaanyr had not been careful with his aim, but he did not care. The sword tumbled past the flank of the creature's human torso, grazing one of its four arms and raking a gash along it. Purplish energy crackled outward in a spiderweb mosaic, radiating from the wound.

The beast screamed and flailed, its deadly strike against Aliisza disrupted. The axe slipped from its grasp as the abomination staggered to one side.

Kaanyr did not wait to see the effects of his attack. Reaching inside his tunic, he stumbled toward the thing. He pulled a wand free and prepared to utter the powerful arcane phrase that would trigger its magic.

The beast turned toward him, and Kaanyr's words died on his lips.

Micus's fevered eyes bore into the cambion.

"You!" Micus screamed, spinning to fully confront Vhok. "Damn you back to the Hells from whence you came!" He lurched toward the half-fiend, and Kaanyr spied Myshik's face jutting from Micus's gut. The half-hobgoblin's mouth slavered as it stared gleefully at him.

Kaanyr recovered his wits and leveled the wand at the onrushing abomination. He activated the magic imbued in the device and flinched as blinding lightning burst from its tip. The charge arced across the distance and engulfed Micus and Myshik in a shower of crackling energy and sparks. To the cambion, the discharge of magic felt . . . off.

The flash left afterimages in Kaanyr's vision, but he could make out enough to watch the monstrosity stagger to one side and go down.

Vhok held the wand steady for a moment, watching to see if the fused creatures remained a threat.

Micus's eyes stayed closed, but he still breathed. Likewise, Myshik's head appeared unconscious. Once or twice, the wings upon the flank of the odd, centaur-shaped abomination twitched, but that was all.

Kaanyr approached the immobile form of the thing and nudged it with the toe of his boot. When it still did not move, he let out a sigh of relief and pocketed the wand. He turned toward Aliisza.

The alu still crouched near the column, her long, dark ringlets plastered to her pale, narrow face. She stared up at Kaanyr. Her eyes, so often smoldering in sultry delight, were instead wide and fearful. Her mouth, usually formed into a cunning smile or petulant frown, trembled. She kept her graceful, batlike wings folded snugly against her body. They matched the shiny black luster of her tight leather armor. Even in that moment of chaos and crisis, Kaanyr admired the form-fitting garment and how it accentuated the alu's shape.

"Kaanyr," Aliisza said, her voice quavering. "You're alive. I thought—"

"Don't ask me how," Kaanyr replied, moving to the alu and kneeling down. He took her face in his hands, drew her close, and kissed her. He could feel her still trembling, and she resisted at first, rigid, as though afraid. Then she melted into him.

"I tried to stop you," Aliisza said into his shoulder, her voice faint, desperate. "I tried to stop you all."

At her words, Kaanyr remembered how she had brought Micus to the rotunda. The cambion's joy at having the half-fiend safely back with him vanished, driven from him like a punch to the gut, as he recalled her betrayal.

"We were on the verge," Kaanyr said as he stiffly untangled himself from her embrace. "I was this close"—as he stood up, the cambion held his thumb and forefinger, almost touching, in front of her face—"to winning my freedom from Tauran's control. And then you went and sabotaged everything." And to think how I grieved, believing I'd lost you within the Eye of Savras's vast caverns of knowledge. Weak, he thought. He wasn't sure if he meant it for Aliisza or himself.

The alu struggled to her knees. She looked like a street waif begging for coin. "I wasn't the one," she pleaded. "It was Zasian. Please understand. I was trying to stop him!"

Zasian!

Kaanyr's memory flooded with thoughts of the hated priest and his treachery. New anger coursed through him, an unrelenting desire to rend the man.

With a snarl, Vhok turned from the alu and stalked toward his sword. It lay in the shadows, crackling with its malevolent energy.

"I don't understand a thing that's happened since you returned from the caverns," he said, "but I *will* free myself of Tauran's control. I *will* slay that damnable priest!" He jerked the sword off the ground and turned back toward the center of the rotunda. "And I *will* not be stopped this time!"

"Wait!" Aliisza cried, trying to rise to her feet. She had to brace herself against the column to keep herself upright. "Something's happened." She reached toward him. "To all of us. Can't you feel it?"

Vhok ignored the alu and stepped between the columns, into the light. He drew up short when he spied Zasian Menz across from him, standing with his arms folded protectively.

A glow emanated from the priest.

Zasian spotted Vhok and smiled, but it was not the treacherous grin the cambion remembered from before. The expression on the priest's face showed a mixture of confusion and hope. It came across as pure and warm, like the uncertainty of a child who has just been praised by his father after doing something for which he expected to be punished.

"Well met," Zasian said. He looked around for a brief moment, frowning, then he gestured. "What is this place? Where are we?"

Kaanyr's mouth opened and shut several times as he worked to form the words. He could not.

"Everything's different," Aliisza said, appearing beside Kaanyr and taking his arm. "Something happened."

Kaanyr clenched his teeth and shrugged free of her grasp. "He tries to fool us both," he growled. He took another step toward the priest. "His clever tricks will not dissuade me!" He drew back his sword and closed the distance, intent on driving the blade through the priest's chest.

Zasian's eyes grew wide with fright and he flinched back. "Please don't!" he pleaded. Then he turned and ran, darting behind the nearest column.

Kaanyr strode forward. "You cannot dupe me with your theatrics, priest," he said. "I will not be denied!"

Zasian's face peeked out from behind the pillar, watching the approaching half-fiend. "Stop!" he pleaded, backing away as Kaanyr got closer. "What did I do? I don't know you. I don't remember!"

Kaanyr shook his head and snorted in amusement. "Weak, Zasian. Very weak. I thought you could do better than that." He reached the column and tried to circle it, reaching for the priest. He remained wary, expecting the man to drop his foolish pretenses and assault him.

But Zasian Menz continued to shy away and retreat, using the columns as protection from the enraged cambion.

"Kaanyr!" Aliisza shouted. The tone of her voice caused a cold pain to form in the pit of his stomach. There was more to her call than mere worry for Zasian's well-being. Something far more sinister troubled her.

Kaanyr turned and faced her, keeping Zasian visible in the corner of his eye. "What is it?" he demanded.

The alu did not answer, but she pointed at something to the side, just out of Kaanyr's view. Her expression matched the fear in her voice and gave him pause.

Kaanyr took a pair of steps toward Aliisza and then turned and peered in the direction she indicated.

A great hole had appeared along one side of the chamber.

To Kaanyr, it looked as though a massive blade had cleaved the rotunda, severing a portion of the wall from the rest of the chamber. Beyond the hole, where the cambion expected to see the great cavern of Azuth's abode within Dweomerheart, nothing but a silvery void existed.

"What is that?" Kaanyr said, feeling confusion and fear grip him.

Beside him, Aliisza shuddered. "I told you, something happened. I felt it." She stepped toward the edge of the hole.

"Don't," Kaanyr warned. "Stay back." He imagined some unseen force or power sucking his consort away through the gaping opening into the nothingness beyond.

Aliisza did not stop, though. She moved right to the edge of the hole and craned her neck forward. A small gasp escaped her.

"What is it?" Kaanyr asked, moving a step closer despite his fear.

There was no sign of Azuth's caverns in the expanded view. The silvery void stretched in every direction. But it was not empty. Islands of material bobbed in the distance, like debris on an argent ocean. Some seemed distant, tiny, while others floated near enough for Kaanyr to discern that they were spherical, bubbles of solidity. Inside those spheres the cambion could see chunks of stone or rock, or hunks of earth, grass- and tree-covered tracts of a world. Based on their contents, Kaanyr got the distinct impression that some of the bubbles of matter were quite large, while others were meager, perhaps only a few paces across.

The spheres of matter slowly moved into and out of view, as though they orbited his tiny refuge. Then his frame of reference shifted, and he realized they did not move after all. Instead, his mind's eye accepted that he was spinning. He could not feel it, but he somehow knew it to be true.

Suddenly, Kaanyr understood.

The cambion stared down at the stone beneath his own feet. He could see then that the edge of the hole was curved, shaped like the edge of a sphere.

They, too, were in a bubble.

"Gods and devils, what happened?" he asked, his voice faint. Terror made him feel dizzy, tiny. "Where are we?"

Aliisza did not answer. She had her hand to her mouth and her eyes were still wide as she stared at something outside Kaanyr's field of view. When he leaned forward, cautiously, to catch a glimpse, he felt his heart skip a beat.

The most gargantuan bubble that Kaanyr could imagine floated there.

A milky cloud of something filled the massive sphere. A thousand thousand sparkling motes of light swarmed and danced inside. A figure hovered within the vapor, vaguely human in shape but only faintly visible, sprawled like some cadaver entangled in the filth of an inner city canal.

The colossal bubble and its cargo gently undulated, and Kaanyr had the impression that they were not stationary. The monumental figure instead drifted, floating on some unseen current within the silvery void. All the other, tinier bubbles bobbed and weaved along with it, as though caught in its eddy.

What has happened?

Fighting vertigo and panic, Kaanyr spun away from the scene. He sought Zasian, certain the priest was behind the chaos. Vhok would make him answer for his duplicity, would force him to return them to somewhere sane.

The cambion took two steps toward the middle of the chamber and froze. Other holes had opened along the periphery of the rotunda, as though the stone itself had melted away. Each breach appeared knife-edge smooth, perfect, and growing. Their bubble was shrinking, eating away at the reality of the rotunda as it did.

Panic shot through the half-fiend.

Before he could react, Aliisza called to him. Her voice conveyed alarm. No, barely controlled terror.

The cambion turned to look back and saw her still staring out at the endless argent sea beyond. A great shadow had fallen over the opening in the wall.

Kaanyr dashed to the edge and peered out.

An enormous creature drifted into view, its body a ponderous, bloated sac of blanched flesh. Kaanyr could see no eyes, but numerous segmented tentacles dangled from it, lazily sweeping the space around itself. The thing reminded Kaanyr of a huge octopus, or perhaps a bloated insect.

It made his stomach churn.

When one of the tentacles came near a bubble of reality, the behemoth gathered the sphere up and drew the material toward a beaklike mouth on its underside. The thing consumed its catch in a single gulp.

Then it turned and began drifting closer, tentacles stretched out toward the remains of the rotunda.

❖ ❖ ❖ ❖ ❖ ❖ ❖ ❖ ❖

The Court of Tyr teetered on the brink of chaos.

In one corner of her mind, Eirwyn recognized the sheer magnitude of the very existence of that thought. Imagining such a fate for a heavenly domain dedicated to the most solemn and steadfast ideals of law and order bordered on blasphemy. It would have been unthinkable only a few short tendays before.

It did not change the angel's assessment one iota.

She had flown back to the great mountains with Viryn and Oshiga—the trumpet archon from Erathaol's court—as fast as the three of them could move. They traveled so quickly there had been no opportunity for the other two celestials to further explain the situation to Eirwyn. Thus, when she arrived, the shock of seeing the entire plane in such a state shook her.

I should not be surprised, she thought, standing in the hall of the High Council. *Magic itself died*—she felt profound grief at such a crime, and more than a little rage toward Cyric—*and no one seems to know what other consequences may befall the multiverse. Tyr and Torm have their hands full, just maintaining the integrity of the House, and no one seems to know where Siamorphe has gone.*

But the unsettling feeling sweeping through the Court went beyond the mere death of a god, and its source played out before her, within the High Council itself.

"I did not authorize such a pardon!" the High Councilor insisted, rising to his full height and snapping his wings angrily. "No one else may grant such a stay of sentence. This is inexcusable."

"On the contrary," one of the six dissenters argued, "the other council members can override the High Councilor's edict with a two-thirds majority, and we have it. You cannot win this fight, Honorable One, and you know it."

"Point of procedure!" the High Councilor interjected. "There was no submission of disagreement, no call for a vote. You cannot override my edict until you have formally petitioned for a review."

Weary already of the bickering, Eirwyn's thoughts drifted

back to her cottage, away from the crowded, frenzied chamber. It would not take much more of the councilors' antics to make the lonely abode a preferable escape.

This is what Tyr's dedication to justice and law inevitably leads to, she thought, grimacing. *Blessed Helm, I miss you. Serving as an ever-watching sentinel might be a lonely job to some, but at least it gave me ample opportunity to contemplate my divinations. And compared to this . . . the angel almost shuddered.*

That's all in the past now, Eirwyn reminded herself. *And you must help in whatever way you can. Countless souls scattered across the planes may depend on your wisdom and foresight.*

Eirwyn returned her attention on the proceedings.

"In the interests of urgency," another of the six councilors was saying, having risen to his feet, "there was no time, and we waste more of it here with this foolish debate. We acted in such haste because we must know the right course moving forward. The entire House depends on us making sound, rational decisions. Point of procedure or no, the outcome is inevitable, and you do no one any favors by clinging to rigid codes in these circumstances."

"I disagree," the High Councilor said hotly, "and I further submit to you that you do irreparable damage to this august institution by circumventing time-honored—and very necessary—practices."

He turned to Eirwyn and stared down at her coldly. "It appears I no longer have the authority to incarcerate you for your indiscretions on behalf of Tauran the outcast and against this body. A pardon has been rendered, although on the most flimsy of evidence and in the most inexcusable manner." The

High Councilor drew a deep breath before he continued, turning to face his peers again. "Therefore, I will not be a party to it. I remove myself from this seat under protest. I will be reporting directly to Tyr these farcical proceedings at once. And as for you," he finished, turning back to Eirwyn again, "I still find you guilty of numerous crimes against Tyr's law and right to rule. You may have escaped justice today, but do not for one moment consider yourself free of guilt!"

With that final declaration, the solar winked out. A moment later, the other two members of the council who had sided with the High Councilor also vanished, leaving the rest of the court deathly silent.

Eirwyn blinked and stared around the chamber. Other stunned expressions stared back at her. *Has it really come to this?* she thought. *Have my own actions become so consequential that the High Council itself has fractured? Truly?*

The angel swallowed down her shock and dismay. *What have we wrought, Tauran?*

"Well," the female solar who had been first to argue with the High Councilor said, breaking the strained silence, "it seems we have resolved and closed this matter. You are indeed free to do as you see fit, Eirwyn. I hope, in your wisdom, you will choose to aid us."

Eirwyn raised her hands helplessly. "I still know so very little about what has happened," she said. "What can I offer that you cannot perform ten times more effectively than I?"

The solar nodded. "In truth, we know not. But the matter is beyond our purview, anyway. We"—the solar gestured at the other five councilors around her—"are but the facilitators of your freedom, at the behest of Erathaol's emissary, here." She pointed to Oshiga. "It is the Seer who believes he can make use of you. You must parley with him to learn more."

The discussion was over. Eirwyn understood that she and her companions had been dismissed. The council, even down three members, had other urgent issues to address.

Outside the chambers, Eirwyn turned to Viryn. "So my overturned sentence was not initiated by a servant of Tyr?" she asked.

The solar shook his head. "No," he admitted. "Though I am sure that your case would have been brought up in short order, regardless. These dark times have compelled the leadership to consider reinstating many who had fallen from grace in the hopes that they might lend aid where it is desperately needed."

Eirwyn tried not to let that fact annoy her. To Oshiga, she asked, "So, what would the Seer want from me? How could I be of unique assistance?"

The archon bowed slightly. "To understand fully, you must travel to Venya with me. I have been instructed to invite you to Xiranthador, Erathaol's library-fortress, to become an instrument of his divination."

Eirwyn cocked her head to one side. "Me?" she said in a meeker voice than she had intended. Still reeling from the alarming proceedings within the council chamber, she wasn't certain what to make of such an offer. She drew a deep breath and tried to gather her wits. "An instrument? That doesn't sound very charming. On the other hand, my prospects at the moment aren't terribly promising."

"I assure you, it is a great honor," Oshiga said, inclining his head again. "The Seer rarely finds others who can serve in such a capacity. You must be a great diviner, indeed, for him to wish to engage with you in such a fashion."

For the first time since the moment that Helm had died at Tyr's hand, Eirwyn felt a thrill of purpose, of true responsibility, course through her.

She nodded to the trumpet archon. "Very well," she said. "I accept. Lead on."

CHAPTER THREE

Aliisza couldn't stop staring at the gargantuan monstrosity floating toward them. No matter how much she wanted to tear her gaze away, no matter how hard she tried to convince herself that none of it was real, she couldn't make her body function. The world had gone mad.

The alu didn't snap out of it until Kaanyr shook her by the arm, and then she realized he had been calling her name.

"Look!" he insisted, pointing at the floor near their feet, at the edge of the stone. Then he spun her away from that and gestured at other holes forming in the opposite walls and the ceiling of the domed chamber. "It's shrinking. The bubble is shrinking!"

Aliisza could only blink, not comprehending.

With a sigh of exasperation, Kaanyr forced her to look at him. "This place is dissolving," he said, staring directly into her eyes. "Whatever is holding it together cannot keep at it."

Aliisza nodded once, vaguely. I didn't do it, she thought. I tried to stop the battle, not betray you.

"Aliisza, focus! Listen to me!" Kaanyr demanded. "There's

no time. You have to figure out what keeps the bubble here while I try to drive that, that *thing* away. Now!"

Somewhere in the back of her mind, Aliisza suddenly heard the old Kaanyr, the ruler of the Scourged Legion, her lord, master, and lover. They were on the field of battle once more, he issuing commands, she obeying them. She remembered who she was then.

The alu blinked again and finally saw her consort's face, perceived the urgency in his voice and expression. "Yes," she said. She took stock of the chamber. "Yes," she repeated, more resolutely. "Keep it away from us. Do whatever you have to. I'll find the source of the bubble."

"That's my girl," Kaanyr said, releasing her arms. "Go!" He moved back to the opening where the monstrous octopus-thing lurked. He had his hand inside his tunic, fumbling for something as he reached the edge of the room.

Aliisza stepped back and oriented herself. She turned her gaze back and forth, assessing the various holes. She wanted to find the center point, figuring that would be where the source of the bubble originated.

There, she decided, turning her attention toward one side of the round chamber. The area was masked by darkness, but even as she made the decision to close the distance, dim light radiated from her left.

"What's happening?" Zasian asked, stepping cautiously out from behind a column. "Where are you going?"

Aliisza halted and turned to stare at the priest. His face, once so filled with expressions of cunning and smug secrecy, looked innocent and childlike. He remained standing several paces away from her, as if frightened that she might lunge at him and he would be forced to duck behind the safety of the column again. The glow still emanated from him, and it seemed to the alu that it might have grown just the tiniest bit stronger and steadier.

She wondered if it truly was just another trick, as Kaanyr suspected, or if the priest had somehow changed as a result of . . . whatever had happened. Either possibility seemed reasonable to her at that moment. Wisdom dictated that she expect the worst from Zasian, but even so, he might prove useful.

"Do you want to help me get us out of this mess?" she asked, watching his eyes carefully.

They never betrayed any sense of treachery as he replied, "Yes. Are you angry with me like your friend is?"

Aliisza tried to keep her face smooth and emotionless. "Do I have reason to be?" she asked.

"I don't know," Zasian mumbled. He stared down at the stones and ran a toe along one seam. "I don't remember."

"Don't remember what?"

"Anything," the priest admitted. He seemed ashamed.

Guilty? Aliisza wondered.

"I will only be angry with you if you don't help me," she said. "We have to find something."

"Very well," Zasian said, and he took a step closer. "What?"

"Whatever is keeping this place whole," the alu answered. She turned part of her attention back to the gloomy periphery of the rotunda, though she kept half an eye on the priest, too. She moved toward the spot she had chosen and passed between the columns. Zasian tentatively followed her.

The alu discovered a pair of doors set into the outer wall of the round chamber, a portal that must have led to an exterior hallway when the rotunda was intact. A lone figure lay sprawled within the opening, facedown and unmoving. Even in the near-darkness, Aliisza could see that it was a celestial being, a green-skinned, bald-headed creature half again as tall as she. Its white-feathered wings lay draped across its still form, but she could make out the armor encasing its body. A greatsword rested near the being's hands.

Zasian moved up cautiously beside Aliisza and stared down at the creature. "What happened to it?" he asked, his voice filled with awe. "What is it?"

Aliisza knelt down next to the celestial being. "A planetar," she said as she ran her hand gingerly along the green skin, checking for signs of life. "A type of angel." She glanced up at the priest's face to see his reaction.

Zasian merely stared at the angel with a wondrous look. "Is it dead?"

Aliisza's answer was cut off as the rotunda bucked to the sound of a powerful blast. She pitched sideways, striking the floor hard and sliding a few feet along its surface. The alu grunted and tried to rise, but a second lurch of the chamber sent her tumbling again.

"Aliisza!" Kaanyr shouted from the other side. "Help me!"

She struggled to her hands and knees and looked over at Zasian, who had been sent sprawling too. He peered around with wide eyes. She turned her gaze toward the planetar as she rose to a half-crouch, expecting another jolt. Magic crawled across the angel's skin and the tremors ceased. The celestial's wings had shifted with the tremors, and for the first time, she could see the wicked gash that ran along the being's chest. Blood leaked from the cut, soaking its wing. The planetar's the one maintaining the bubble, she realized, and he's dying.

"Whatever game you're playing at, we have no more time

for it," Aliisza said, looking at Zasian. "We are doomed unless you can keep him alive while I go aid Kaanyr."

The man opposite her said nothing, but he stared at her with large, frightened eyes.

Aliisza wanted to slap him. "You're the priest, do something!" she yelled, then she turned and sprinted toward Kaanyr.

The hole had grown considerably wider than Aliisza remembered. Worse, the tip of one of the great tentacles was making the gap even larger as it probed the opening, ripping chunks of stone away as it sought its prey.

Kaanyr, on one knee, flinched back from the segmented feeler and raised a wand. He muttered something unintelligible and an arc of lightning burst in Aliisza's vision. Unlike the bolts Kaanyr usually employed, the charge of electricity appeared much more chaotic and unregulated than she remembered. Balls of fizzling energy sprayed out to the sides and careened off every surface, and the main bolt shimmered and shifted oddly in a haze of smoke.

Aliisza threw her arm up too late to ward off the blinding flash. She stumbled and nearly fell, but instead used her wings to hold herself upright. As the shimmering afterimage of the miscast bolt faded enough for her to see, Aliisza spotted two more of the tentacles joining the first, which bore a ragged black streak along part of its length.

All three of the probing appendages flailed wildly, riled by Kaanyr's attack. The gigantic creature seemed more determined than ever to get at its intended morsels, for it rapidly tore huge segments of the wall away and brought its beak in close to the ever-expanding opening. By that time, nearly all of one side of the domed chamber had been rent.

Kaanyr, still down on one knee, raised the wand to fire again, but one of the tentacles located him before he could discharge the magic and quickly latched onto the cambion. He grunted and arched his neck back in pain as the tentacle squeezed him and began to pull him toward the creature's maw.

"Kaanyr!" Aliisza screamed, stumbling forward to aid him. She felt helpless without a weapon, but her sword was on the opposite side of the chamber, still impaling her son.

"Stay back!" Kaanyr ordered her through clenched teeth. "Hit it with this!" He tossed the wand to her. "Say, 'Galvanos!' "

The wand skittered across the floor to the alu, who snatched it up. Even as she prepared to use the device, a second tentacle snaked its way toward Kaanyr and joined the first in constricting the cambion. Kaanyr's cry of anguish reverberated through the chamber.

Aliisza engaged the magic and the wand spit forth another misshapen bolt of lightning. She flinched as she uttered the magical phrase, sparing her eyes the worst of the flash. The alu's aim was effective; the arc of energy ripped into one of the tentacles and split it nearly in half. It trembled and uncoiled from Kaanyr, then withdrew with a sudden jerk.

Aliisza was on the verge of firing the wand again when yet another tentacle grazed her leg. It flapped in a frenzy, hunting a firmer grip. Shuddering in revulsion, she leaped into the air to evade the probing appendage, using her wings to hold herself aloft. The tentacle continued to flail violently as she moved farther out of reach.

"Aliisza!" Kaanyr screamed.

During her distraction, the great beast had dragged the cambion closer to its mouth. The maw snapped in anticipation.

Kaanyr had his feet wedged against its beak, scrambling frantically to hold himself back.

Heedless of the three new tentacles that writhed within the ruined chamber, Aliisza darted in close and aimed the wand. The burst of lightning struck true, crackling against the creature's mouth.

The thing let out a horrid, hissing scream and shook violently, making the whole rotunda rock and shake.

"Again!" Kaanyr screamed, his voice cracking in panic. "Hit it again!"

Aliisza lined up for another attack, but a shadow of movement in the corner of her vision drew her attention.

The Micus-Myshik aberration reared up and into the alu's view as he galloped forward. Micus held the war axe high as he charged into the fight. It looked to her as though he intended to cut down Kaanyr. She opened her mouth to scream a warning, but she knew she was too late to help.

The war axe sliced down.

The blade severed the tentacle holding Kaanyr.

As the rest of the appendage whipped around and retracted, Micus used his other two arms to grab hold of Kaanyr and drag him backward, out of the way. At the same time, Myshik's mouth opened wide, and another burst of lightning shot forward, engulfing the exposed mouth of the octopus-thing. That bolt formed true, but it flashed a deep blue color.

With another angry hiss, the monstrous beast released the rotunda and retreated.

Aliisza sighed in relief and exhaustion and dropped her hands to her knees, breathing hard. She watched Micus-Myshik carefully, wary of what he would do next.

The fused creature set Kaanyr down. The cambion wriggled free of the limp tip of the tentacle and rolled away. He came up in a crouch, his wicked sword free of its scabbard. Purple magic danced along the length of its blade.

Micus turned toward the half-fiend and swished the war axe through the air. "Is that how you choose to repay your savior?" he asked, panting. He strained to form the words. "Perhaps I should have let the astral kraken devour you, after all."

"I do not trust you, creature," Kaanyr answered. "Aliisza, stay on his opposite side. Keep him flanked."

The alu did as instructed, but she wondered how much good she could do with the wand.

The Micus abomination danced backward, trying to keep both his opponents in view. His wild-eyed expression worried her. "If we are to escape this dire predicament, we must do so together," he said. "That is why I saved you, half-demon. Do not make me regret it."

"What has happened?" Aliisza asked. "How did we come to be here? How can we possibly trust you?"

She wanted to add, How did you come to be as you are?

"I do not understand all of it," Micus replied, still spinning and watching the two half-fiends as they circled him, "and there is no time for the details." A look of agony crossed the transformed angel's face, and he shuddered and nearly fell. He grunted in pain, then recovered enough to bring the war axe back up in a defensive position.

"Mystra is slain, and all the multiverse reels at her destruction," Micus continued. "Waves of devastation crisscross the Astral and rend the planes. Dweomerheart is no more. Magic has gone terribly awry."

Aliisza gasped at the twisted angel's revelation. She remembered again the vision within the Eye of Savras. Shar had wanted to kill Mystra. No! she silently screamed. I tried to stop you!

"Why should we believe you?" Kaanyr asked. "How do we even know you are still of sound mind, after . . . after—"

"After becoming this monster?" Micus finished for the cambion. "I would think my twisted form would be evidence enough for you. But we must hurry! There is no more time for debate. Every moment, I feel the savage rage of the half-dragon grow inside me. Soon, it may overwhelm me, and then I will no longer be interested in helping you."

"And just how do you intend to help us?" Kaanyr asked, his expression wary. "What do you want of us?"

"Come with me, back to the House of the Triad. I can take us there, all of us. My control over my power grows weaker by the moment, but I can still transport you, save you from this oblivion."

"And then?" Kaanyr asked. "Once we have returned?"

"Then you will stand trial for your crimes," the angel answered, his breath coming in gasps as he fought to maintain his senses. "You must answer for your role in Mystra's death. But it is a better fate than remaining here, trapped, until the astral kraken—or something worse—comes for you."

"I think not," Kaanyr replied, an unkind grin spreading across his face. "I will not be your prize, angel." He raised his sword higher.

"So be it!" screamed Micus. "I will take your corpses instead!" He reared, intending to charge.

Aliisza watched as the wretched thing that once had been an angel and a draconic hobgoblin charged her lover. She

THE CRYSTAL MOUNTAIN • 41

saw Kaanyr step back, intent on using the columns as a line of defense.

An idea formed.

"Kaanyr, to me, quickly!" she cried, conjuring the magic of a spell she had never conceived of before. She began the incantation, only distantly thinking about where it had come from.

A blue glow formed around her, brighter than the emanation from Zasian. It turned the chamber a brilliant azure. For a heartbeat, Aliisza faltered, stunned by the peculiar effect. She regained her senses just before the energy of her magic evanesced and she managed to continue the enchantment.

The cambion performed a drop-step to slide out of the way of the charging abomination and let Micus's momentum carry him past. Then he retreated toward Aliisza.

Perfect, Aliisza thought. She flung the completed spell forward, shaping it with a thought.

A cage appeared, a shimmering barrier of bright blue bars that pinned Micus-Myshik within. Aliisza formed it in such a way that it confined the abomination where he stood. At the same time, she felt sharp sickness erupt in her belly. She doubled over from the pain of it.

Micus roared in anger and defiance. She looked up as he battered the barrier with feet and weapon, but it resisted his efforts. He grew still, and Aliisza saw him close his eyes in concentration. Sweat poured from his face.

She could feel the angel test the limits of the magic she had woven into the arcane cage. She could feel him try to shift, to leave the place, to travel elsewhere in the multiverse.

The cage held Micus fast. When he realized he was truly trapped, he screamed and threw himself at the barrier.

Beside her, Kaanyr kept shifting his view between the caged abomination and the alu. "What did you do?" he asked. "What's wrong?"

She shook her head, feeling the sickness recede. The strange blue glow faded with it. She rose upright and attempted to smooth her features. "I'm fine. It's nothing," she lied. "Magic has been behaving oddly ever since . . ." She left the thought hanging and shook her head to dismiss it.

"But that's not a trick I ever remember you performing before," Kaanyr said quietly. "And you looked like you were in pain. What's happening?"

Aliisza reached a hand up and touched Kaanyr on the lips. "I said I'm fine," she replied with a faint smile. "Just too much excitement. And you should know your girl well enough by now to understand that I'm still full of tricks."

The cambion stared at her a moment longer, then shrugged and turned to examine the cage she had created.

He did not see her troubled expression as she contemplated what had just occurred. What in the Nine Hells is happening to me? she wondered.

❖ ❖ ❖ ❖ ❖ ❖ ❖ ❖ ❖

Eirwyn felt like she and Oshiga had been climbing forever. Up and up she flew, following the trumpet archon, ascending past the endless slopes of Mount Celestia. The pair winged their way through numerous layers of clouds, emerging each time above yet another realm with yet another great slope rising before them.

The angel had never traversed so far up the sides of the majestic peak, and she had never fully realized how incredibly large it was. Once, as they had stopped for a rest upon a small tropical island with a beautiful beach of white sand and palm trees, Eirwyn asked her guide if the mountain was truly so massive. Oshiga had assured her that they were taking a shortcut between layers and would reach Venya soon.

The two of them passed through yet another large bank of clouds, and Eirwyn shivered at the damp, cool caress of the water vapor. She concentrated on staying close to her guide, as he had instructed her, for he had warned that to fall behind or lose her way could result in being lost forever within the heavenly realm.

She kept the archon firmly in sight.

Eirwyn burst from the cloud cover abruptly and found herself soaring over rich, green farmland far below. The route Oshiga followed took them over a ridge of forest and then across the shoreline of a vast, blue lake. The angel stared down into the clear water as she kept pace with her companion, spying unusual shapes along the bottom.

Seashells, she realized, and massive ones at that.

It made no sense to Eirwyn, having seashells within a mountain lake, but she shrugged it off as the whim of the archon ruler of the place.

Oshiga changed course, diving toward the surface of the water. Puzzled, Eirwyn followed him, noting that he angled toward a particularly deep cleft in the lake floor. At first, the angel thought perhaps her eyes were playing tricks on her, but eventually she was certain that faint light glowed from something within that cleft.

Eirwyn took a huge breath and held it, then braced herself as the two plunged into the crystal-clear lake, expecting the water to be icy from mountain runoff. She was surprised when the jolt of crisp cold did not hit her.

At first, the angel tried to swim, but she caught on quickly that Oshiga still "flew" with his wings, coursing through the water at incredible speed, and if she did not attempt the same mode of travel, she would lag behind. Shrugging, Eirwyn unfurled her own wings and tested them.

It felt no different to her than gliding through the air.

"You need not fear drowning here," Oshiga called to her over his shoulder as they moved deeper into the depths. "You are a guest of Erathaol's. He has made the way more welcoming."

Eirwyn, her chest already aching from holding her breath, released it, and was surprised to find no bubbles escaping her mouth. Tentatively, she drew in a breath. She did not choke on the water. How wonderfully odd, she thought, and began breathing normally.

As the light from above grew dimmer, the glow from below increased. Eirwyn found that she could see just fine the entire way down. More than once, they startled a school of fish as they passed, sending the creatures scurrying with a flash of silver.

Before long, they reached the bottom, and Eirwyn stood before a massive edifice made of huge seashells. It rose before her like a great castle, with countless levels towering overhead. The glow she had seen before emanated from within, shining out through windows and doorways scattered all across the imposing structure's surfaces.

Oshiga led her to a large portal made from a matching pair of shells. It fanned open like the angel's own wings and covered the entrance. The twin valves parted before the archon, and

Eirwyn followed him into a long hallway beyond. The shells sealed themselves shut once they had passed them, leaving both standing in a corridor filled with air rather than water.

Eirwyn was perfectly dry.

"What a fascinating journey," she said with a smile. "It's not every day you get the opportunity to fly through the water."

"As I said," Oshiga replied, "Erathaol welcomes you and wished to make the way easy. Come." He led his charge deeper into the castle.

Eirwyn followed her guide through numerous hallways, passages, and rooms, marveling at the decoration. Every surface not covered in bookcases featured smooth white stone, perhaps marble, covered with finely etched imagery, often visual tales that stretched for many paces with one scene flowing seamlessly into the next. Sculptures of dainty coral, delicate gold and silver filigree, or highly polished wood, bone, and stone separated the graphic stories, while rich tapestries divided large chambers into smaller, more cozy sections. Luxurious divans, end tables, and throw rugs completed the furnishings, while the entire place glowed with the warmth of faint but soothing amber light that seemed to come from nowhere and everywhere all at once.

Eirwyn hardly noticed the grand extravagance of the place, though. The sheer volume of written works completely captivated her.

She stopped in one great oval room through which they walked, staring awestruck at row upon row of tomes, scrolls, and tablets. They sat upon great bookcases that stretched from floor to ceiling and covered every wall, with more standing free in rows through the middle of the chamber.

"So many," the angel breathed, gawking. "Never have I seen so many."

"And they shall be yours to peruse as you desire," Oshiga said, taking Eirwyn's hand and gently pulling her along. "But first, you must meet with the Seer. He has much to discuss with you."

A shiver of delight went down the angel's spine as she turned to follow the archon toward another set of double doors. Even as an immortal, she thought, I could never finish reading all of these.

The two of them passed through the portal and into an inner sanctum. Eirwyn followed Oshiga past more stacks of books and toward what she could only think of as a very sumptuous den. Several divans framed an open area with a large table in the middle. Smaller tables with faint glowing orbs set like lamps rested between the couches, providing rich, comfortable reading light. An assortment of books, many open, lay scattered across the central table. Others teetered in rickety stacks, ribboned bookmarks spilling free of the pages.

A figure stood with its back to the two visitors, bent over, studying something Eirwyn could not make out. She could tell that her host stood considerably taller than either her or her guide. Lustrous golden hair cascaded down the figure's back, draped upon rich blue robes adorned with finely wrought silver thread and hundreds upon hundreds of pearls. A pair of white feathery wings sprouted from the middle of the figure's back, folded tightly against the robes.

At the sound of Eirwyn and Oshiga's approaching footsteps, the figure straightened, turned, and faced them. The wise and serene face that regarded them was human, faintly male in attributes, and pearly white.

He smiled warmly and gestured for Eirwyn to come closer. "Welcome, deva," he said, and his voice resonated throughout the chamber like the deep echoes of a whalehorn. "I am so pleased you decided to visit me."

Eirwyn blushed despite her years. She curtsied once and smiled back. "Thank you for inviting me, my lord Seer," she said, "and for sparing me the fate of loneliness and inactivity that had been thrust upon me."

"Please," the figure across from her said, "address me as Erathaol. And it is I who must thank you, Eirwyn, for choosing to accept my hospitality."

Eirwyn nodded again, but she frowned. "I am grateful, but I am puzzled too. I cannot fathom why you would possibly need my services. Your powers of divination are vast compared to my own."

The archon pursed his lips and nodded. "Indeed, my insight is great. But even one such as I cannot foretell every possible bit of the future. There are things that remain hidden from me, or that are simply beyond my scope to research and discover. Time is my enemy in many ways, Eirwyn."

She nodded.

"However, I did not ask you here because I need your help, strictly speaking."

Eirwyn cocked her head to one side. "Oh?" She cast a sideways glance at Oshiga. "Your messenger claimed otherwise."

The trumpet archon looked confused and a bit uncomfortable.

Erathaol smiled. "Yes," he said. "Because I did not choose to reveal my true intentions to him. I hope the deception does not sour your enthusiasm for your visit."

Eirwyn raised her eyebrows. "That depends on the real

reason you asked me here." She felt uncomfortable speaking to a paragon archon in such a manner, but at the same time, she did not care for being deceived.

"Truthfully, I cannot explain it all to you," the Seer admitted. "For I do not know all, myself. I only understand that you have locked within you a great secret, a glimpse into the future that must be revealed, lest dire happenings come to pass."

"Inside me?"

"Indeed," Erathaol said. "Something you yourself cannot yet see. Something quite dark and dangerous."

Eirwyn's thoughts turned to her dreams, forgotten each morning when she awoke.

"Yes," the Seer said, "you struggle against remembering. We must find a way to calm you, to allow them to come to the surface. I believe you will recall them during your stay here."

Eirwyn was suddenly terrified.

CHAPTER FOUR

Satisfied that the abomination of Micus and Myshik could not escape the cage Aliisza had formed, Kaanyr turned his attention back to their surroundings. He eyed the edge of the gaping hole where the astral kraken had tried to make a meal of him and noted that the edges remained rough, irregular, just as the beast had left them.

"The bubble no longer seems to be shrinking," he said. When Aliisza did not answer, he turned to find her kneeling over the prone form of Kael. The sight made him grimace. Would she be that concerned over *my* injuries, he wondered, or has Tauran filled her head with too many foolish thoughts of nobility?

Despite his anger, the image of her worrying over him pleased Kaanyr. There was a time, not so long ago . . .

Memories of the sultry alu, teasing him as she nursed him back to health after some battle or another, filled Kaanyr's mind. She had always managed to find creative ways to keep him in bed, he recalled with a chuckle.

But now perhaps *she's* the one who needs healing, he

thought. Despite her assurances that she was fine, Kaanyr could see her pain, had seen the bizarre blue glow that had radiated from her. He knew her too well to believe her dismissal.

She's not telling me everything. I'm not sure she knows what's going on herself. Just one more outlandish thing to add to the list. Either the multiverse is going mad, or I am.

"He's dying," Aliisza said, her voice cracking. "We must do something."

"Do?" he asked. "Neither of us is a healer. That wound . . . Don't take the sword out." He regretted his words immediately. If only I could get her to do something foolish, he thought.

His hatred of Kael seethed to the surface again, and Kaanyr imagined killing the fallen knight of Torm. He struggled against the compulsion placed upon him by Tauran, but the angel's magic stayed his hand.

"Zasian can heal him," Aliisza said. "Find him."

Zasian! Kaanyr had almost forgotten about the priest, with the commotion of the huge astral kraken and then Micus's strange appearance.

An outlet for Kaanyr's anger had presented itself.

"Oh, I'll find him," the cambion snarled and reached for his sword. "I'll gut him!"

"Wait!"

Kaanyr ignored her and stalked off, hunting for the man who had become his mission, his sworn enemy. It wouldn't be hard to find the priest; the gleam emanating from his body was still the only source of light in the ruined chamber, other than the odd silvery illumination from beyond the rotunda's walls.

Aliisza reached Kaanyr's side, grabbed his arm, and tried to slow him down. "You cannot do this! It isn't him anymore!"

Kaanyr jerked free of her grasp. "Your mind is addled, fool girl," he said. "Between the bilge you spew about gods slaying one another and all the time you spent suffering from the angels' tender mercies, I'm not surprised Zasian has you so befuddled. But I still see him for what he is—the last barrier between me and freedom."

They found the priest. He knelt on the stone floor on one side of the chamber, hunched over the unmoving form of another figure. It took Kaanyr only a glance to discern that the unconscious one was the green-skinned planetar that had given Kael and him such fits outside, in the corridor.

Before everything went to pieces, he thought. Before Aliisza fouled it all up by bringing Micus here.

Zasian saw Kaanyr approach. He flinched as the cambion raised his sword, ready to do the man in. "Wait!" he pleaded. "I didn't do anything! He's still alive!"

"The Hells you didn't!" Kaanyr shouted. "You damnable priest, you double-crossed me so many different ways, it makes me dizzy to think on them. Now you will pay for it!"

Kaanyr drew back his arm, preparing to deliver the death strike.

Aliisza grabbed Kaanyr's arm and held it. "Don't," she said, her voice low and angry.

"If he dies, the bubble will pop," Zasian said, cowering. "I'm doing my best. Please don't kill me!"

Kaanyr wanted to yank his arm free, wanted so desperately to vent his frustration and anger upon the pathetic, cowering priest who had been the source of so much trouble. But something made him hold.

"He's right," Aliisza said. "He's the only thing keeping us all alive at the moment. *All* of us. Harm him, and you put Kael and Tauran in jeopardy. If you can't believe that he's lost his memories, than at least accept that."

Kaanyr could see the glimmer of smugness in her eyes. He understood what she was trying to do, and he tried to block it out, but the thought was already there. Her words took hold of him, stayed his hand against destroying the priest. If what Zasian said was even remotely possible—if the priest's efforts at keeping the planetar alive were the only thing between everyone within the remains of the rotunda and oblivion—then dispatching the priest meant putting Tauran and Kael at risk. Tauran's magic denied him once more.

The cambion narrowed his eyes in fury at Aliisza's treachery. He wanted to smack the alu and drive her from him, but he merely yanked his arm down in disgust. "You're just not content unless I'm squirming in misery, are you?" he said, turning away. "What a fine mess you made of this. Just when Tauran, Kael, and I were on the verge of finally defeating this wretch, you burst in with Micus to muck it all up. And now, when I can finish this once and for all and be rid of angels and half-drow and priests of Cyric forever, you weave me into a snare impossible to untangle! I'm beginning to think you loathe me, wench."

"It's the only way to get through to you, you bull-headed idiot!" Aliisza retorted. "You're so damned eager to let blood, you never think. I'm beginning to wonder why I try so hard."

Kaanyr's eyes bulged. "Try? Is that what you call it? So far, everything you've *tried* has caused me untold trouble. And if I so annoy you, just leave! Quit making my life so complicated and just go!"

Aliisza stared at the cambion with a mixture of fury and sorrow and said nothing for several moments. She pursed her lips and glared at him. He thought she was on the verge of crying.

Wonderful, he thought. She's going to become a weeping mess again. "What?" he asked, his voice softer. "What are you trying to prove?"

The alu drew in a long breath and took hold of both of Kaanyr's arms. "First," she said, trying to keep her voice steady, "I never meant to betray you. You must understand that."

"Then why in all the Hells did you bring Micus?"

"Because a battle here was just what Zasian wanted. He needed the distraction so that Kashada could steal Azuth's staff. That's the vision I saw in the Eye of Savras."

Her voice sounded so earnest, Kaanyr wanted to believe her. He suddenly felt guilty. "Why didn't you come back sooner?" he asked. "Tauran wouldn't wait, and I—"

"I don't know. Just know that I hurried to you as fast as I could to try to stop you." She looked down, then, sounding defeated. "I wasn't fast enough."

Kaanyr began to understand. "But you believed it strongly enough to work with Micus to stop us?" he asked. "You were willing to surrender to our enemies just to keep us from realizing your vision?"

Aliisza nodded. "Yes," she said. "I didn't want to, but it was the only way to reach you in time, to stop you. I have hated myself for it every moment since then." She gave a forlorn laugh. "And despite my betrayal, it all happened anyway." She turned and gestured at their surroundings. "Everything is destroyed. We're lost, adrift who-knows-where. And he"—she pointed at Zasian—"has the only means of keeping us alive right now."

The sight of the man still boiled Kaanyr's blood, but he saw the wisdom in his consort's words.

"So save your vengeance for when the rest of us are safely somewhere else," Aliisza said.

Kaanyr sighed. "So be it," he said, making up his mind to see the whole thing through. "If what you say is true, then all we need to do is get Tauran awake and on his feet. Once he is recovered, we *resolve* this." He glared at Zasian. "I don't trust you. Whatever games you play, I will be watching you." He turned and strode away, slamming his blade back in its sheath.

❖ ❖ ❖ ❖ ❖ ❖ ❖ ❖

Garin surveyed the woods from his perch upon a branch high above the forest floor. He listened for the sound of upheaval, but for the moment, all was quiet.

He grew tense with expectation.

Smoke wafted through the trees below him, thick black stuff that stung the angel's eyes and made it difficult to see more than a few paces. Much of it came from the remains of the trees that had already burned, guttering embers that lay strewn all along the coarse, loamy ground. Some, however, spewed from the odd chasms and fumaroles that kept splitting the earth.

Below Garin, several hound archons waited, watching. They sniffed and coughed occasionally, but they were dedicated to their duties and would not leave their posts. One turned in his direction and gave an all-clear signal. The angel acknowledged the gesture then swung his gaze out across the treetops in search of other devas. He spied a few, watching as he did from the crowns of their own trees. Their expressions were every bit as wary and dire as his.

This cannot go on much longer, Garin thought. Tyr must regain some control over the region soon.

A howl came from nearby, a haunting sound nothing like the call of one of his faithful archon servants. Garin whipped his head and stared through the smoke, trying to spot the source. Below him, the hound archons stirred, raising their weapons.

Something came crashing through the trees, stampeding along the forest floor. Garin could feel it vibrating all the way up to where he sat.

"Get ready," he called down. "Hold the line."

The archons directly below him shifted, setting themselves.

The trees on the periphery of Garin's vision shook and thrashed in a course directly toward him. As the thing drew nearer, he got a better look at it.

What he spied made him catch his breath.

A huge bear made of plants and vines burst through the foliage and charged the hound archons. It was not the largest specimen Garin had ever seen—not nearly as massive as the one he and Micus had found slain near that spot when they had been pursuing Tauran and the half-fiends—but the grotesque way the backlash of magic had warped the creature made the angel cringe.

Madness, Garin thought. Magic has fallen into madness, and it's taking the whole plane with it.

The angel spied several eladrin caught up in the growth

that formed the creature's body. They appeared as a jumbled mess, with arms, legs, and heads poking out at random directions. They weren't merely entangled with the creature. They had somehow been fused with it. Garin could see vines piercing the chests, thighs, and even mouths of the hapless eladrin. When he did spy a face, the expression of horror and misery made his heart weep for them.

The nearest hound archons exchanged nervous glances as the warped beast rushed closer. One or two took a step backward.

"Steady," Garin commanded. "It's almost caught."

When the creature got within ten paces of the closest of the hound warriors, the trap sprang.

Concealed netting ripped up off the floor of the forest. It engulfed the creature, wrapping it and confining it. The net closed tight, hoisting the beast up off the forest floor and sending it swinging lazily back and forth between the stout trees.

Garin sighed as the beast howled and thrashed. *Thank Tyr it's just a small one,* the angel thought.

He leaped from his perch and glided on feathered wings to the ground, near the front ranks of the archons. He offered a few of them praise and encouragement for their service. As the other angels landed near him, he began issuing commands. "See what we can do to aid those trapped within it," he said. "And we must try to spare the beast too, if possible."

The other angels and their archon assistants nodded and began their work. The process of separating creatures from the bizarre fusing they had experienced required both physical and spiritual efforts. The celestial creatures would be at it for quite some time.

A lantern archon appeared a pace away from Garin and

hovered there. "My pardon, holy one," it said, "but your attention is needed—"

The glowing ball's last words vanished in a roaring blast as wild magical energy surged through the forest all around them. Garin launched himself skyward as the ground tore apart. Curtains of color slashed across huge swaths of ground, shredding soil, tree, and creature alike.

Not again, Garin thought as he maneuvered to escape the deadly fields of raw arcane force. Please, Tyr, stop this madness!

Below Garin, several archons screamed and went silent. The rest managed to teleport themselves out of harm's way. The rippling, shimmering walls of magic churned across the landscape, tearing apart the forest like some terrible multi-hued tornado. Garin sped away from what he thought of as the "edge," where the astral shock waves slamming into the plane steadily consumed, bit by bit, the reality of the House of the Triad.

Just as abruptly as the outburst began, it stopped. In its wake, acres of the world had been obliterated. Where forest once vanished into the haze of distance, it simply ended. A roiling, rumbling barrier of silvery-blue clouds shot through with crackling deeper blue lightning marked the border between the House and . . . whatever lay beyond.

By Garin's estimation, the forest ceased to exist nearly half a mile from where the portal to the World Tree once stood. The waves of energy had chewed up that much of the land. He hated to think of what the other side of the gate was like.

If this keeps up, there won't be anything left of the House, Garin thought. Surely Tyr must know this!

A small voice in the back of the angel's mind began to

question whether Tyr was, in fact, capable of stopping the horrific waves of destruction crashing against the plane. Garin chastised that voice and silenced it. Tyr knows what he is doing, even if you don't.

Garin turned his attention back to the aftermath before him.

Hound archons and other devas moved through the woods, seeking some sign of others in need of help. Based on the initial reports, they had lost several of their number—four or five hound warriors and two devas—as well as the corrupted bear.

"Garin," a voice called from behind him.

He looked up and back and spotted the lantern archon. "Yes?"

"As I was reporting before, your attention is needed farther south, along the Springflow Trail. It appears to be even more urgent now, after . . . that upheaval."

"I'll get there promptly."

A cry of agony rose up from the distance. The lantern archon vanished. Garin turned and sped in the direction of the forlorn sound.

A hound archon had been caught in the whirlwind of magic. The tumult had melded him with a tree. His face, arms, and feet protruded from the warped, twisted trunk. The creature was still alive, but Garin was uncertain for how much longer. The tree had become animate and was expanding, threatening to engulf the archon, to absorb him.

Angels and hound warriors worked feverishly to halt the growth of the tree and save their companion.

"Take over here," Garin ordered one of the devas. "I'm needed elsewhere."

The other angel turned his attention to the desperate rescue.

"And be careful," Garin added as he went aloft. "If another of those arcane maelstroms erupts, get everyone out of here."

The other angel nodded and returned to the task at hand.

Garin soared above the treetops, opting for a higher view of the terrain as he sped toward his new problem. To his right, the great wall of roiling Other continued to churn.

Garin spied another maelstrom nearby. He increased his speed, angling to get near the storm without getting so close that he was in danger of being affected by it. The veils of color and light sliced through the forest like a barrage of whirling blades. Everywhere they touched, reality changed.

We're losing this fight, Garin realized. We cannot slow it down.

Shoring up his resolve, he dived toward the place the lantern archon had indicated. He could already see another crew of devas and archons scattering before the churning, obliterating maelstrom. Garin sought out the commander.

The fleeing angel heard Garin's shout and changed his course. They met in midair, well back from the surging power of the wild magic. "It's too much," the other angel said, panting. "That's the fourth one just since I sent word to you. We can't do any good here."

Garin gave the other angel a stern look. "We have our responsibilities," he said, chastising the deva. "You will hold your position and work to cure the damage done until you receive new orders. Is that clear?"

The other angel glared back. "You would sacrifice us all to this madness just because that was the instruction handed down to us? You're as foolish as Tyr himself."

Garin, dumbfounded at his counterpart's insurrection, could only gape.

"Perhaps Torm has a more level head on his shoulders and can think of better ways to use those loyal to him. If you wish to die needlessly, then you and your rigid commands are more than welcome to do so. I leave you to it." With that, the deva turned and flew away.

Garin watched the traitorous angel depart, sadness filling his heart. *Please act soon, Tyr. Your followers begin to abandon you. Hope is dwindling.*

Below him, another eruption of magic roared. He looked down to see the very land turn inside out, blossoming like some bizarre, nightmarish flower. When the upheaval abated, a strange seedlike object twenty paces across bobbed in the ground as though it sat upon the surface of water.

Several archons approached the peculiar object cautiously. As they drew near, it shimmered and shook, then began to crack along the top.

"Get back!" Garin screamed. "Stay away!"

He soared closer, yelling at the remaining celestials to stand clear. He had no idea what it might be, but he would not sacrifice more of his followers until it was necessary.

The seed-thing split in two, each half flopping to the side. A horde of vile creatures from some nether plane spilled out, accompanied by a gagging stench. Their pasty bodies oozed pus and drool dripped from their slavering fangs. They gibbered in delight, chattering to one another in some fell tongue Garin did not understand. They raised wicked weapons—dark, serrated blades and barbed, blood-soaked hooked polearms—and screamed a challenge.

Demons, Garin realized, stunned and sickened. Demons in paradise. It cannot be.

With cries of glee the wretched things swarmed outward from their broken cocoon and raced toward the celestial denizens.

❖ ❖ ❖ ❖ ❖ ❖ ❖ ❖

Eirwyn stared at the game board before her, frowning. She could see several possible moves that might create an advantage for her position, but none of them felt right. She could gain no insight into her path.

No, that's not quite right, she admitted. I can't focus.

"You seem restless," Oshiga commented, sitting across from Eirwyn. "Have I backed you into a corner?"

Eirwyn smirked. "Not yet, but I can't seem to concentrate. I'm not certain this is working."

Oshiga nodded. "Perhaps we should rest."

Eirwyn shook her head. "That's not it. I know Erathaol wants me to relax and get back in the habit of divining in small ways, but this doesn't feel right."

"How so?"

Eirwyn frowned and shrugged. "I shouldn't be here," she said finally. "All this"—she gestured around herself at the sumptuous chambers that had been prepared for her stay—"is too . . ."

Oshiga gave her a puzzled look. "I do not understand. The rooms are not to your liking? How can we make you more comfortable?"

Eirwyn sighed. "No, the accommodations are wonderful. That's the problem. They are too nice."

Oshiga looked more confused.

"Something terrible is coming," Eirwyn said. "Something I need to be a part of. I shouldn't be here, enjoying such luxuries, when trouble is brewing."

"Erathaol believes that you cannot find yourself until you release this anxiety. You will not know your role until you stop fighting it."

"I know," she said. "It's quite a conundrum. The more I remove myself from the threat—the more I escape my troubles and cares in order to make peace with my unconscious and unearth this mystery—the more confused I become."

"I will speak to Erathaol about this at once," Oshiga said, rising. "Perhaps he can offer you some sense of how better to proceed."

"No, do not trouble the Seer with this," Eirwyn said. "I will muddle through it somehow." She stretched and rose. "But let us leave off from playing board games for a while. I must seek some other ways to relax."

Oshiga bowed. "As you wish." He turned to go. "If you have any need, I am at your disposal."

"I know," Eirwyn answered, and she smiled in appreciation. "You are most kind, generous, and patient with me."

Oshiga bowed again and departed, leaving the angel to her thoughts.

Eirwyn peered around the chambers once more, trying to decide what she wanted to do. Fly away, she thought. Return to the surface. Find something meaningful to do. Help.

She threw her arms up in frustration and decided to swim. She moved to the pool. As she entered the water, Eirwyn thought of Tauran. She remembered how he rarely chose to swim in the Lifespring merely for pleasure. She could see him, in her mind's eye, diving from high above the enchanted waters, honing his skills, practicing.

He never let up, the angel recalled. He was always preparing for the next development. That's what I should be doing.

Much later, Eirwyn awoke in darkness, panicked. She fumbled to rise, could not, and finally realized she had become entangled in the covers. She was drenched in sweat, and her heart pounded.

Another nightmare, she thought. About what?

She sat in the darkness of her chambers and concentrated, trying to remember anything at all.

Images flashed through her mind. Pictures of danger, of dark creatures. Of prisoners. There!

Eirwyn focused on one particular image, a place that seemed somehow familiar, yet not a place she recognized. I must go there, she understood. But what—and more importantly, where—is it?

She rose from her bed and dressed. I must do some research, she thought. Somewhere in this massive library is the answer I seek. I need Oshiga.

Eirwyn left her chambers and went in search of the trumpet archon.

CHAPTER FIVE

Aliisza watched Kaanyr pace from one side of the rotunda to the other. She could see the cambion's mood grow fouler with each lap. Beyond him, barely visible in the dim light, her arcane cage still stood, holding the creature that had once been Micus and Myshik. The aberration had finally ceased his attempts to batter his way out. He sat near the back of his enclosure, watching Kaanyr.

Aliisza rested against one of the columns between Tauran and Kael, with the planetar nearby. Zasian stood over all three of the wounded companions, watching over them.

Aliisza and Kaanyr had decided to move the three unconscious forms into the center of the chamber, where the priest could tend to them more easily. Kael bucked and groaned when they removed Aliisza's sword protruding from his gut, but he did not otherwise awaken, and Zasian managed to close the wound with his unusual healing power. The half-drow seemed stable, but Aliisza refused to leave his side until she was certain he wasn't going to succumb to his injuries.

From time to time, the priest would place a hand upon

one or another chest, close his eyes, and murmur something Aliisza couldn't quite make out. He had been at his vigil for quite some time, and Aliisza marveled at how he kept it up. Her own body ached with fatigue.

"Is he ever going to waken?" Kaanyr asked, standing in the middle of the chamber and staring at Zasian.

The man cringed and shook his head. "I don't know," he answered. "I'm trying. This one"—he pointed at the planetar—"is badly hurt and I can't seem to heal him. But those other two are much better. They should be awake by now, but for some reason, they just aren't. I don't understand."

Kaanyr's sigh echoed through the room. "This is ridiculous! We're getting nowhere!"

When Aliisza didn't answer him, he returned to pacing. Aliisza glanced over at Zasian. He was watching Kaanyr with a mixture of fear and curiosity, his eyes wide. The strange childlike innocence that the priest exhibited continued to intrigue Aliisza. Beyond her distrust of the man, the youthful attitude belied the maturity of his face. If it was a hoax, he was carrying it off perfectly.

"I just wish I could remember," Zasian said as he returned to monitoring Kael. "I must have done something very bad to make him so angry at me."

Aliisza just watched the man next to her. Finally, when he looked up, she said, "Be glad that you can't."

She turned her attention back to Kaanyr. He returned her stare, but his mind seemed far away. Aliisza rose to her feet and crossed the floor.

"Hey," she said, taking Kaanyr's hand in her own. The preternatural warmth of his skin felt good. She had forgotten how much she used to seek out his touch. "What is it?"

Kaanyr shook his head. "It seems like we've been out here for days. Who knows? Maybe we have."

"And?" she prompted, pulling the cambion around to face her squarely. "What of it? We already agreed that waiting for Tauran to wake up was the best choice. Perhaps Tyr will have seen fit to grant his blessings to Tauran once more. But even if he hasn't, we won't be any worse off. Just be patient."

"I'm just so tired of feeling . . . helpless."

Welcome to my world, Aliisza thought, but she resisted the urge to snort in derision. Standing close to him, sharing that moment, felt familiar and comfortable, and she didn't want to lose it. Instead, she just watched him. Her mind flashed through a series of memories, of a happier time for the two of them, back in Amarindar, when they were master and mistress of their world. A lifetime ago, Aliisza mused. Several lifetimes, perhaps.

When she turned her attention back to Kaanyr, she was surprised to find him smiling at her. She could tell by the twinkle in his eye that he was thinking lascivious thoughts.

Aliisza returned the grin, though she felt slightly embarrassed. Must have been thinking the same things I was, she thought. "What?" she asked him.

"I was just remembering when you used to come find me in the throne room," Kaanyr said. "How you used to sit on my lap and squirm, trying to distract me, and I'd pretend not to notice just to aggravate you."

Aliisza chuckled and punched Kaanyr gently in the arm. "Infuriate me, is more like it," she said. "I should have known." She rolled her eyes playfully, then stepped into his embrace and snuggled there. "Mmm," she purred.

"Let's go," Kaanyr said abruptly, that old mischievous

tone in his voice. "Just you and me, right now. Let's just take off into that silver void and find our old lives again. What do you say?"

Aliisza felt her smile turn sad as she pulled back to look him in the eye again. "You know I can't do that," she said, "and neither can you."

Kaanyr nodded and said, "I know, but would you if we could? Is there still enough of the old you in there somewhere that you could see yourself slipping away with me, starting over again, without . . . without all this?" He gestured around the two of them. "We didn't have such a bad life together, did we?"

You're just figuring this out now? Aliisza fumed. Only now, after using me as your personal skeleton key? She looked away and fought her frustrations at her lover's misguided ambitions. Instead of answering his question, she asked, "Where would we go? How would we escape this?"

Kaanyr shrugged, and a look of consternation crossed his own face. "I don't know," he said. "Does it matter? I just thought—"

"I'm sorry," Aliisza said, realizing she was spoiling the moment. "Yes, of course I would go with you. If none of this was happening, if there weren't other lives dependent on us for survival, and we could just slip away, steal back our place in the world, I would go with you." Maybe.

Kaanyr's smile returned. "I miss us," he said. "I really do."

That time, Aliisza couldn't help herself. "Then why in the Nine Hells would you do what you did to me?" she asked, her voice plaintive. "Why would you put me through all this? I never crossed you. I deserved better." She looked down, biting her lip.

Kaanyr laughed, then, a deep, long chuckle that made him shake. Aliisza glared at him, but she knew why he was laughing. That didn't make her any less angry about it.

When he finally caught his breath, he said, "You may never have crossed me, but you were hardly loyal, wench. You plotted your own course all the time, my instructions be damned." He saw her fury and softened his tone. "But that's exactly why I loved you so much," he said, taking her face in his hands. "That's what always drew me back to you, time and again. You may have kept your own counsel more than I would have liked, but you always had spirit."

Aliisza tried to cling to her anger, but his praise made her blush, and she couldn't help but smile. "You always knew how to flatter a girl," she said. "You know, maybe, after all this"—she gestured around the ruined chamber—"is over and we get away from everything, we can—"

A thump in the floor interrupted Aliisza. Kaanyr felt it too.

"What was that?" he asked, spinning in place.

"Let's find out," Aliisza said and walked to the opening in the wall.

As she strode to the hole and peered out, another thud, stronger than before, reverberated through the rotunda. It came from overhead, and it dislodged a chunk of stone from the fractured ceiling that landed very near Tauran's head before bouncing away.

"What is that?" Kaanyr demanded, moving beside her.

The other bubbles that had been drifting along beside their refuge had gathered together. They all jostled one another as they bobbed and flowed in the wake of the massive bubble with the mysterious figure inside. To Aliisza, it felt as though the current they followed had picked up speed, and the wash streaming behind the massive form had grown more turbulent. She had nothing by which to judge it, of course. No landmarks drifted by to give her any sense of speed or scale. It was just a gut instinct.

"I think we're getting close to something," Aliisza murmured, trying to stare in the direction she thought they were traveling. The effort was made more tricky due to their constant rotation in the void—it hurt her head too much to try to imagine the rotunda doing the spinning. "It feels like we're about to go down a drain or something."

"Wonderful," Kaanyr grumbled.

He turned and cast a withering glance at Zasian. "Is the bubble going to hold?"

Zasian shrugged. "He's dying. I can't stop it, only slow it down."

"How much time do we have?"

The priest shrugged again. "I don't know."

Aliisza could sense that he was afraid of saying the wrong thing. "Leave him be," she admonished when Kaanyr started to stomp toward Zasian. "We've got enough to worry about without you putting him in a panic again."

Kaanyr stopped, but he continued to glare at the priest. "He's lying. I know it. I just can't figure out what he's up to."

Aliisza sighed. She had long since given up trying to figure out the veracity of Zasian's behavior. If it was a trick, nothing they had said or done yet had caused him to slip up.

She turned back to the view beyond their little shelter. They had stopped spinning, and everything beyond her jagged little window remained in view. When she spotted something dark on what might have been a horizon, she blinked in a double take.

Could it be?

She waited and watched, not trusting her own vision enough to call Kaanyr over. After a few more moments, though, she was certain.

"Kaanyr," she said. When he joined her, she pointed. "What is that?"

Kaanyr stared at the darkening line for several long moments before he spoke. "It looks like land," he said. "And we're drifting right toward it."

❖ ❖ ❖ ❖ ❖ ❖ ❖

"This doesn't make any sense!" Eirwyn shouted, slamming the book down upon the table. Her voice echoed through the great chamber and came back to mock her. "In my mind, I can see this place as clearly as the Court, and it's not to be found anywhere in these books. Why not?" She closed her eyes and pressed her hands to her lids, rubbing them.

Beside her, Oshiga shifted. "Perhaps we are simply not meant to find this information," he said. "Not all divinations are meant to be."

Eirwyn lowered her hands and glared at the celestial being. "You're not helping," she said crossly. "I know this is part of the dream I've been having. Even though I can't recall anything else about it, I know it has something to do with this place. Maybe we're just not hunting for it the right way. Are you sure you know what you're doing?"

Oshiga drew himself up and said haughtily, "Quite certain. But let's start again, from the beginning. Describe the place you see in the most exacting detail as you can muster. Leave no feature out."

Eirwyn sighed and calmed herself. Yelling at him isn't helping either, she told herself. "Very well," she said. "Up close, it appears to be a crystalline fortress, roughly formed. It sits dark and brooding upon a plateau. Although it is night, a green glow fills the sky. It's very eerie. The glow comes from what I can only describe as a snowstorm composed of jagged green shards or flakes. The place feels very sinister and . . . alive. It's hard to explain any better than that."

"Go on," Oshiga said, furiously scribing into a blank book that rested before him. "Tell me more."

"From a greater distance, the plateau is actually a floating island, much like many of the places here in the House. But this feels dark and sinister. It also feels abandoned, or . . . incomplete."

"Which is it?" Oshiga pressed. "Abandoned or incomplete?"

Eirwyn sighed. "I'm not sure. I can't tell. It's just not clear enough. But I know it has something to do with my lost vision!"

Oshiga held up his hand to forestall another outburst and continued to write. Finally, when he was finished, he set down the quill he had been using, held his hands over the page, and began to chant.

Eirwyn watched the archon, careful to remain quiet to avoid disturbing him. He had used that method three times already to attempt to discern where in Erathaol's great library they should research her mysterious fortress, but every time, they had hit a dead end.

Oshiga finished his chant and turned the page. A listing

of texts and their locations within the library appeared on the page. The archon scanned them for a moment, frowning.

"We have three new sources to examine, plus five more that appeared previously. I'll retrieve the new ones." He rose from his seat. "You should begin again on the sources we already have."

Eirwyn tried not to sigh. I'm doing that too much of late, she decided. She nodded and pulled the magic book toward her, selecting the first resource from the list and flipping through it.

❖ ❖ ❖ ❖ ❖ ❖ ❖ ❖

"I think he's very near death," Zasian said from behind Aliisza.

Aliisza had been watching as the landform had steadily grown larger. The priest's words sent a chill down her spine, and she turned away from the gap in the wall. She saw Zasian kneeling over the planetar, with his ear pressed to the celestial creature's mouth.

"He's barely breathing," Zasian said. "I don't know how much longer. Not long."

From across the room, Kaanyr rose from the spot where he had been brooding by himself. His brief moment of affection with Aliisza had not held his bad mood in check for long, and she had left him alone. Kaanyr moved toward Zasian and his three patients and stared down. He was not frowning quite as much as he had been before.

Aliisza knew what he was thinking. If the planetar dies, the bubble pops. One way or another, we're forced to act. She grimaced at her consort's impatience.

The alu turned away and checked the confines of the bubble. It was definitely shrinking, she saw, and she took a step back from it where it formed a "window" in the broken wall that allowed her to see into the Astral beyond.

Can we breach it and survive? she wondered. Even if we can, how do we travel?

Aliisza wracked her brain for memories of tales of great sorcerers and demons traveling the plane. She had heard the stories, but rarely did they explain much about the magic involved in moving through the silvery void. And she had done no research at all in her years of magical training.

And with magic behaving so erratically, who knows what's even still true anymore?

Another jostling bump made her stumble a step toward the border of their safe haven. She caught herself easily, but the glance she got beyond the confines of the ruined rotunda startled her.

The argent void had vanished, replaced by a shimmering curtain of color that rippled all around them. The strange multi-hued veil blocked the alu's view of anything else. It flashed and shifted, and it reminded Aliisza of the first moments after she had regained consciousness.

A storm of magic, she thought, frightened.

Then the curtain was gone, and they were falling.

The bubble was no more, and the Astral Plane had vanished. In its place, brooding red sky met black water at the horizon. The rotunda, reduced to a collection of unstable stones no longer held together by the planetar's magic, began to crumble apart as it tumbled toward that murky sea.

Zasian shouted in alarm.

Aliisza used her wings to rise up and hover, then she

whirled to see the priest flailing as the floor beneath his feet broke apart. He, along with the three comatose figures he had been tending, became four more bits of debris falling from the sky. Near them, Micus thrashed and howled as his prison careened downward with him still trapped inside.

In a panic, Aliisza shot forward, winging toward all of them, desperate to save them.

Before she had time to contemplate the consequences of her act, she conjured magic. It began as a welling of energy deep in her gut, a swelling of power that blossomed and burst from her. The ominous blue glow accompanied it, swathing her surroundings in azure light. She sought control of the potent energy, shaped it and guided it, all the while bracing herself for the pain she feared would accompany it.

Aliisza created an invisible surface beneath the four tumbling figures. It held them aloft. At the same time, she willed the magical cage surrounding Micus to vanish. The abomination took flight, veering away from the ruined chamber. The remaining stonework of the ruined rotunda plummeted away, reduced to little more than a rockfall.

Pain and sickness filled Aliisza's limbs. Intense cramps wracked her muscles, and she nearly curled into a ball from it, fighting the urge to retch. She panted from the agony. She thought of releasing the arcane energy in order to bring blessed relief. Can't let them fall, she thought, gritting her teeth and fighting the urge.

Micus soared past Aliisza on his mismatched wings. He glared at her, hatred filling his eyes. He still had Myshik's powerful war axe, and he gripped it tightly as he swooped by. Aliisza watched him bank into a wide turn. He was coming around for another pass.

To her left, a tremendous splash threw inky water in a torrent into the air. Some of the cascade drenched Zasian and the others. When the waves subsided, a great mass floated within the darkened sea. Aliisza thought it looked like a huge man, but she couldn't take the time to get a good look at it.

Kaanyr, hovering upon his own innate magic, descended into view near her. "Can you get them to shore?" he asked, pointing.

Aliisza looked to where he indicated and saw a rocky stretch of gray beach not far from where they all hung in the air. Fighting the exertion of maintaining her magic, she nodded. "Just keep Micus away from me," she gasped.

She guided the invisible platform toward the beach. Zasian crouched upon it, hands and feet splayed apart for balance. He looked at her, wide-eyed with fright, then he whipped his head around, staring at everything else. The three prone figures remained sprawled at his feet.

Kaanyr unfurled the magical cloak he had acquired in Dweomerheart and pushed himself forward into flight. He angled his direction to head off Micus, who had climbed to a higher altitude and was starting a dive toward them. Aliisza wanted to watch the impending clash, but the pain racked her body too much. She clenched her eyes shut to fight it and focused all her concentration on getting the rest of them to safety.

Flying behind her conjured conveyance, Aliisza steered the magical surface to a bare spot of beach and set it down as gently as she could. Even with her efforts, though, her control faltered from the pain and sickness she felt, and the arcane platform winked out when the figures upon it still sat a few paces in the air. They all went tumbling to the soft sand in a heap.

Aliisza dropped to the beach nearby and crumpled, retching. Gods and devils, she thought as she emptied her stomach. Must . . . never . . . do that again. She panted for a moment until both the pain and the ominous blue glow subsided. When her stomach ceased heaving, she flipped over onto her back and caught her breath, staring up at the carmine sky.

Blood red clouds roiled across it, churning and obscuring whatever sun lit the place. A hot, foul wind blew over the gray sand, carrying a stench of something decayed with it. A vague sense of distaste, something strange yet oddly familiar, filled Aliisza's senses.

Kaanyr settled to the ground beside her and furled the magical cloak. He knelt down next to her and placed his hand upon her shoulder. "You look awful," he said, his tone gentle. "There's something you are not telling me, Aliisza. What is it?"

Aliisza shook her head. "I'll be fine," she said, surprised at how weak her voice sounded.

Kaanyr's face grew stern. "Don't lie to me," he said. "This strange power of yours is killing you. I want the truth."

She tried to give her consort a defiant stare, but his expression never wavered. "Very well," she said at last, closing her eyes in defeat. "I'll tell you what I can. Just let me rest a bit, first. What happened to Micus?" she asked, changing the subject.

"Gone," Kaanyr replied, "but not for long, I fear."

"Good," Aliisza said, thankful for even a brief chance to rest. "Just give me a moment."

"We may not have a moment," the cambion said.

When Aliisza opened her eyes again and looked up at him, Kaanyr was staring at something in the other direction, down the beach. She stood and peered that way, too.

In the distance, a small band of beings moved toward them. Aliisza squinted and saw the muscle-bound ebony creatures spread broad, leathery wings and take flight. Wicked black horns sprouted from their heads, and they waved vicious weapons overhead as they closed the distance. Whatever they were, they were spoiling for a fight.

The hulking beasts followed a somewhat smaller but no less fearsome leader, also black and winged, although its body shimmered as it flew, the effect of shiny black scales. A tail fluttered behind it.

Aliisza swallowed hard, recognizing the source of the foul ambience of the place at last. "Devils," she murmured. "Not good."

"Hey!" Zasian said from behind Aliisza. "Look!"

She turned, expecting to see that Zasian had spotted the same group of interlopers, but the priest pointed in the opposite direction.

The black waves of the sea had pushed the form of the great human figure Aliisza had seen before up onto the beach. The figure was indeed a man, though larger than any giant Aliisza might have imagined. The top of his head, resting on the gray sand, appeared so gargantuan that she imagined it rising fully three times her own height. A bedraggled, graying beard covered his wizened face, and his once-fine clothes marked him as noble.

Or a god, Aliisza thought, suddenly terrified, for she recognized that face from her vision within the Eye of Savras.

Azuth.

Is he slain too? she wondered. Can such possibly be? What is happening to the universe?

Aliisza turned away. Somehow, looking upon the face of a god, even one that might be dead, hurt. "We need to go," she said, trying to rise. "Now."

"I agree," Kaanyr said, standing beside her and still looking at the gargantuan deity, "but where?"

"Anywhere. Let's just get off the beach."

"How are we going to move the others?" Kaanyr asked. "We'll never outrun those fiends trying to carry them, and there's no way you can muster that magic trick again. You're exhausted as it is."

"I'll just have to," she said.

"No," Kaanyr said, grabbing her shoulder. "Don't."

"What choice do we have?" she demanded. A part of her beamed at his concern.

Kaanyr looked at her helplessly and shrugged.

"Very well, then," Aliisza said. She grimaced as she prepared to conjure the magic once more. She dreaded the pain and suffering. For a moment, she wasn't certain she could muster the willpower to subject herself to it again, but all it took was a glance down at Tauran and Kael's still forms to convince her. She drew a deep breath and braced herself.

A howl from a ridge of rock higher up the beach interrupted her.

A second horde of creatures swarmed into view.

Dozens of muscular, pasty-skinned humanoids took flight on matted feathered wings. Aliisza could see three red eyes blazing on each of their faces, and rows of sharp teeth filled their gaping mouths. Each thick arm ended in a deadly barbed claw that reached and grasped ahead as the creatures swooped toward the oncoming black-skinned fiends.

A crimson-skinned humanoid with a howling, feral-eyed hyena head led the newcomers. A snake protruded from the side of the monster's neck. The creature held a massive axe aloft as it screamed a war cry and commanded its charges to attack. He spoke in a language Aliisza understood all too well.

"Demons," she breathed. "Where in the blazes are we?"

The white-skinned things outnumbered the ebony fiends two to one, and they flew at the other creatures, who appeared just as eager to join the fray. In a matter of moments, the sky above the six castaways swarmed with white and black bodies clashing, screaming as they fought and died.

The crimson demon rushed to attack its own counterpart, the scaly-skinned devil. They slammed into one another with a vicious clang of weapon on weapon and became embroiled in a fierce battle of their own, whirling and slicing at one another as the war between their subordinates raged in the background.

For the moment at least, neither collection of fiends paid any attention to the six castaways sitting on the beach below.

"It's the Blood Rift," Kaanyr murmured, staring at the fight in awe. "How did we end up here?"

"What difference does it make?" Aliisza said, scrambling to her feet. "Once the fight's over, whoever wins is going to turn on us. We must leave!"

As if to punctuate her point, one of the ebony devils darted out of the swarming maelstrom and swooped close to where Zasian and the unconscious bodies of Kael, Tauran, and the planetar lay. The priest shrieked and cowered. The devil pulled up and hovered, staring down at the still form of Tauran. Recognition gleamed in his eyes, and he gave a shout of triumph as he drew his trident back for a killing thrust.

At that moment, two of the white demons swooped in and bowled the devil over. He went tumbling through the air and flopped into the shallow water along the shore several paces away. The two white demons jumped on him and shredded him with their claws. Black blood and chunks of flesh spurted and flew everywhere as they rent the devil. When their prey was nothing but a pulpy mess, the two demons took to the air again and went back into the battle, seeking new opponents.

"Come on!" Aliisza said, conjuring a magical doorway. She hardly noticed that the outline glowed a deep blue instead of the familiar red. It matched the emanation shining from her own body. "Push them through!" She bent down to hoist the planetar up and carry the celestial through her portal. "We have to get out of here!"

Kaanyr shook his head as Aliisza instead staggered, overwhelmed by the gut-wrenching sickness that slammed into her. "It's no use," he said, pointing. "The fight's over."

Aliisza coughed and nearly vomited, but she managed to peer in the direction Kaanyr showed her. The demons were all but finished with the devils. The last few black-skinned creatures were down, overwhelmed by the pasty, hairless fiends. To one side, the crimson hyena-headed thing slammed its axe into the shoulder of its foe, taking the devil's arm off. Another stroke removed its head. When its enemy fell dead, the demon turned and sped straight toward the six stranded observers.

"Then you'd better hope," Aliisza said, crumpling to the ground and gasping for breath, "that they're interested in negotiating."

Kaanyr cocked his head to one side. "That's not a half-bad idea," he said.

The crimson demon settled to the sand in front of Kaanyr. His white-skinned followers gathered around them and formed a circle to prevent anyone from escaping.

Beside Aliisza, Zasian curled up into a tiny ball and cowered.

"You are far from home, lord," the crimson demon said. "And you consort with wretched angels." The demon pointed at Tauran's form. "I shall enjoy flensing you for your treachery."

"Do that, and your own lord will gut you like a pig and roast your innards. I come with important news."

"Come?" the demon asked, looking at Kaanyr warily. "Why here?"

"We are lost, trying to return to the Abyss. Help us, and you shall be rewarded."

"Lies," the crimson thing said, smiling. He looked to his underlings. "Let us feast upon their tender flesh!"

"I have been to the angels' plane," Kaanyr said, backing up a step as the demons closed in. "I have spied on them. They are fools, and I know where they are weakest."

"Kaanyr!" Aliisza growled under her breath. "Don't!"

"Hush, fool alu," Kaanyr whispered back. "I know what I'm doing!"

"Tell me," the demon leader said, "and I will let you live."

"Oh, no," Kaanyr said. "It is for your master's ears only. Kill me, and he will not receive my report, and you will be the one he punishes for it."

The demon cocked his head, considering. The snake growing from his neck writhed and hissed. Finally, the red-skinned beast nodded. "Very well," he said. "We will take you to meet *Her* Eminence. And when *she* has finished torturing you for everything you know, I will teach you not to speak to me in such a manner."

Chapter Six

"With me!" Garin shouted at three archons following him through the forest. "It went that way!" He pointed toward a tangle of underbrush. One of the surviving demons had plunged through a narrow gap in the snarl of brambles and weeds, fleeing the angel and his servitors. Garin could hear the wretched thing crashing through more distant foliage, and the faint smell of its stench still hung in the air.

Garin pushed himself aloft, soaring upon his wings over the barrier of undergrowth. He spotted the demon farther ahead, its pasty pale flesh glowing in the gloaming light. The creature forced its way through a stand of saplings, snapping smaller branches and sending a hail of leaves fluttering to the ground.

The three hound archons with Garin worked in unison, using their innate magical abilities to teleport ahead. They surrounded the demon in the blink of an eye and closed in. Garin tried to glide closer, to aid them in destroying the fiend, but he got his wings caught up in a low-hanging branch and had to drop to the ground to free himself. He turned in place, drew the branch free from his feathered appendage, and released it to snap back up over his head.

A flash of light burst behind Garin, from the direction of the archons and their quarry. It filled the forest with an instant blaze of blue. The flare vanished just as quickly as it had come, replaced by a howling, chill wind. Stinging fragments of ice rode upon that gale, and a roaring storm filled the forest.

Garin brought one wing up to shield his eyes and staggered away from the wind. He sought shelter on the leeward side of a large tree and crouched, pressing his hands to his ears. His heart pounded in his chest. He was certain that he would, at last, succumb to the magic run amok.

After the initial violent burst of sleet, the storm settled to a dull roar. Snow mixed with the ice pellets and coated the ground. The air became more frigid and a deeper darkness settled over the forest. With every passing moment, the certainty of his death seemed to recede, so Garin opened his eyes and peered through the maelstrom. The angel couldn't make out more than the nearest trees, themselves already rime-coated.

Emboldened, the angel rose to his feet and took a few steps in the direction he had last seen the others. He stared hard into the gloom, hunting for the spot where the three hound archons had surrounded the demon. He listened for signs of the creatures. The howl of the wind filled his ears, but he detected nothing else. A few steps brought him to an abrupt end of the world. The ground, the trees . . . everything simply stopped. He stood upon a precipice, and beyond, he saw only storm.

Damn this insanity! How much longer must this go on? How many good soldiers must we lose?

Garin offered up a quick and forlorn prayer to Tyr for the three servants. He beseeched his lord to lend his deific strength to the land, to bring to an end the devastating magic tearing the House apart.

Then Garin turned and trudged back the way he had come.

He found the hike much easier with the wind behind him. He dismissed the notion of flying, and he refused to use magic to shift elsewhere when soldiers under his command might still need his aid. He wasn't sure where he was going, exactly—he could see little beyond a few paces and certainly no distinguishing landmarks—but he knew that those loyal servants of Tyr had been fighting all through the woods, and he trusted that he would come upon them in due time.

From the angel's left, the faint sound of a branch snapping accompanied shadowy movement. Garin spun and barely dodged the thrust of a massive black sword with coarse, fractured edges. The fiend wielding it stumbled forward, over-balanced in the expectation of connecting with its strike. Garin took two quick steps back and swung his heavy mace at the fiend's weapon, knocking it to the side. The wind muffled most of the clang of metal on metal.

The demon, a bulbously fat green thing with slavering fangs and webbed fingers, looked to be more at home in fetid swamps than snow-bound forests. It had a hard time getting traction on the icy ground and slipped down to one knee.

Garin used the advantage to leap high, intent on winging himself behind the fiend and finishing it off. But the storm betrayed him, for he failed to notice some low-hanging branches. The boughs snagged and tangled in his wings right at the apex of his jump. He grunted in pain as his appendages bent back at an awkward angle, and he had to flip halfway backward to avoid spraining the limbs. The maneuver spared him any serious damage, but he didn't clear the demon and instead wound up landing on top of it.

The fiend thrashed beneath Garin and pitched him off to one side. The angel tumbled away, wary of an attack. As he completed a roll, he brought his mace up to swipe away any blade thrusts. The wicked black steel of the creature's ill-formed sword whipped through the air and drove the mace wide. Garin grunted from the exertion of hanging onto the weapon and sprawled backward on his rump.

Before Garin could regain his balance, the demon leaped atop him. It brought its sword down hard, and Garin was forced to brace his mace with both hands to ward off the blow. The fiend used the opportunity to drive its weight onto both weapons, ramming them toward Garin's face.

Garin grunted as he resisted the onslaught. Enough of this, he decided. He opened his mouth to utter a holy word, but the abyssal fiend must have been expecting that, for it vomited a foul-smelling thick sludge right into Garin's face, choking and blinding him.

The angel coughed and shook his head from side to side, trying to fling the vile substance from him, all the while fighting to keep the demon from crushing him.

A low growl emanated from Garin's right, and he felt a powerful concussive force slam against the fiend. The weight of the demon toppled to the left. Canine snarls of rage mingled with reptilian hissing. Garin could feel thuds in the ground beneath him as the fiend wrestled with a new adversary.

Garin rolled away from the fight and dropped his mace. He frantically wiped the sludge from his eyes and spit the disgusting stuff from his mouth. He scooped up handfuls of snow and vigorously scrubbed his face clean of the noxious goop. When Garin could see again, he turned toward the commotion.

A hound archon perched atop the demon, pummeling it with his fists. He went tumbling head over heels as the fiend bucked and pitched him off. The dog warrior landed with a splat into the wet snow and immediately went into a roll. He sprang to his feet and spun to face the demon. He gave a shake, flinging leaves and ice from his fur and spared Garin one quick nod.

Garin grabbed his mace and moved to circle the demon so that he and the archon could get it between them and gain the advantage. He was forced to move wide, however, due to a particularly large tree. As he raced around the thick bole, a deafening roar burst from the other side. Blue flames shot everywhere, engulfing the entire forest and blinding Garin once more.

The angel sank to one knee, shielding his eyes with his forearm and wing. The heat of the fire scorched his skin and melted much of the snow from the storm. A torrent of it splashed him as it cascaded off the tree branches overhead.

Just as quickly as the fire began, it vanished again.

Garin opened his eyes and found that he had been spared the worst of the inferno by the tree. Everything to either side of him was blackened to a crisp. On the far side of the tree, he discovered a large rift in the ground, perhaps ten paces across, still smoking and smelling acrid. The angel moved warily to the edge and peered down, but he could see nothing but darkness.

Of the demon and the archon, there was no sign.

By Tyr, he thought, mourning the loss of yet another celestial. This madness must stop!

Garin took to the air, anger and purpose driving him. He rose above the tree line, where the roaring winds became stronger and buffeted him. The icy storm had passed, and he could see clearly. Clouds that glowed a deep blue filled the entire horizon to the west of him, and flashes of green, red, and yellow lightning crackled through them.

Garin put his back to that terrible field of arcane insanity and began flying home, toward Tyr's Court.

Tyr must do something, he fumed. This destruction, this loss of life, cannot continue.

No, he insisted to himself. Questions, doubts, and anger are the signs of a faith beginning to waver. That is not who I am. I am a good, devoted follower.

But I harbor disloyal feelings. I presume to know what is in Tyr's heart. I presume to wonder why he leads in the direction he does. Down that path lies sorrow, ruin. Micus knew this. Micus was strong. Micus was not afraid to confront those who question Tyr's ultimate wisdom. Would he challenge me if he were here?

He would if he could look into my heart, Garin decided. I am an imperfect being. For the sake of Tyr, I must try to right my course.

By the time the Court was in view, Garin had vowed to redouble his determination. He would *not* stray from the path set before him by those wiser than he. He would serve to the best of his abilities, especially in the most trying of times. He was a dedicated and devout soldier, loyal to Tyr.

The angel's resolve lasted until he reached the outer plaza.

The entire mountain roiled in chaos. Petitioners filled every open surface. Devas and even a few planetars and solars worked hard to keep order, but the uproar consumed everything. As Garin got near enough, he could tell that many of the citizens of the Court argued. In several instances, pushing and shoving broke out.

Blasphemy, he thought. Never has such behavior been contemplated, much less tolerated, within Tyr's domain.

He landed atop one of the higher plazas and had to dodge numerous folk shouting to him to help them before he could slip inside. He hurried down and across an open courtyard toward the Hall of Requisitions. Even before he reached it, though, he could tell the angels there were barely able to maintain order.

The whole House has lost its way, Garin realized. There's too much disruption.

Then another thought slipped unbidden into the angel's thoughts. Tyr is losing control.

Garin wanted to shake those impure notions loose, cast them away from himself, but the unease he felt prevented him from completely ridding himself of them.

Is this what it comes to? Is this how a deity finally succumbs to the ravages of chaos? Is even Tyr bound to the strictures of time and change? Am I witnessing the end?

Garin did not want to think such thoughts, and he staggered momentarily under the weight of his own trepidation. His vision blurred and he found it hard to breathe. The thought came that perhaps Tyr sensed his lack of loyalty and was sending a harsh reminder of the price of faithlessness. He fought his own despair and stood straight again.

Don't think about any of that, he told himself. Just do

your job. The rest will work itself out. Have faith.

The inside of the Hall of Requisitions was in no better shape than the courtyard outside. Though no petitioners milled within, celestials filled the place, all clamoring for assistance. Most of them were devas, like himself. From the snippets of conversation he caught, Garin realized they had been on the outskirts of the House, battling untamable magic too. No one's tactics were effective. They all needed reinforcements and new instructions. They were all trying to fight the good fight, as he had been, and they were all beginning to lose hope.

Garin spied an angel he recognized off to one side. He did not know the deva well, though they had served Micus together on a few occasions. Nilsa was young but competent, if Garin's memory served.

He worked his way through the crowd, trying to reach Nilsa. When he finally got near enough for her to hear him calling above the din, she looked up. Garin motioned for her to join him, then he slipped outside again.

They found a relatively quiet spot atop a wall dividing two sections of the Court that looked out over several lower levels. When they were both seated and comfortable, Garin took a deep breath and spoke.

"I hadn't expected to see things this bad. I've been near Deepbark Hollow—or rather, what's left of it. I came back for reinforcements, but that doesn't look very promising."

Nilsa sighed. "It's the same all over. Everyone is trying their best, but there just aren't enough of us. And the numbers dwindle every moment."

"What?" Garin asked, looking up into the younger angel's face. "Why?"

Nilsa looked carefully at him. "You haven't heard, have you?" she asked. "You *have* been away."

"Tell me," he insisted, fearing the news.

"Many are abandoning Tyr," the other angel said, her voice cracking with emotion. "They are leaving his banner and flocking to other gods. Mostly Torm."

Garin pursed his lips. "I had a subordinate do that today," he said. "I would not have dreamed so many would abandon the Blind One."

"I can't say that I blame them," Nilsa continued, drawing a sharp stare from Garin. "No, wait." She held up her hands to forestall his admonitions. "I do not agree with them, but I do understand. What with Tymora's departure, and the—"

"What?" Garin interrupted, unsure he had heard correctly. He stared at her, shocked. "Tymora has left the realm?"

Nilsa was silent for a long moment. "I do not know everything," she finally said, "but whispers have suggested that, in light of Cyric's manipulations, Tymora cannot be certain of what is real and what is contrived between Tyr and her, and she is departing to spend time in contemplation."

Garin could only shake his head. "Blessed Tyr," he breathed.

"That's not all of it, though," Nilsa said. "The High Council has dissolved."

Garin felt his eyes widen. That cannot be! He opened his mouth to protest, but he could not find the words.

"The membership was too sharply divided on many things, and once the High Councilor quit in protest over some of the other members' actions, everything else crumbled."

"This must not be allowed to continue," Garin said, but he felt weary, without hope. "The law of Tyr must stand supreme.

If Micus taught me nothing else, he taught me that. Tauran was a pale imitation of him, and unworthy of his status. He and those fiends brought much of this upon us."

"If you truly believe that, then I need your help," Nilsa said. "I came here hoping to find a companion or two to aid me in a very important task, but I was on the verge of giving up and going alone when you spotted me."

"What is it?" Garin said, giving the other angel his full attention. "What are you talking about?"

Nilsa studied his face for a moment, perhaps judging his sincerity, then she said, "Come with me."

Intrigued, Garin nodded. "If there is a way to honor what Micus fought for, then I am ready to serve."

Together, they took flight, and Garin followed Nilsa toward another part of the Court.

❖ ❖ ❖ ❖ ❖ ❖ ❖ ❖

Tauran remembered scouring, burning pain.

Zasian would succeed because Tauran had failed.

The priest's schemes would come to fruition because Aliisza had betrayed Tauran.

Cyric would triumph.

All was lost.

No. It must not happen that way, Tauran thought. He flailed helplessly, felt the searing fire consuming him.

No!

Tauran awoke with a start. He heard himself screaming. His voice was raw.

The angel drew a ragged breath and willed himself to relax.

Foulness assaulted him in every conceivable way. He could sense the taint of evil hanging in the hot, fetid air. He felt it in the very stones beneath his body, tasted it on his parched and swollen tongue.

"I am forsaken," he gasped. The words were barely more than a croak.

"Just about," came a reply in a familiar voice.

Tauran turned toward the sound. A dim glow filled the otherwise dark space around him. He lay upon hard ground, uneven rock that poked and dug into his shoulder and thigh. Overhead, the jagged ceiling of a cave hung low, with several stalactites dangling even lower.

Beside him, another figure sat slumped in dejection. The figure looked at him, ebony skin and red eyes framed by silvery hair.

Kael.

"My friend," Tauran tried to say, but the words got lost in a choking cough. He was desperately thirsty.

"Easy," Kael said, scooting toward the angel. "It will take a while for you to recover."

Tauran could tell that the half-drow was bound, shackled at wrists and ankles. He realized his own body was similarly restrained, and that bands of tight, constricting material wrapped around his torso, pinning his wings to his back.

Kael moved until he was right next to the deva, then he helped Tauran rise into a sitting position. "There," he said. "Now you can see our guest chambers a little bit better."

Tauran peered around the cavern and spotted a third figure on the opposite side of the room, cowering. The odd glow that filled the room came from that figure. Long flowing hair and mustaches warned the angel of imminent danger, but the shaking, timid body language was at odds with that assessment.

"Zasian," Tauran said, his voice still hoarse. It stung to speak. His thoughts screamed at him to beware, that the priest of Cyric would immolate him, would bring every last bit of his foul, unholy magic to bear against him. In panic, Tauran tried to roll away, to escape before the searing pain struck him.

"Easy," Kael said, reaching out with his bound hands to take hold of the struggling Tauran. "Where do you think you're going?"

"Zasian!" the angel repeated, trying to wriggle free. "Must stop him!"

"Stop," Kael said, his voice soft. He pressed his hands down, holding Tauran still. "He's no threat to you, my friend. His mind is gone."

Tauran continued to fight his bonds for a moment longer, until the words at last sunk in, and he quieted.

"Here," Kael said, reaching down beside him. "Drink this. It's foul tasting, but it's just water, and you need some." He held out a badly dented bowl with both hands so that Tauran could take a sip.

Tauran leaned forward as best as he could and took a whiff of the water. It smelled tainted with disease. He made a disgusted noise and flinched away.

"I know, but you must drink," Kael said, still holding it out. "You've been unconscious for days. Your body is in bad shape. Help it heal."

Tauran wondered if the damage of drinking such sickening water would offset any benefits it might provide, but he took a deep breath and leaned forward once more to gulp the proffered substance.

The taste was ten times worse than the smell and it made Tauran want to gag. It felt slimy in his mouth. He could sense the evil essence of it, and he was sure he was being poisoned. He jerked his mouth away and spat out what he had not already swallowed.

"Oh, that's awful!" he complained, but already, his throat felt better, and his voice sounded clearer, stronger.

"Well, don't waste it," Kael grumbled, righting the dish before any more spilled out. "This is all we have!"

"Sorry," Tauran said. He shuddered at the disgusting aftertaste. "But it's truly unpalatable to me. The stench of evil wafts from it."

"I imagine it does," Kael said. "Maybe it's no good for you," he added, sounding pensive.

Tauran tried to rise up straighter, but his bonds made it impossible for him to do much more than worm back and forth ineffectually. Kael set the bowl down and helped him.

"Where are we?" Tauran asked after he had gotten more comfortable. "What's happened to us?"

Kael drew a long breath before answering. "I think we're somewhere in the Blood Rift," he said. "I heard Vhok and Aliisza discussing some battle between these demons and a host of devils they ran into."

Tauran's mind reeled. It could not be! "No," he gasped, his voice a gurgle of panic. "No!" he repeated.

"Be still!" Kael growled softly, reaching out and holding Tauran down again. "Let me finish explaining."

Tauran used every bit of his willpower to calm himself. If he was to suffer the tortures of a horde of demons, as must surely be his fate, bound as he was, he would show Kael the bravery he knew the half-drow deserved to see. "I'm sorry," he said at last. "Continue."

Kael nodded and released the angel. "I awoke some time ago. Vhok and my mother were still here."

Images of Vhok and Aliisza flashed through Tauran's mind. He remembered clearly the devastated emotions that washed over him when the alu had appeared with Micus in tow within the great rotunda. Everything that had gone wrong in that battle had been because of her. Tauran's heart sank deeper, but he realized Kael was speaking again. He refocused his mind on the words.

"They were bargaining with a wretched creature who seemed to distrust both of them a great deal. Something about providing his lord with information gained from tricking you. I didn't quite get all of it, but it sounded like they were debating what could and couldn't be done to us until it was time to meet." The half-drow's voice quavered the tiniest bit as he finished.

Her betrayal had run much deeper than he had suspected, Tauran realized. The High Council had been right; she and Vhok *had* been manipulating him all along. They had used him to see Zasian succeed. That thought sapped any remaining will Tauran had left to fight for his life. His sorrow was complete. He had failed miserably.

"Before they left, my mother leaned down to us and whispered to me not to worry," Kael said, interrupting Tauran's lamentations. "She said it was all a ruse to save our skins and that she and Vhok would be back soon. She seemed unsure of herself, but she also seemed sincere."

Tauran tried to make sense of the knight's revelation. Too much was at odds. How did we come to be here? he wondered.

What's happened to Zasian? Can I trust Aliisza? That last question stuck with him. He feared allowing himself to hope that she had been forthright with her son. To do so was to invite even more pain and suffering later. And she had brought Micus with her. Hadn't that been a betrayal?

But didn't you yourself try to teach her that the essence of goodness was to trust, even when it put you in danger of grief? he asked himself. Can you practice what you preach, Tauran?

He honestly wasn't sure.

"Where's Micus?" Tauran asked.

"I don't know," Kael admitted. "I haven't seen him."

"He became cursed," Zasian said from across the room. His voice, so shaky and filled with fright, belied every sense Tauran had of him as a dangerous, cunning foe.

"What?" Tauran asked quietly, suspicious of the priest's motives. "What do you mean?"

"He and the dragon creature were fused," Zasian said, sounding uncertain. "A terrible thing. He was mad, filled with unreason."

Tauran leaned forward and spoke his next words very carefully. "How do you know?"

Zasian began to explain everything that had happened to them, to all of them, since he had awakened. He told his tale in a simple, straightforward way, detailing events as a child might. From time to time, Tauran or Kael would prompt him about some piece of information or another. Always, the priest expounded on his story to the best of his ability.

Through it all, Tauran listened with half an ear toward catching Zasian in a lie or sly trick. He expected the priest to slip up at some point, reveal that he was, in fact, still the dangerous enemy Tauran knew him to be.

When Zasian finished recounting what he had witnessed since awakening—a point before which he could remember absolutely nothing—Tauran felt tears running down his cheeks.

"The planes have shattered," he mumbled, letting the despair overwhelm him. "We are all lost."

CHAPTER SEVEN

C an you conjure some impressive magic, if need be?" Kaanyr asked in hushed tones. "Something fancy that will intimidate these fools?"

He and Aliisza stood near the entrance to a large cavern, waiting for a chance to talk to the powerful demon who controlled the forces with whom they had become entangled. Hot, wet fumes wafted through the natural chamber, disgorged from fumaroles scattered across the uneven rock floor. A channel of glowing, viscous lava tumbled from a hole near the ceiling along one side and vanished again through a sloping, narrowing crevice a few paces away. In the darkest recesses at the edges of the chamber, fungi and mosses sprouted from damp rock, fed by both the heat and the minerals seeping from the stone. Some gleamed with their own innate light.

A huge marilith remained on the far side of the chamber, towering over her servants. She swayed as she moved, half woman and half snake, her back turned to her guests. Her six arms, constantly in motion as she worked at something Aliisza could not see, seemed to perform a bizarre, synchronized dance. The hyena-headed demon with whom Aliisza and Kaanyr had first negotiated stood at her side, waiting for her to acknowledge him.

Aliisza considered Kaanyr's request for flashy magic. "Maybe," she said, "but I'm still not certain this is the best idea. You are risking Kael and Tauran's lives with this gambit, and we are not negotiating from a strong position." *Not to mention the fact that I might pass out from the strain of it,* she thought. *How quickly you forget to be worried for me, lover.*

"Leave that to me," he said. There was a smugness to his tone that made her uneasy.

Aliisza wanted to roll her eyes, but she kept her features neutral.

Her thoughts instead strayed back to a time that seemed lost in the mists. She remembered when Kaanyr had come to power within Hellgate Keep. He had engineered his ascension by playing the trio of mariliths in command, one of which was his mother, against one another. It had been a grand day for him, and for Aliisza at his side, as he took control of the demonic armies imprisoned within the labyrinthine tunnels beneath the ancient tower. Kaanyr eventually led that collection of fiends to freedom, and they formed the basis of his army, the Scourged Legion, when he later occupied dwarven Amarindar.

But that had been lifetimes ago, Aliisza thought. Then another thought struck her, and she grimaced. *Did I bring this on?* she wondered. *Is this my fault? Did our reminiscing in the rotunda trigger some of Kaanyr's old urges?* Aliisza felt consternation mingle with guilt. *He is his old self again. He thinks he can outwit another marilith, just because she reminds him of his mother. His dealings with the Triumvirate* all those years ago have made him cocky and too certain of his own success now.

But he doesn't have other demons to turn against her this time.

Kaanyr nudged her, drawing her out of her thoughts.

The marilith had finally given her subordinate her attention. The creature spoke quietly to her and pointed at Aliisza and Kaanyr. The massive she-demon turned to face the pair, and Aliisza could see an expression of mild curiosity, mixed with wary concern, grow on the fiend's face. With a gesture and a word the marilith dismissed the hyena demon, who grimaced as he departed the cavern through another tunnel.

The marilith turned and glided across the stone floor, her snake body rippling behind her.

Aliisza sized up the creature. The demon's torso was slightly larger than her own. If she had been a human woman, most men would have considered her thick-boned and ugly. Her face was unusually round, with puffy cheeks and lips and a slightly crooked nose, possibly broken once or twice. She had pulled her hair, a dull gray-brown in color, into half a dozen braids that hung limply down the sides and back of her head. She wore a cuirass of hammered bronze, and a set of matching broad-bladed scimitars dangled in their sheaths on a belt draped low across her hips.

"I am Vhissilka. Who are you?" the marilith demanded.

Aliisza craned her head back in surprise. *Not the usual tack I would have expected,* she thought.

Kaanyr bowed slightly. "I am Kaanyr Vhok, the Sceptered One, ruler of the Scourged Legion and son of Mulvassyss. This is my consort and lieutenant, Aliisza. Thank you for granting us an audience."

The marilith continued to look at them with suspicion. "What do you want?"

Kaanyr grimaced and said, "In truth, we want nothing from you, other than safe passage from this place so that we may travel on to our own destination."

The demon stared at Kaanyr, her eyes narrowing. "Grekzith says you consort with angels," she said.

"Ah, not true," Kaanyr said, "though we do have one as a prisoner. We are taking him to visit others who would be most interested in what he knows about his homeland."

Vhissilka brought one of her six hands up to her chin and stroked it. "I think not," she said. "Give me the angel and you can leave. I will take him to others who will want to hear his information."

Kaanyr shook his head. "No, no," he said jovially, but Aliisza could see that his eyes glittered with subtle anger. "That would not work at all. You see, the angel trusts me. He believes I have his best interests at heart."

Aliisza glanced over at Kaanyr in alarm. How much truth is he going to weave into his lies? she wondered.

How much is he lying?

Kaanyr continued. "Should you take him from me, he will never divulge what he knows. This is a very delicate matter."

The marilith hissed. "I am not a fool, cambion. Whatever you think you can extract from the angel, I can squeeze from him, too. You are not so important that I cannot just kill you and keep the angel for myself." Vhissilka pulled several scimitars free and twirled them casually.

Aliisza's heart thumped madly in her chest. This isn't going well, and Kaanyr knows it. She considered a bit of magic and prepared to conjure it.

"You can certainly try," Kaanyr replied, stepping back and placing a hand on the pommel of his own blade, which glowed purple with its magic, "but we are not foes to be taken lightly. I can promise you that you will die before your lackeys can reach us to finish us off."

The demon swayed back and forth, and she twirled her scimitars more rapidly as she considered the threat. Aliisza took a few steps to the side, not wanting to give Vhissilka two targets right next to one another. She had just about decided to create a magical portal and dash through it back to the cave where Tauran and Kael waited when Kaanyr spoke again.

"What do you lose by honoring our request? How does it harm your own goals to grant us safe passage from here?"

The marilith spun away and slithered across the room as though dismissing the two visitors. The scimitars she had brandished before had been returned to their sheaths. "I cannot help you," she called over her shoulder. "You must find your own way."

Aliisza chuckled once, softly to herself. Called her bluff, she thought, looking at Kaanyr.

Kaanyr was frowning. He followed the demon. "Abandoning us to our fate in this hostile place is little better than turning on us," he said. "It is in your best interests to ensure that we are well beyond the Blood Rift before you send us on our way."

Aliisza groaned inwardly. Kaanyr, no! She gave us our freedom to leave. Let's just do it!

Vhissilka laughed, and the shrill, screeching sound made Aliisza cringe. "The Blood Rift!" the marilith chortled. "Is that what you think this place is? Then you are a bigger fool than I thought."

Kaanyr stopped in his tracks. "What do you mean?"

The demon turned and swayed as she glided back toward them. "This wretched chunk of rock is no longer part of anything! I commanded a horde of demons ten thousand strong. I led them in wave after glorious wave against our devilish foes, driving the hated enemy before us, securing my status in the annals of time. Victory was to be mine!"

Aliisza, her hands trembling at the vehement explanation she was hearing, stepped up next to Kaanyr. "What happened?"

The marilith shrugged. "I don't know," she said. "But this wretched chunk of rock got ripped away from the Blood Rift. One moment we were driving the hated devils before us, and the next, I and my personal honor guard, along with the foes we were destroying, went spiraling away as the sky shook and turned a million colors."

"So you're just as lost as we are," Kaanyr said to himself, so softly that only Aliisza could hear him. Then, louder, he said, "You seek the means to return to your glorious battle, and we seek passage to the halls of the great demons who commanded you. I think I see a perfect union in the making."

"Your clever words and double meanings bore me, cambion." Vhissilka spat, slithering around him. The scimitars were back in her hands. She let her tail curl just a bit at his feet as she circled. "I will rend you to pieces soon, whether it costs me my life or not. Speak plain!"

Kaanyr spun in place, facing her squarely. "Our problems have a single solution," he said. His hand twitched over the hilt of his sword, but he did not draw it. "We both need to get someplace else. Why not work together?"

"How can you help me?" the marilith asked, a look of

doubt filling her fiery red eyes. "You don't know where you are, either. And you said before that your destination lies elsewhere. You do not desire to visit the Blood Rift."

"Yes, but you do," Kaanyr said, spreading his hands wide in a gesture of supplication, "and we have ways of finding a path back. We will aid you as we aid ourselves. In exchange for protection until we get where we need to go, of course."

"You did not answer me. How can you guide us?"

Kaanyr opened his mouth to speak, but the marilith held up her hand, gesturing for silence. The cambion snapped his mouth shut, and Aliisza could see the frustration and impatience in his mien. Vhissilka cocked her head to one side, as though listening. She held that pose.

Aliisza was just on the verge of reaching out to Kaanyr to urge him to give up the dangerous negotiation when Vhissilka spun away and said, "No more discussion on this now." She glided rapidly toward the far end of the chamber. "Right now, we must fight."

"Why?" Aliisza asked. "What's wrong?"

"The devils," the marilith replied. "They have found our caves and are invading."

"Invading?" Kaanyr asked, sounding doubtful. "In what strength?"

"Kaanyr," Aliisza said under her breath, "This is our chance. Let's get out of here now, while we still can!" She took the cambion's hand in her own and gave it a squeeze. "Please?"

Kaanyr disentangled his fingers from hers. "No," he said. "This is the best opportunity we have. If we leave, where will we go? Back to the beach? Over to the devils' camp? Don't be so timid, Aliisza. We stay."

More demons arrived while the two half-fiends argued, and the chamber began to fill up. The demons crowded in and pushed toward the front, where the marilith had taken her place. The chamber filled with nervous excitement as the host of creatures grew in size. The denizens chattered and snarled at one another as they strained to get close. A pair of fiery red insectlike demons near Aliisza and Vhok got into a squabble, pushing and shoving, before a much larger fiend with extremely broad, fur-covered shoulders and the face of a great hunting cat lashed out at the two with a spiked club. One of the insect-demons sank to the floor, its carapace cracked and fluid leaking from it. The other, cowed, scrambled away to another part of the room.

Aliisza followed Kaanyr as he headed toward a shelf of rock near the back of the chamber. He scrambled up to it and then reached back to offer her a hand. She joined him. From there, they could see over the throng to where the marilith slithered back and forth, as though pacing.

From somewhere along one side of the gathering, the sound of war drums boomed. A rhythmic cadence reverberated through the chamber, slow at first but growing more rapid. The demons chanted and howled in time with the drumming, and many began a strange, frenzied dance, thrashing back and forth and pounding the hilts of their weapons against the stone floor of the cavern. The energy level built. Aliisza pressed herself back against the wall. The whole chamber seemed to strain to contain the savage eagerness of the crowd. They were ready to burst in fury, to kill, destroy. Only Vhissilka's fierce stare, raking across the crowd, held them entranced.

"Go!" the marilith at last screamed at her underlings. "Kill everything that stinks of the Hells!"

The roar that erupted shook the very stone. The throng rushed toward the exits, every demon scrambling to be the next one out into the passages beyond. Their bloodlust had completely overcome them, and they hacked and stabbed at each other just to make room for themselves. Those that managed to force their way through went howling on their way, seeking enemies to rend. Those that did not splashed the floor and walls with their blood.

Finally, only Vhissilka and the two half-fiends remained. "We will join you in the fight," Kaanyr said. "We help drive the devils from the tunnels, you return the favor by granting us safe passage with you. What do you say?"

The marilith frowned. "I will consider it, but I make no promises. I don't trust you, cambion."

"Fair enough," Kaanyr said. "We'll just have to prove our sincerity, won't we?" He gave Aliisza a smirk.

"Suit yourselves," Vhissilka replied. She slithered away, leaving Kaanyr and Aliisza by themselves.

"Kaanyr, let's just go," Aliisza pleaded again. "Let's get back to the others and flee. This will not end well. Even if her forces win, you cannot trust Vhissilka to uphold her end, and you're making a mistake if you think you can outwit her."

The cambion glared at her. "Why? All I have to do is convince her I'm sincere. How hard is that? What better way to do it than to fight for them?"

"What if she demands that you sacrifice Kael to prove your loyalty? What if she insists on torturing Tauran before giving him back to you? There are a hundred ways she can circumvent your desires while sticking to any sort of agreement she makes. Hells, she could agree to anything you want today and change her mind two days later. She's a demon. She can't be trusted."

Kaanyr chuckled. "Maybe that's the point," he said.

His smile said he was joking, but Aliisza wasn't sure. "That's not funny, and you know it. You're playing with fire. Let's just slip away in the confusion!"

"I can't," Kaanyr said. "I'm convinced that this is the best way to save Tauran's life. Fleeing without Vhissilka's protection seems a greater risk to me, so thanks to Tauran's infernal compulsion, I couldn't do it even if I tried. Sorry, lover. We're staying here and fighting until she does something to convince me otherwise."

Aliisza groaned. "Fine," she said. "What do you want to do?"

Kaanyr smiled, and it looked almost feral. He slipped his malevolent purple-hued sword free of its scabbard and said, "Let's go hunt some devils."

❖ ❖ ❖ ❖ ❖ ❖ ❖ ❖

Eirwyn sighed as she glided through the warm, scented waters of the pool. The bath was supposed to help her relax, but she could not shake off her anxiety. Time was slipping away, and she was no closer to understanding her visions and dreams than she had been when she had arrived.

Get it out of your head for a while, the angel told herself, but the order was easier thought than done. The image of the strange, crystalline fortress surrounded by green bits of glowing snow dominated her thoughts day and night. No matter how carefully she examined it, no matter how many tiny bits of detail she could ferret out of the mental picture, she had gotten no closer to figuring out what—or where—it was.

She had been toying with the idea of departing from Xiranthador, of leaving the Seer and Venya and returning to the Court, or even setting out . . .

To where? she asked herself. Where would you go? What path would you follow? What clues would lead you? You are lost, and this is your best hope for finding the way once more.

The angel sighed again and paddled through the water, letting the scents of the soothing oils permeate her body and mind. She paused near the center of the pool and flipped onto her back. She stretched herself out and floated there, her face protruding above the surface while the rest of her seemed to get lost in the gentle caresses of the bath.

Eirwyn had no idea how long she had drifted there when she became aware that she was not alone. She jerked upright and shook water from her silver hair, which cascaded all around her neck and shoulders. She wiped the water from her eyes and peered around the room.

"I'm sorry to disturb you," Oshiga said, standing near the entrance to the chamber. "I wanted to let you know that there is news."

Eirwyn smiled. "You're not disturbing me," she said, climbing from the bath. She dried herself and began to dress. Oshiga pointedly stared elsewhere while she did so. "I'm trying to relax, but this whole doing nothing business doesn't suit me." When she had donned her white tunic, she began to braid her hair. "So, what do you know?"

"Tyr, Lathander—who has revealed his true form to be that of ancient Amaunator, incidentally—and Sune have imprisoned Cyric. His own plane has become his prison."

Eirwyn waved that bit of news away. "That was inevitable," she said. "What else?"

"The backlash from Mystra's demise swept through the Astral Plane. Waves of raw magic crashed against many shores. No one knows the extent of the destruction yet, but it appears that several planes vanished, while others merged together."

Eirwyn frowned. "Though grievous, that's not really news," she said, finishing with her hair. She straightened and looked at the trumpet archon. "Of course there were aftershocks. The goddess of magic was slain." She motioned for Oshiga to lead the way. "Unless there's more to your message than that."

Oshiga nodded as they strolled down the hall. "There is. Erathaol has been receiving reports for quite some time now. I haven't been privy to all of them—and I don't know the details contained within any—but apparently, these waves of magic are different." He paused. "They are having a strange effect on the places they touch. The edges of the House have even felt their impact, where the passage to the World Tree once stood. We are receiving news that the fabric of reality is changing there. Not just the land, but those caught up in it."

"I see. And what is happening to these poor unfortunates?"

Oshiga sighed. "A few grow very sick. Many perish." He paused, grimacing, as if what he had to add was too distasteful for him to repeat. "And the rest suffer strange transformations."

"A plague?" she asked. "A plague of magic?"

Oshiga nodded. "Yes. These transformations are often gruesome, from what I have heard thus far."

"Can they be aided?" she asked. "Healed or restored? Should I venture somewhere where I can be of more help?"

"I do not know," Oshiga said, spreading his hands apart helplessly. "I truly cannot counsel you on what this means, or what you might choose to do about it. I just thought you'd want to know."

Eirwyn frowned. "Thank you. Perhaps there is something useful for me in the—" A thought whirled through her head. "You said that planes are vanishing. Correct?"

"Yes." He tilted his head to one side, giving his counterpart a puzzled look. "Why?"

"Suppose some of them aren't merely vanishing, but disintegrating? What if this place I have been seeing in my dreams didn't yet exist, until this immense tragedy broke something free, created the crystalline fortress?"

Oshiga caught her meaning. "If we were trying to ascertain the identity of something that we assumed already existed, but it did not, then the seeking book would have a difficult time revealing useful results. Everything we came up with must exist now, but have some connection with the future and your mysterious site."

"Precisely," Eirwyn said, growing excited. "We've been searching wrong. We need to project this fortress as something that will be, rather than something that is."

"Unless it has come into being since we last attempted to focus on it."

"There would be no way to tell," she admitted. "We would need to tease the book into 'guessing' for us. Can you do that?"

"I believe I can," the archon replied.

Together, they hurried to the library chamber to commence their new search.

Much later, after they had worked to produce a new list and had poured over the resulting collection of books, Eirwyn uncovered a telling bit of information. She reread the entry, wanting to make sure. Satisfied that what she had found was both accurate and useful, she showed it to Oshiga.

The trumpet archon nodded. "Yes," he said. "I think that must be it." He sat back and looked at Eirwyn. "Now the question is: what must you do about it?"

Eirwyn took a deep breath and said, "I must go there. I can feel it. Whatever the terrifying dream I have been experiencing is trying to tell me, the answer lies there."

"Yes," Oshiga said, rising from his seat. "I believe you must." He began to pace. "But you cannot simply set out blindly. This is no ordinary journey, even for an angel of your extraordinary talents. With the chaos rampant everywhere, it would be folly to journey there unprepared, by yourself."

Eirwyn fanned her hands. "Perhaps, but I have little choice. My patron is no more. I cannot call on others to accept this task alongside me."

"That may be," Oshiga replied, smiling. "But I do not think your prospects are so slim. You have demonstrated a remarkable level of perseverance in the face of such adversity. Other patrons will welcome you into the fold, should you wish it."

Eirwyn felt a rush of nerves course through her. She had kept the debate over accepting patronage from another deep inside herself, not wishing to confront the issue of whether to change her allegiance after Helm's demise. It was too painful to contemplate. She felt like a traitor, betraying everything she had dedicated herself to serving.

"I cannot," she answered softly. "Not yet. It's too soon."

Oshiga tilted his head. "Is it? I cannot tell you what the right course is in this matter, but perhaps you should ask yourself whether you are truly best serving your cause by permitting your grief to render you impotent, immobile. In this time of need, do you do the just thing, or the selfish thing?"

Eirwyn glared at Oshiga, who sat across from her. How dare you, she thought. You know nothing of the pain and tragedy of losing your deity. But she let the anger subside and stared down at the surface of the table. "Your insight may be accurate," she said softly. "However, it does not change my reluctance. Helm was as selfless in his love for me as any I could imagine, and I fear the disservice I do to him by tarnishing that love."

Oshiga pursed his lips. "Even Helm would see you move beyond such a relationship when duty and others had need of you."

Eirwyn knew he was right, and she felt a little part of herself being wrenched free, torn from her heart. She wanted to weep. "I know," she said, "but I know of no power I wish to swear my allegiance to. I cannot bear to think of it."

Oshiga smiled. "I do not think you need to," he said, his tone filled with compassion. "You have already done so much in the service of so many. The mountain itself has embraced you, Eirwyn. You are a child of the heavens, a celestial creature heart and soul. Why not draw your spiritual energy from the entirety of the plane? Why not refill your heart with the love of Celestia itself?"

Eirwyn considered his words. It was not unheard of for

certain angelic beings to dedicate themselves to the righteousness of ideals, and the lands from which they flowed, rather than to a divine creature. She had forsworn obeying Tyr's law because she believed it was more important to uphold the values under which even he lived.

How would it be any different? she wondered. I have pledged myself to this philosophy. Can the philosophy not grant me strength and power in return?

Slowly, as the realization filled her that she had been living her life dedicated to Celestia all along, Eirwyn began to smile. In that moment of recognition, Eirwyn felt hope and energy wash over her again.

It felt good.

"I thank you," she said to Oshiga, who smiled.

"I am deeply proud to be of service." He stood and looked officious. "Now," he continued, "we must prepare you for your journey. It will not be an easy one."

Later, as the trumpet archon led Eirwyn away from the Seer's domain and back into the skies of the House of the Triad, they did not notice the pair of figures that followed them.

CHAPTER EIGHT

Fuming, Aliisza squeezed through a narrow gap in the tunnel. *Gods and devils, Kaanyr, what were you thinking?* "Let's find another route and flank them." *Brilliant if you know the tunnels well, but I'm so turned around now, I've got no idea where we are. And now they're chasing us, and you've gotten too far ahead. Wait for me, you thrice-damned—*

She cast a quick glance behind her and spied the bearded devil that was chasing her. He caught up to her and swung his heavy polearm, topped with a thick, serrated chopping blade, at her head.

She ducked and the blade whistled over her.

A sharp ring of steel on stone reverberated just behind her ear. Chips of stone sprayed the back of her neck. Aliisza pushed past the bottleneck in the passage, then she turned to face her pursuer again. He grinned at her, licking his cracked, blackened lips, and thrust his blade through the gap for another attack.

Aliisza grimaced, shook her head in disgust, and lunged

away. The stretch of tunnel before her opened up into a wide path, and the smooth floor was devoid of obstacles. She took off running.

As she retreated, Aliisza went back over Kaanyr's final conversation with her. Did he really get trapped by his own logic? she wondered. Then another idea struck, and it horrified her. Maybe he has begun to figure out a way to manipulate his own thoughts, convince himself a certain course of action is in Tauran's best interests. Can he deceive himself and thus circumvent the spell? Surely not.

But newfound doubt lingered in the back of her mind.

She neared a turn in the tunnel and could sense the bearded fiend behind her closing the distance once again. She marveled at how fast he could move.

Time for a little surprise, she decided.

As she reached the bend in the path, she planted her foot against the rocky surface. She leaped into the air and pushed herself backward. She flipped over so that she faced downward again and unfurled her wings enough to glide. The alu sailed over her pursuer, who stared up as his momentum carried him past her.

Aliisza landed behind the creature and slashed at him with her long sword. The blade bit into the fiend's moist, scaly flesh and drew black blood, but the cut did little to slow the devil. He snarled, turned around, then rushed at her again. He swung his nasty, serrated glaive with both of his clawed hands. The foul odor of his breath wafted from him, making Aliisza gag.

Another fiend arrived at the far end of the stretch of tunnel and rushed pell-mell toward Aliisza. She spied him raising a saw-toothed blade to strike at her. She kicked out with her booted foot and caught him squarely in the chest before he could land his blow. The impact drove the creature backward, but it also distracted her enough that her original opponent got inside her guard with his longer weapon and nicked her shoulder.

Aliisza grunted from the wound. It burned, and hot blood ran down her back inside her leather tunic. She tried to ignore the pain and refocus her attention on her two foes, who had her pinned between them in the narrow tunnel.

This killing things isn't as fun as it used to be, she decided. Where in the Hells is Kaanyr? Is he going to figure out he left me behind?

She knocked away a swipe aimed at her head.

She leaped a second, lower attack from the opposite side and summoned a collection of magical darts. The whistling, streaking blue missiles shot from the tip of her finger and burrowed into the devil's chest in rapid succession, leaving four scorched, smoking holes in the howling creature. He fell back, screaming in agony and clawing at his wounds.

Aliisza tried to ignore the painful twisting of her insides from the tainted magic.

The first devil slashed at Aliisza with his glaive again, and when she parried, she struck her foe's weapon hard enough that she jarred it loose from his hands. The loss of the glaive didn't seem to faze the creature one bit. He simply smiled malevolently and lunged at her with both his clawed hands extended.

"Pretty meat to tear and eat," the devil crooned as he grappled with Aliisza and pinned her arms to her sides.

She struggled free and fought to keep him at bay, slashing at his arms to prevent them from reaching her. Each time her blade struck, it cut into the fiend, but she simply wasn't having much of an effect on the devil.

"Begone!" she screamed as she brought her foot up between herself and the devil. "Go back to the hole from which you crawled!"

She shoved the devil away before he could get any closer. As he stumbled back and fell on his fleshy tail, she willed another set of the arcane missiles into being and flicked her fingers, flinging them from the tips so that they rushed at the thing. Three of the four blue projectiles pounded him, while the fourth fizzled out with a mild pop. Still, the magic did the trick. The devil fell, twitched, and writhed upon the stone.

Aliisza whirled back around, fighting not to hunch over in pain. The other bearded fiend was struggling to regain his feet. He staggered unsteadily but would not stop coming. She spied three more of the things scampering toward her from the far end of the tunnel, along with another devil covered in wicked-looking barbs. It reminded Aliisza of a cross between a lizard and a porcupine. The four of them crowded together, bumping and jostling one another as they tried to be the first to reach their target.

Aliisza sighed in exasperation and chose another spell. The magic came almost unbidden to her then; she no longer had to think about what she needed to do, only brace herself for the accompanying pain each casting inflicted upon her.

Whatever else may have been wrong with living under Tyr's shadow, at least I didn't have to put up with the vile stench of devils all day, she lamented, only half in jest.

She waited until the horde of devils closed to only a few paces away. Then she gestured at an area directly behind them and let fly the magic. At the same time, she opened one of her magical doorways. The moment the conjuration was completed, she fell through her doorway and let it wink out before any of the foul creatures could follow her through.

She reappeared further up the passage, back in the direction she had originally come, and crumpled to the floor in agony. Her blade slipped from her hand as she writhed. She fought to catch her breath. She managed to glance back over her shoulder to catch a glimpse of her handiwork. A thick sheet of ice filled the passage from wall to wall and floor to ceiling, sealing the devils on the other side of it.

Aliisza could hear the fiends slam against the icy barrier from the other side. She clutched her stomach and willed the pain to dissipate. The blue glow emanating from her subsided, and she felt the gnawing of her insides ease at last. As she grabbed the hilt of her weapon and rose from her hands and knees to her feet again, two or three more thumps shook the thick slab, but it did not budge.

That ought to hold them, she thought as she managed to stand upright. I'll just return to the last intersection and wait for Kaanyr. When he realizes he left me behind, he's bound to come back looking for me.

Isn't he?

Before she could turn to retrace her path, though, the devils materialized on the near side of the ice.

Aliisza groaned. Not this again, she thought, turning to sprint away. I had enough of this with the archons!

She ran back down the stretch of tunnel and slipped past the narrow gap, rushing through the winding, twisting passage. She fought against the urge to employ more magic to aid her in escaping.

Not unless absolutely necessary, she told herself.

She could hear the devils behind her as she darted around one bend and then another, racing to reach the intersection where she believed she had taken a wrong turn and lost track of Kaanyr.

Ahead, more sounds of fighting reached her ears. She feared running into a hornet's nest of trouble in that direction, but she knew she was outrunning certain difficulties behind her, so she resisted slowing down. The sounds of clanging steel and screaming combatants grew louder.

Aliisza turned another corner and nearly collided with a hulking froglike demon. A hezrou demon. The stout creature towered over a dead devil, nearly filling the tunnel with its broad, slimy body. Body parts and blood from its deceased foe splattered much of the floor. It opened its wide, teeth-filled mouth and growled at the half-fiend, then drew back a claw to strike at her.

"Wait!" she gasped, cringing back from the impending strike. "I fight for your mistress! Grekzith brought me before her! We're on the same side!"

The beast snarled again and pushed her aside.

"Then get out of my way," it rumbled.

"Several devils coming," she said as the behemoth demon stalked past. "Stinking, filthy barbed things."

The hezrou snorted and said nothing, but it sat back on its haunches and maneuvered its hands in front of itself in what Aliisza recognized as arcane gestures. She waited and watched, and as the first of the devils careened around the corner, the big frog-thing flung its spell. The barbed devil slipped and stumbled as it tried to halt, clearly surprised at the unexpected blockage in the passage.

The demon had timed its magic well, and a cascade

of bouncing, multi-colored energy burst forward from it, ricocheting off the floor, walls, and ceiling like balls of madly flashing light. The globes of power pummeled the devil and the two that slid to a stop next to it, buffeting them and knocking them backward with considerable force. The devils howled and tried to swat the swarming attacks away.

Relieved that the hezrou had slowed the devils down, Aliisza turned back to her journey. *I forgot how disgusting those things are,* she thought. *I must have grown soft while a guest at the Court.*

She reached the three-way intersection a few paces later and turned down the only remaining path she had not yet traversed. She listened for sounds of threats or anything else that might give her a notion of where Kaanyr was, but the tunnel ahead was silent. Only the mad fight between the hezrou and the devils reached her.

Aliisza came to a slight incline in the path and followed it up. As she rounded another sharp bend in the passage, she found herself near the ceiling of a much larger cavern. She stood upon a small outcropping, much like a balcony, that overlooked a roomier chamber below.

A vast collection of prisoners stretched out before her.

Aliisza could see that the captives were not fiends. The humans and humanoids hailed from faraway places, and their shredded rags and bruised bodies gave her the distinct impression they had been incarcerated for a long while. Someone had chained them together in cruel ways that rendered them virtually immobile.

Demonic guards stood watch over them, brandishing weapons and viciously poking and prodding their hostages for the pure glee of watching them squirm. More than a few prisoners cried out in anguish, but those were silenced again with a well-placed kick or punch. Sometimes permanently.

Aliisza grimaced at the display, but she had no time to feel sorry for them. *Their own lot in life,* she thought. *I have problems too.*

A commotion erupted from one side of the room. A throng of devils rushed in, swarming over prisoners and guards alike. They attacked viciously, striking to kill the demons and steal the prisoners. The demons, caught off guard for a moment, recovered and struck back, battling the devils with depraved abandon. The chamber became a whirlwind of screaming, thrashing fiends carving one another up with furious hatred.

To prevent the devils from making off with their prizes, the demons began slaying the prisoners. The panicked wails of the hostages made Aliisza cringe.

I was that brutal once, she realized. *Does that make it worse to watch now? Can I simply no longer abide the wretched cruelty of fellow fiends, knowing I was once that cruel, or do they behave more mindlessly, more ruthlessly than I remember? It seems I can no longer tell the difference.*

Aliisza wanted to rush forward, to swoop down upon both devil and demon alike and scour them from the room with her magic, but she knew she would succumb to the backlash of her curse long before she could destroy them all.

And then I could not aid Tauran and Kael to return ho—

Aliisza gasped. *They are in danger!* she realized. *The fiends will find them and kill them, just because they can. I've got to reach them first!* She hesitated a moment, pulled between her worries for Kaanyr and the other two.

She turned and sped back the way she came, hoping to find the route that would return her to her companions.

◆ ◆ ◆ ◆ ◆ ◆ ◆ ◆ ◆

"I can hear them fighting ahead," Kaanyr said, increasing his pace. "Come."

He raced up a steep slope to a point where the passage became a narrow chimney. They would have to climb up. He glanced back as he reached the vertical shaft to see if Aliisza needed help.

She was not there.

Kaanyr stopped and peered back down the ragged stone tunnel, watching for the alu, but she did not appear. Frowning, he called to her.

She must have gotten lost, Kaanyr thought. He shrugged and turned away. She can take care of herself.

He continued forward, toward the sound of fighting. The ring of weapon on weapon, the death cries, quickened his heartbeat. Once he reached the top of the chimney, he slipped his sword—he had taken to calling it Spitefang—free and grinned. Time to shed a little blood, he thought.

The path took him down and around two more bends, and then he was in an open chamber filled with furiously battling fiends. He had entered the vast cavern along one side, away from the main swirl of melee. The demons and devils battled on the far side, across a strange irregular floor filled with large holes of various sizes and shapes. Kaanyr stepped close to the nearest one and peered down. He could see no bottom; it descended into absolute blackness.

The demons and devils screeched and howled as they

slammed into one another, desperate to rend and crush their foes with tooth, claw, and weapon. Kaanyr could see that the opposing creatures outnumbered the abyssal fiends by a substantial amount, and the battle was not going well.

Long years of military instinct took over, and Kaanyr assessed the situation with an eye of how to improve the situation. He spied a small patrol of demons that had just charged into the chamber from another entrance not far from him. Acting quickly, he rushed over to cut them off, navigating his way between the odd craters that filled the floor. It was like traversing a series of narrow stone bridges, but he did not fear falling in.

"You, come with me," Kaanyr ordered as he reached the group of perhaps a dozen tall, gaunt, ram-headed demons. He had to step in front of them to keep them from rushing forward into the battle.

They glared at him, and one, holding its overly large spear-headed polearm in one hand like a staff, half-walked, half-hopped to stand before the cambion and rose up to its full height. "Skewer you!" it snarled, spraying spittle from its thin, fanged mouth at him. "We take no orders from a half-breed."

The other demons grumbled in agreement. To punctuate its defiance, the first whipped its long, bristle-tipped tail back and forth and drew the long weapon back to strike at Kaanyr.

He sighed, smirked, and levitated up into the air by means of his innate magic. He slashed Spitefang through the air in one clean motion. The demon's rheumy eyes widened in surprise as its head separated from its body in a spurt of black blood. Both head and carcass toppled over and plummeted into one of the strange craters in the uneven floor.

Kaanyr gave the rest of the band of demons a hard stare as they watched their companion disappear into the fathomless blackness. "Anyone else want to debate?" he asked.

The creatures snarled and grumbled, but none of them openly defied him.

"Excellent choice," he said. "Now let's go."

It felt so *good* to assume command again. It had been far too long.

Kaanyr led the troop of fiends forward, navigating through the maze of holes, toward where the rest of the demons still struggled to hold their position against the invading devils. They had been overrun, separated into isolated groups surrounded by their foes. If Kaanyr did not act quickly, the entire fight would be lost.

He sent half the new demons accompanying him to flank the horde of devils on one side. "Wait for my signal," he instructed the creatures. "I mean it," he added, giving them a pointed stare. "We must strike as one, together."

The other demons grimaced and gnashed their teeth, but none of them argued. They turned and scurried in the direction Kaanyr sent them.

He suspected they would only hold off for a few moments before battle-lust overcame them. *Their fear of me won't stay their weapons for long,* he thought, *but we'll make sure it's enough.*

He led the other contingent of reinforcements to the opposite side and surveyed the battle once more.

"We must hurry," one of the creatures near him growled. "There is blood-letting to be done."

"Indeed," Kaanyr replied, "but if we do not hit them in

the right place, the blood will be ours." He raised an arm and pointed to a location where several devils were milling in confusion. "There," he said. "Go."

With shrieks and howls of glee, the half-dozen or so creatures rushed forward, thrusting their polearms at their targets. They slammed into their enemies and skewered the first few of the devils. It happened so fast, the devils did not have time to react. As the first fell, the demons swarmed and overwhelmed the next rank. Then the devils turned to fight back, and the fight grew hot.

Kaanyr rose into the air to get a better view of the overall battle. The demons he had sent to the far side were just joining in the fray from there. Somehow they had managed to time their attack as Kaanyr wished.

Excellent, he thought, smiling. This might work out well after all.

He spotted an enemy commander that stood a bit apart from the others and directed their forces. Half-human like himself, the leader stood upon a large protrusion of rock. A fine breastplate adorned the half-devil, beneath which he wore fancy clothing. A pair of small, curled horns protruded from his forehead, and his skin was tinged red. He wore an oiled black goatee and wielded a pair of falchions that dripped with a vile, greenish substance.

Kaanyr engaged his magical cloak and headed toward the opposing commander. The half-devil spied him approaching and gave the cambion a smile and a mocking salute with one of his blades, then took to the air himself.

The two half-fiends swirled toward one another in the air above the larger battle. Kaanyr launched a thrust with Spitefang and watched to see how his foe would react. His counterpart spun and blocked the strike with one of his own weapons and then sliced low with the other. Kaanyr kicked the blade with his boot to deflect it. That drew a second strike from the half-devil's first falchion that the cambion was forced to duck.

"Not bad," the other commander said, smiling still. "I will enjoy this."

"Not for long," Kaanyr answered.

With that, the half-devil twirled in place and slashed at Kaanyr with a rapid succession of strikes that came from different angles and targeted various points on the cambion's body. Kaanyr gasped at the speed of the attacks, but Spitefang was well balanced and up to the task, and the cambion parried them all.

The two parted and circled again.

The half-devil's smile deepened as he surveyed Kaanyr's defensive stance. "You seem a bit unsure," he said. "Would you like a moment to collect yourself?"

"Thank you, but no," Kaanyr replied. "I'm just relishing the chance to dispatch such a worthy foe. It's been a while."

Kaanyr twirled Spitefang and beckoned his opponent to come. The half-devil obliged, and they began a dance of blades in earnest.

The ring of steel clashing against steel created a bizarre song above the swirling melee of demon and devil on the floor below. Kaanyr and his foe jabbed and blocked, swirled and circled, each trying to find a weakness in the other's defenses. Kaanyr had to work hard to keep the twin falchions at bay. More than once, a poison-coated edge got dangerously close to creasing his skin. Each time, he managed to evade the deadly strikes, but he was breathing hard with the effort.

Fortunately, Kaanyr's opponent was exerting himself just as much. The two of them separated and hovered in the air, taking a moment to catch their collective breath.

"You fight well," the half-devil said. "It's a shame you fight for the wrong side."

"That's a matter of perspective," Kaanyr replied. "I could say the same about you."

The half-devil grinned. "True, but I was not referring to your demonic kin. You stink of the taint of angels."

Kaanyr blinked in surprise. Had his association with Tauran rubbed off on him that much?

"Yes," the half-devil said, his grin growing more mocking, "I can see by your sudden meek expression and quivering lip that I am right. Fall in with the wrong crowd, did you?"

Kaanyr glared. "Hardly," he said. "Not that it's any of your business, but I found it necessary to deceive a few and associate with them in order to further my own agenda."

"Which is how you came to be ensnared in one of their magical compulsions, is it? How's that working out for you so far?"

Kaanyr snarled and lunged at the half-devil. He slammed Spitefang at his foe's head, smashing the magical blade against the falchions.

The half-devil laughed as he defended himself against Kaanyr's enraged attacks. "I must have hit a nerve, cambion," he said gleefully. "You let me know sometime how that agenda is coming along."

The half-devil began to use Kaanyr's own rage against him, redirecting his momentum as the cambion slashed and hammered at him. Kaanyr's fighting became frantic and sloppy and it was only when he got nicked on the forearm by one of the poison-coated falchions that he recovered his wits.

Kaanyr backed out of the fight and hovered out of the half-devil's reach. As the other commander approached him again, Kaanyr reached inside his tunic and grabbed a handful of colored sand from a small inner pocket. He flung the sand toward his opponent and uttered a quick arcane phrase. The sand burst into light and sent a spray of dazzling color right into the half-devil's face.

The magical burst startled the half-devil. He threw an arm up to protect himself from its effects. Kaanyr used the distraction to shoot higher into the air, above the half-devil. By the time his opponent had recovered from the arcane attack, Kaanyr was swinging his sword down.

The cleaving blow sliced the half-devil's head in half. He seized up and then dropped like a stone from the air, nearly yanking Kaanyr down with him. Kaanyr wrenched his blade free of the half-devil's skull and watched his corpse plummet into a crater in the floor.

Kaanyr sighed in relief and cast a quick glance around. The battle between demon and devil had ended. Two demons still stood, both wounded but still able to fight. They had been watching the aerial combat from below.

"Go," Kaanyr ordered. "Find more devils to kill."

The two demons grinned and took off, heading toward another tunnel. Kaanyr turned his attention to his injury.

The wound was slight, but it burned terribly. He saw that it was already festering and that pus seeped from it. What was worse, discoloration in the skin was spreading from it along his arm.

Blast, Vhok fumed. I let him taunt me into making that

mistake. Been around too-noble angels for too long. Must not let that happen again.

Wondering if Tauran had at last awakened and might be able to heal the poisoned wound, Kaanyr turned and sped from the chamber, seeking his way back to the angel.

CHAPTER NINE

The two demons that had been left behind, presumably to watch over Kael, Tauran, and Zasian, turned suddenly and departed. Kael watched them disappear up the gloomy passageway just beyond the cramped cave where he and his fellow prisoners waited. He didn't know whether to feel relieved or worried. Kael certainly felt better, not having the vile creatures looming so near, but he wondered what would have drawn them away so abruptly.

He jerked again on the chain that kept his manacles connected, knowing he could not break it but needing to keep trying. To do otherwise felt too much like giving up.

Kael stole a quick glance at Zasian. The glow surrounding the priest had grown slightly brighter, more steady. He wondered why that might be, but he didn't dwell on it. The human just sat, staring at nothing. He had grown very quiet after recounting their ordeal, and the half-drow wondered if he was beginning to suffer from the grimness of their predicament.

He can't be doing well in this hellish place, Kael decided.

Kael tried to imagine what it must be like to have the sum total of his memory be only a few days old. He had grown convinced, based on the priest's odd behavior, that his new personality was not an act, but a genuine transformation.

At least he's not in as bad of shape as Tauran.

Tauran lay curled up nearby. His breathing was mostly slow and even, as though he slept, but occasional coughing fits interrupted his rest from time to time, and he tossed and turned as much as his bonds would allow, groaning or even whimpering. He had not said anything after Zasian's recounting of what had happened, either.

Torm, Kael thought. *This place is killing him. We've got to get out of here.* He yanked on the chains holding him captive once more.

In a moment of desperation, Kael managed to get to his feet and, taking small steps because of the restraints holding his ankles, walk toward the tunnel leading out of their chamber. He reached the passage and peered down it as far as he could see, until it turned and disappeared from his view. Kael debated continuing, seeing what he could find out about their prison, but the way was rough and uneven, and with his chains, it would be difficult to maneuver. Plus, he loathed leaving Tauran behind.

It's not like he's going anywhere, he decided, taking a few steps farther along his route. He braced himself against a stalagmite and used it to aid him in scrambling up a small incline. *And if I get close to something I'd rather avoid, I can always scoot back here.*

Still, Kael felt vulnerable. The weakness stemmed not just from wearing shackles, but also because he did not have his sword with him. It was a rare occurrence for him to be without his blessed blade easily within reach, if not in his hands outright.

No, Kael realized. *It's more than the sword. I am afraid that Torm is beyond my reach, too.*

The half-drow had uttered a prayer or two to his patron in the time since he had come awake in captivity, but they were throwaway offerings made out of habit. He had not dared beseech his god to intervene on his behalf, granting some power or energy to aid him in his escape.

What if he cannot hear me? What if this place is too far removed . . . or too tainted?

Get over it! he snarled. *Do I really need that comforting connection so badly? What would Tauran think of such timidity? Use what you have. Be the power that's inside you. Act!*

With his fears of being cut off from Torm cast aside for the moment, Kael cast a glance back at Tauran and set out again, ready to face whatever might be lurking around the next turn in the tunnel if it meant the possibility of escape.

Kael did not get too far before he heard the sounds of commotion ahead in the distance. He froze in place, slowed his breathing, and listened.

It sounded like battle. And it was coming closer.

Kael's fingers itched to be holding his greatsword. He fought to keep his hands still as he tried to ferret out some sense of who was fighting whom. He strained to hear more clearly, but whatever was happening was still too far away. Nonetheless, he did not want to get in the middle of some conflict with who-knew-what bound as he was.

He needed an advantage.

Ambush, he decided.

Kael turned and headed back the way he had come, returning to the small chamber where Tauran still lay in a troubled sleep and Zasian sat in a stupor.

I won't get much help from either of them, Kael decided. No matter.

He surveyed the chamber carefully, taking note of every feature and protrusion of rock. There wasn't much. The floor was rough but relatively flat. The ceiling overhead hung pretty low; near the edges of the room, he had to duck to avoid cracking his skull on some bit of sharp, jutting stone.

Kael decided his best option was to position himself near the exit to the chamber, flat against the rock wall, and watch for anyone coming in. With their attention on the other two occupants, particularly Zasian and his bizarre glow, he might go undetected. It wasn't much of a hiding place, but he had nothing else.

He got into place by bracing his feet against a short, stumpy stalagmite and lifting himself high against the cave wall. Use the high ground, he thought. Take every advantage you can. He pressed his back against the rock and waited.

So, what do I do when something *does* come in? he wondered.

He considered the chain between his manacles. He could use it like a garrote, perhaps even lifting an opponent off its feet and swinging it around to dash it against the rocks. It was the best he could do, and it would have to be enough. He wasn't going down without a fight. He owed Tauran that much. And Torm, he reminded himself.

The sound of the fighting increased until Kael was convinced the conflict was just beyond the entry. He fought his own nervousness and waited.

Suddenly, there was a gasp and a dying scream, and the sounds of combat ceased. Kael held his breath, anxious to find out what had happened, worried about betraying his inadequate hiding place. He detected the sound of footsteps, faint but rapid, approaching. Then a shout issued from deeper in the corridor.

Just when he thought he couldn't stand to wait any longer, a figure dashed into the room. It was some kind of fiend, short and squat, with greasy black skin and patches of fur growing everywhere. It held a nasty looking saw-tooth-edged blade in one hand. A foul odor filled Kael's nostrils, a mixture of feces and acrid smoke. The creature skidded to a halt, stared at the two occupants, and the obvious dead-end. He let out a howl of frustration.

Zasian cried out in alarm and scampered backward from the intruder. Tauran didn't move, seemingly oblivious to his own danger. Kael prepared to lunge at the thing, knowing he only had one chance to get behind it and get his manacles over its neck, but he hesitated. He sensed something else coming, following the fiend through the tunnels.

The creature turned, and Kael could see its grotesque face and ratty, caked beard as it caught sight of him. The bearded devil snarled and took a step toward Kael, but then it froze in place, its attention turned back toward the entrance again.

A second, hulking figure emerged from the tunnel. The new arrival filled the entrance with its bulk, and it could not stand upright in the cramped chamber. It looked much like a gorilla from Kael's vantage point. The smaller devil let out a nervous growl and began to back away, brandishing its serrated weapon.

The gorilla-demon snorted and roared, then it punched at

the bearded devil with one massive fist. The smaller creature yelped and tried to retreat further, but there was nowhere to go. It took a swipe at its enemy's fist with its weapon, slicing open a gash across the knuckles. The gorilla-demon howled and yanked its fist back, sucking the wound into its mouth, but it used its other hand to swat at the devil.

The sweeping strike caught the smaller creature and sent it sprawling. It gibbered in terror and tried to roll out of the gorilla's reach, but it was truly trapped and got another punch for its troubles. The devil slammed against the wall with a sickening thud and slid down limply to the floor, leaving a dark smear on the stone. The gorilla demon loomed over the devil and pummeled it several times with both fists, reducing it to a mass of pulpy flesh.

Kael watched the entire skirmish, frozen in awe and unable to react. In the back of his mind, he knew that, even if he had been able to jump on the demon from behind, its head and neck were much too thick and muscular for him to be able to do anything with his makeshift garrote.

Without his sword, Kael was no match for the hulking thing.

The creature finished satisfying itself with pulverizing the devil and turned to stare at the other occupants of the chamber. Zasian had managed to scoot away from the fighting and pressed himself as closely as he could to the rock wall of the room, but Tauran still had not moved. When the demon saw the angel lying bound near the base of the wall, it howled in savage glee and reached out to grab him.

"No!" Kael roared, jumping from his position and ramming his shoulder into the creature's ribs. Even with his limited mobility, the knight managed to generate good thrust with his powerful legs, and the metal of his shoulder armor struck bone.

The gorilla-demon grunted and staggered to the side. With a snarl, it spun away from the angel and swatted at Kael with its big, meaty fist.

The half-drow had been expecting the attack, and he managed to sag backward as the powerful punch sailed over his head. As soon as he landed on his back, Kael rolled the rest of the way backward and flipped himself onto his feet. The problem, he quickly realized, was that he had backed himself against the wall in the process, so there was little maneuver room left for him.

The gorilla-demon grunted and closed the distance, aiming another punch. Kael tried to dodge to one side, but in his haste, he forgot how limiting his ankle restraints were, and he tripped, dropping to his knees. He caught the brunt of the blow on his shoulder and the side of his head.

A blaze of light flashing in his vision, the half-drow sank to the stone floor, woozy.

The demon roared in triumph and scooted closer.

Kael tried to clear his head of the cobwebs, but his eyes wouldn't focus right.

The big ape-thing smacked him with an open palm and sent him tumbling across the floor.

Kael struck his hip against a sharp protrusion of rock that sent shooting pain all through his midsection. He knew the demon was toying with him, and that one more blow like that would probably knock him unconscious.

No more stalling, part of Kael insisted. Call to Torm.

What if he does not answer? The thought terrified him.

Then die like a true servant of the Loyal Fury.

A peace settled over Kael in that instant, the thought filling him that he would represent his god in the best way he could, even without the deity's comforting presence to guide him. No one would know, perhaps, but he needed to prove to himself, one last time, that he was worthy of Tauran's trust in him. In grim resolve, Kael began a prayer to Torm, asking the deity for the strength and discipline to face the demon, no longer terrified that he would not be answered.

The gorilla-demon loomed over Kael again, raising both fists high, clenched together, ready to bring them down in a final, crushing blow. Kael realized he would not complete his prayer in time. He did not want to die, but he braced himself for it and hoped it would be with honor.

A flash of blue light filled one corner of the room.

Aliisza stepped through a magic doorway, her slender long sword in hand.

"Hey!" she shouted. "Get away from my son!"

❖ ❖ ❖ ❖ ❖ ❖ ❖ ❖ ❖

It took Kaanyr quite a while to find his way back to the small chamber where he and Aliisza had left their other companions. In the confusion and thrill of battle, he had become turned around in the catacombs, and he couldn't remember which route to take.

Along the way, he encountered a few other knots of demons and devils doing battle, but the invasion appeared to have been thwarted and the diabolical fiends were being destroyed or were fleeing. Kaanyr was pleased. He did not relish the idea of having to negotiate with devils, even though they were more willing to stick to their bargains than chaotic demons. He had double-crossed more than a few of them in his time, and he feared that his reputation might precede him in any dealings.

Kaanyr reached a series of tunnels that looked more familiar to him, and he followed the one he believed led back to the cave. He hurried down it, checking his wounded arm as he did so. The poisoned cut had turned a nasty shade of purple, and his entire arm was swollen and stiff. Whatever had coated the half-devil's scimitar, it was not treating him nicely at all.

As he drew closer, he could hear the sounds of fighting.

Not yet, he thought, increasing his pace. Don't kill the angel yet. I still need him.

Then another thought crossed his mind.

If I am too late, at least I would be free of his confounded *geas* upon me. The thought both pleased Kaanyr and forced him to sprint. He would not mind at all escaping the compulsion magic, but it would be by his own hand. The celestial bond required him to attempt to save Tauran.

Kaanyr turned the last corner and dashed into the chamber in time to see a huge, brutish bar-lgura with its back to him, flailing at some target he could not see. To one side, Zasian cowered against the wall, the illumination that surrounded him providing the only light in the cave. Next to the priest, Kael struggled to rise to his hands and knees, but the knight appeared woozy and was having trouble staying upright. On the opposite side of the chamber, Tauran also tried to move, but the angel, bound as he was, could not do much more than thrash around on the hard stone floor.

Kaanyr ran to Tauran. "Can you heal this?" he asked, thrusting his wounded arm in the angel's face. "I've been poisoned by a devil's blade."

The deva blinked and stared at both the wound and Kaanyr's face. "Help Aliisza," he croaked, his voice hoarse. "Hurry!"

Kaanyr saw that Aliisza was the object of the big ape-demon's wrath. She brandished her weapon but could do little more than poke and prod defensively at her foe's ferocious punches and swipes. Kaanyr grinned and felt an old, familiar stirring at the thought of fighting alongside her. Watching her lithe, black-clad body glide so smoothly from one battle stance to another always thrilled him. But his wound was pulsing in time with his heartbeat.

"I can fight better with both arms healthy. Can you do it?"

Tauran shook his head. "Not bound like this," he said, and his voice cracked. "But there's no time to free me. Aid her first!"

Sighing in exasperation, Kaanyr rose to his feet and slid Spitefang free. He swished the blade through the air and then closed the gap with the crazed demon. He tried to ignore his throbbing arm as he swung the blade with all his might, aiming toward the bar-lgura's flank.

The blade bit deep into the demon's flesh and sent crackling purple energy crisscrossing over the beast's body. The demon howled and spun away from Aliisza, turning its glittering red eyes on Kaanyr. With a roar, it tried to smash Kaanyr with one of its fists. Kaanyr stepped neatly out of the way and sliced at the wrist of the creature. Once more, the keen edge of his sword sliced deeply into demon flesh, and the malevolent magic of the blade scoured the demon.

The ape-thing yelped, but before it had time to react, Aliisza stabbed her own sword into its shoulder, then she flung a handful of glowing, magical missiles at it. As the familiar azure glow erupted around the alu, her whistling blue darts hit it in the head, and the creature dropped to the ground and writhed in death throes. Kaanyr finished it off with a quick thrust into its chest, directly into the demon's black heart.

When it was clear the fight was finished, Kael said, "That was fortuitous timing, Vhok." He attempted to rise on unsteady feet that were still restricted by steel. "I thought we would all meet our end here."

Kaanyr nodded, catching his own breath. "Glad I could be of service," he said absently, not even mocking the knight. His arm burned with an inner fire. He turned to Tauran. "My arm is about to fall off. Do you think you could possibly take care of it *now?*"

The angel closed his eyes as though in pain, but he nodded. "Yes," he said. "I will heal you with what little power I have left."

"No," Kael said.

Kaanyr spun to face him, angry. "What?" he asked. "Why not?"

"Let Zasian try, first," Kael said, pointing at the priest. "He has a healer's touch and isn't suffering the effects of this place like Tauran is."

Kaanyr smirked, but he didn't argue. He moved over to where the priest sat, a vacant look upon his face. "Can you leech the poison out of my wound and heal me?" he asked. When Zasian didn't answer, Kaanyr squatted down in front of him. "Hey, you!" he said, raising his voice. "Can you hear me?"

Zasian finally turned his gaze toward Kaanyr, but there was little recognition there. Kaanyr sighed but held his arm out in the hope that perhaps the man who had once been his adversary might understand. The priest looked at the wound and finally, some sense of awareness blossomed in his eyes.

"You're hurt," he said, reaching out to touch the open sore, which by then had become a festering gash oozing greenish pus. The touch sent fiery pain shooting through Kaanyr's arm, which was otherwise growing numb.

"Yes," Kaanyr said, trying to remain patient. "I've been poisoned. Can you do something about it?"

Zasian did not answer, but he dabbed at the infected cut with the tip of his finger. The cambion clenched his teeth and tried not to wince.

Zasian closed his eyes and let his fingers caress the wound. Where he touched, Kaanyr felt cooling sensations, and the swelling seemed to go down the slightest bit, while color returned to the skin. Kaanyr let out a deep, satisfied sigh, not realizing until it was made better just how bad his arm had felt.

Zasian continued to work for a few moments more, magically leeching all of the poison and infection from Kaanyr's arm. When he was finished, the priest smiled vaguely up at the cambion, then turned his gaze away again, lost in his own stare.

Kaanyr stared at the place where the wound had been. His arm felt perfect, and there was nothing to denote that he had been injured at all other than a very narrow white scar that was already fading. The cambion flexed his arm a few times, testing its mobility. Satisfied, he rose to his feet and turned toward the others.

It was only then that he realized what a sorry state Aliisza was in.

Her body looked beaten and battered, and blood poured from several wounds. She had balled herself into a knot and was retching blood. She gasped for breath as she writhed on the hard stone ground, even as the blue glow around her faded.

Kneeling down beside her, Kaanyr said, "You look like death warmed over. Do *not* tell me you aren't hurt."

"I am hurt." She coughed again, and more blood dribbled down her chin. "I think my newfound arcane power is devouring me."

"What?" Kaanyr asked softly. All his recent thoughts and memories of their happier times together surged through him, jumbled in a painful revelation. He felt sudden fear. "Why would that happen?"

Aliisza drew a deep breath. "The backlash of Mystra's death," she said. "I felt it course through me when I first came to, back in the rotunda. Just as I suspect it is what fused Micus and Myshik together and stole Zasian's memories, it must have imbued me with unparalleled power." She trembled. "But that power draws on me, on my lifeforce, to function."

For a moment, the look on Aliisza's face reflected Kaanyr's own pain. "I don't understand," he said.

"Yes, you do," she said. "Great power. Killing me. Slowly."

Kaanyr felt his chest tighten, found it hard to breathe.

"How bad is it?" he asked. "Can you recover?"

Aliisza shook her head. "I don't know. I dare not—" Another wracking coughing fit hit her. She wiped away the smear of blood from her lips and tried again. "I dare not invoke the magic again," she said. "Each time, it gets worse. I can rest and feel better, but if I cast another spell, it takes me all the way down. And then some."

Kaanyr sagged back against a stout stalagmite. I'm losing her, he realized. Perhaps Zasian could . . .

Kaanyr rose, crossed over to the priest, and grabbed him by the arm. "Come here, you," he snarled, pulling on the man. "Come make her better."

But Zasian didn't react. He merely toppled over onto his side.

"Damn you!" Kaanyr shouted, drawing his leg back to kick the priest.

"Kaanyr, stop it!" Aliisza cried out. Her voice was weak, and she could hardly hold herself upright, but she crawled toward Zasian anyway, trying to reach out and ward off the impending blow.

Kaanyr paused, stunned. You would protect him, even if it meant your own death. You'd defend him even from me. As feeble as a lamb, yet you still—

Then his indignation and rage left as realization struck him. You're a fool, Kaanyr Vhok, he told himself. You've created a mess of massive proportions and stuck yourself right in the middle of it. Well, it's time to fix it. It's time to fix everything you've fouled up. There can be no future for you until you resolve this.

With that, Vhok felt a great weight lift from him. He sensed many tendays' worth of anger and frustration dissipate. It was time to act. No more hesitation, no more succumbing to inaction. It's a new day, Kaanyr Vhok.

Vhok saw Aliisza's eyes widen, staring at him. She's wondering, he thought. She's worried that she's just crossed a threshold, revealed her deepest, darkest weakness to me, and that she can't trust me with the knowledge. Let me show you, lover.

"It's remarkable," he said. "A day or so ago, I would have wanted nothing more than to ram my blade through his gut. Today, he restores my arm without a thought. And I mean that. He literally doesn't seem to have a thought left in him."

Tauran coughed. "He is becoming a Living Vessel," the angel said, still sounding as if he hadn't had a thing to drink in several days. "I've never seen it happen like this, though."

Curious, Kaanyr moved over to the angel and knelt down. "What is he?"

Tauran fought a coughing spell, then explained. "Usually, a celestial creature can make an ultimate sacrifice of itself by making its body an empty vessel for another to inhabit. We don't do it often, but when certain needs are pure and dire, we sometimes offer ourselves in this way.

"Zasian told us a bit about what happened in the rotunda," the angel continued. "It sounds as though, with the strange surges of magic that cascaded through there right after Mystra was slain, his spiritual form and the planetar's somehow merged. Perhaps the planetar invoked his power accidentally when he was so badly wounded, almost like a reflex. But instead of the planetar's body becoming the vessel, Zasian's did. But some small part of a personality—neither the planetar's nor Zasian's complete memories, but some small part—remained behind, which is why he has been behaving so oddly. And over the last few days, as it has perhaps dissipated, he has grown more vacant, detached."

Vhok tried to absorb what the angel was saying. "Why would one of you do this?" he asked. "What can become of the Living Vessel afterward?"

"The mind and spirit of another being can inhabit our

body," Tauran answered. "It's not the same as the powerful arcane magic you are more familiar with. It's more of a divine melding. I cannot adequately explain it."

Already, Kaanyr's mind churned with the possibilities. "That is very interesting," he said. "So what has become of Zasian? Where is his original mind?"

Tauran shrugged as best as he could in his restraints. "I do not know," he said. "Perhaps it's also in there somewhere, buried and unable to react to us. Perhaps it has been eradicated or is cast out on the Astral, adrift and bodiless. I barely understand all of the ramifications of the magical surge that wreaked so much havoc on the universe. The fate of one man no longer seems so consequential."

Kaanyr chuckled, finally at the moment of truth. "Perhaps for you," he said. "But unless you have forgotten, my fate is inextricably tied to Zasian, through you. We have unresolved issues."

Tauran coughed again. "You are right, cambion. I agreed to free you should you successfully aid me in stopping the priest of Cyric—"

"Or should it no longer be relevant."

"Indeed." Tauran drew a deep breath and said, "I gave my word. I free you of your obligation."

Vhok felt the magical shackles fall away from him at last. He wanted to stretch, to crow, to shout "Freedom!" at the top of his lungs. He wanted to draw his sword and run it through the damnable angel who had caused him so much trouble. Instead, he merely grinned.

"Kaanyr," Aliisza said, giving him a warning look. "Do not."

The cambion smirked at her. "I don't know what you're

talking about," he said playfully. "I was merely savoring the moment of release."

"We must help them get out of here," Aliisza said. "They will not survive this place."

"And take them where?" Kaanyr asked, his voice growing cold. "We do not ourselves know where we are, and the odds are not good that we would survive if we tried." He stood and looked down at her. "At least, the odds aren't good for the four of you. The angel is dying, Zasian is nothing but a shell of a human being, hardly more than a halfwit child, and . . ." His anger and glee subsided. "And you can no longer draw on your power, lover. You've become a liability."

Aliisza stared at him. He wasn't sure whether she was on the verge of crying or screaming at him. "No," she said, her voice barely above a whisper. "Kaanyr, don't."

A pang of regret sent a chill through him. No, he insisted, shrugging it off. It's time.

"Vhok," Tauran said. "You have done so many right things. Don't undo all that now."

Kaanyr ignored him. "I thought I wanted what we used to have, Aliisza. When we were talking earlier, and when I watched you fight, I recalled how good we were together, and I yearned for those days to return." His voice had become gentle, but it grew stronger, cold once more. "But I realize now that such can never be again. You are not the cunning trickster I loved back in the dwarven halls. Your time spent in the heavens changed you. Even if I were inclined to try to fight through all that, to guide you back to the crafty minx I remember, magic is killing you. Frankly, I don't want to watch you waste away as your power eats you alive."

Aliisza said nothing, but tears ran down her cheeks, and

she looked as though he had just rammed his blade through her gut.

"No," he continued, tuning Aliisza's soft sobs out, "the odds are pretty low that the five of us could escape here together. I, on the other hand, have many options. I think I will honor the bargain I made with Vhissilka the marilith. I like my chances much better that way."

"You bastard!" Kael shouted, struggling to get to the cambion. "I'll kill you!"

Vhok laughed as he drew his sword once more. "I ought to kill you now," he said, "but it's just too much fun watching you flounder around in those chains."

He launched a series of feints at Kael's head, got the half-drow off-balance, then kicked the knight's legs out from beneath him. Kael went down in a heap and grunted in pain as his head bounced hard against the stone floor.

"Kaanyr!" Aliisza cried out as she struggled to where her son lay panting. "Leave him alone!" she growled as she hovered over him protectively.

"You see?" Vhok said, feeling anger rise. "That's what I'm talking about, lover. Always more worried about them than me. I sure won't miss that."

Then he bent down and looked her squarely in the eye. "Would you sacrifice yourself, use the last of your 'immeasurable power,' to strike the killing blow on me right now? Do you even have anything left to expend?"

Aliisza returned his gaze with a hateful glare. "Yes," she said in a voice barely above a whisper. She reached one hand up toward him. "Come here and let me show—" The strain of her effort sent her into another coughing fit, and she crumpled down again atop Kael.

"That's what I thought," Vhok said, rising again. He saluted the four of them with his blade, eager to get out of there before Aliisza decided to try again to unleash her fury at him. He truly didn't want to have to be the one to kill her. "It's been grand," he said, then he turned and departed.

It was, for a brief moment, very hard not to turn and look back at Aliisza one last time.

CHAPTER TEN

Aliisza remained draped over Kael for several long moments. The agony of Kaanyr's words washed through her over and over again, mingling with the physical pain of her dying body. During all the years she had been his consort and his lieutenant, she had known he might turn on her one day. She had never imagined it could hurt so much.

The prophetic words of a conversation, spoken long before and in a very distant place, came unbidden into her mind. "It's dangerous, caring for others," she had said at the time. "You leave yourself open to . . . to pain."

"Yes," Tauran had replied so long ago. "It is hard to care for others, because you give something of yourself in the process. And you fear that it will come back to injure you if you let it. Everything we do in life, we do out of fear. Fear of betrayal; fear of pain. In the end, those fears materialize despite our efforts."

"Despite our efforts," she repeated, fighting the tears as she buried her face in her hands atop Kael's chest. I've tried it both Kaanyr's way and Tauran's, and despite everything, this is how it ends. In pain and misery. Why did I bother? That had been her reply so long ago, too, when she and Tauran had discussed the vulnerability of caring in that enchanted garden.

She repeated the question aloud. "Why bother living at all? How does making myself vulnerable change anything? It only makes it worse!"

She felt a cool touch upon the back of her neck. She started, at first fearing that Kaanyr had returned, but his touch had always burned with his inner fiendish fire. She shifted around as best as she could and found Zasian kneeling next to her.

"You're hurt," he said. He shifted his hand to her forehead, then blessed comfort poured into her. The pain in her gut faded somewhat, and she felt renewed strength return to her limbs.

Zasian looked pained as he withdrew his hand. "You're dying," he said simply. "But not yet. I've helped."

Aliisza looked back at the priest and smiled. "Thank you," she said. Such kindness from . . .

Zasian sat still and stared beyond her, at nothing.

"You called me your son," Kael said.

Aliisza blinked and sat up. "What?" she asked, sniffing and wiping her eyes.

"When you first arrived," Kael answered. "You told that thing"—the half-drow jerked his head in the direction of the gorilla-demon—"to 'get away from my son!' You've never called me that before."

Aliisza shook her head. "So? I don't understand."

"I think he's trying to answer your question," Tauran said, his voice very weak. "It's why you—why all of us—bother."

"Exactly," Kael said. "I'm sorry for what Vhok said to you. He's a fool. I'm proud to have you as a mother."

Aliisza smiled faintly. Kael smiled back, and gladness welled up inside her, pushing aside some of the hurt Kaanyr had inflicted upon her. He's my son, she beamed. And he's proud of it.

But they were still doomed. Kaanyr had made good on his promise to punish Tauran and Kael for their manipulations. He was free, and they were all trapped, dying in a deep hole in the ground.

"How could you do that?" Aliisza demanded, turning to where the angel panted, his eyes closed. His blond curls lay plastered against his pale skin, soaked in sweat. He looked terrible. "How could you free him like that? You've just sealed our fates," she said, anguish welling up once more.

"I had no choice," Tauran replied. "I gave him my word. A guarantee of my own well-being was not part of the bargain."

"Tauran, that's insane!" Kael said from across the room. "Surely there was some way you could have maintained the letter of the agreement a little longer. Are you that ready to die?"

"Death may be a blessing for me after everything that's happened," Tauran murmured. "The demons will not slay me for a long time, if they can help it."

"No," Aliisza said, fighting to control her emotions. "I won't let that happen."

Tuaran opened his eyes and looked at her. "I welcome whatever intervention you wish to provide, but it is as Kaanyr said. Where are we to go?"

"We can still try, damn you!" Kael said. "If you just want to lie there and wait for them to come for you, then you're not the creature I believed in. That's not the Tauran I know."

Tauran closed his eyes again and sighed wearily. "Would that I could still be that person for you, my friend. But too much has been lost. I cannot muster the strength or will to continue the fight."

"Nonsense," Aliisza said, rising to her feet. "That's this place talking. You're succumbing to it." She tried to adapt a brusque, practical tone, but inside, she fought to avoid falling apart. Kaanyr had everything he wanted, had every advantage. And he had been right; they *were* all liabilities.

Maybe he'll come to his senses, she hoped. Maybe he'll reconsider. Then that false hope vanished. She knew nothing would change the cambion's mind. He had been through too much. Too much suffering, too much humiliation. He intended to extract a heavy toll from everyone who had gotten in his way, everyone who had thwarted even a tiny bit of his ambition. The four of them would be nothing, trying to stand against him.

Something inside Aliisza resolved itself then. Something powerful, something that had lain in wait for her to finally see the universe as it really was. Kaanyr's words had stuck with her. Would you sacrifice yourself? he had asked.

He's a fool, she realized. He will never understand. I'd rather die with these two by my side than waste another moment grieving over him.

Clarity had come.

Aliisza knew what she must do.

She knelt next to Kael and muttered a simple spell, touching the locking mechanism of his manacles as she did. An audible click accompanied the shackles coming apart and dropping from his wrists. A wave of pain shot through Aliisza's gut as her blue glow filled the cave, and she doubled over for a moment, gasping. When the discomfort subsided, she manipulated the spell a second time, freeing the knight's legs.

Kael stared at her. "Is it bad?" he asked, and the gentle concern in his eyes warmed Aliisza's heart.

Aliisza smiled. "No," she lied. She reached out and caressed his face. "I'm fine."

The half-drow snorted. "The Hells you are," he said. "You look like you're about to pass out."

Aliisza shook her head and resumed her officious attitude. "There's no time for worrying about me," she replied. "We've got to get Tauran free and out of here. This place is killing him."

Kael stared at her for a moment, but then he nodded. "I'll do it," he said. "Whatever you've got in mind, get started. Vhok won't be long in returning to finish his betrayal."

Aliisza shuddered, hearing her son's words. *He's not blaming me,* she insisted. *He's just right.* Swallowing the guilt, she stood and headed toward the tunnel leading out. "I'm going to find your weapons," she said softly. "I'll be back soon." With that, she left them.

Kaanyr, she thought as she prowled along the passage, *why did you do this to me? I did still love you, you fool.* She grimaced. *No more grieving! It's done. Deal with the ones who still care.* Swallowing the growing lump in her throat, the half-fiend continued on.

She reached an intersection and slowed, listening. Things had grown quiet since the commotion of the devils' invasion. Aliisza assumed the demons had been triumphant, but she wondered how high a price they had paid for their victory.

The more of them dead, the better, she decided. *Fewer for me to deal with.*

Satisfied that nothing was nearby that would cause her trouble, Aliisza braced herself against a wall and manipulated innate magic once more. The crash of agony lasted only a moment. When the blue emanation subsided and she had caught her breath, she could sense in which direction Kael's sword lay. She scurried around a bend in the tunnel and followed her internal compass.

It took her several wrong turns and a few retreats to avoid being seen by others before she found the chamber where her son's sword had been discarded. The cavern was small, much like the one Tauran, Kael, and Zasian had been imprisoned within, and it had only one entrance. It lay at the end of a narrow passage with a few other, similar chambers lining either side of it. The demons had been using the chambers as refuse storage. They stank of filth and decay.

Aliisza stood at the edge of the chamber and peered around at the trash and bones, the foul sewage and carcasses. Her magical guidance suggested that the blade lay on one side, and when she went to that spot, she found it, carelessly tossed atop a heap of other waste. Tauran's mace sat nearby. In fact, all of the trio's equipment was there.

She began to gather it up, then paused, struck by an idea.

Aliisza stacked her companion's weapons and other gear in a neat pile near the entrance to the chamber, and then sucked in air to prepare herself for the onslaught of pain. She summoned a shimmering blue doorway, gasped at what the magic did to her insides, and then stepped through.

She found herself in the chamber where Tauran, Kael, and Zasian waited. She did not dispel the doorway.

Kael knelt next to Tauran, trying to help the angel sit up. Kael had managed to remove the bindings that had held

Tauran immobile. Even so, Tauran was a sorry sight. Zasian still sat nearby, staring across the room at nothing in particular. The bodies of the fiends that had rushed into the room remained there too.

"Did you find them?" Kael asked, rising to his feet.

Aliisza nodded. "Come," she said. "Let's get out of here before Kaanyr comes back."

The half-drow frowned. "Where are we going?" he asked. "We'll just be trapped somewhere else in this godsforsaken place."

"Maybe," Aliisza replied, "but it will buy us some time to figure out a way to escape. Help Tauran. I'll get Zasian."

Mother and son each took a companion. Aliisza got the priest to his feet and found it easy to guide him where she wished. She steered Zasian toward the doorway, while Kael followed her, supporting the ailing angel with an arm around his waist.

"I hear someone coming down the passage," Kael whispered. "Hurry!"

Aliisza stepped through the magical portal and then moved away from its twin at the other end, making room for the other two following behind. Once Kael and Tauran passed through the door, she released the magic and the doorway winked out.

"Ugh," Kael said, wrinkling his nose. "I didn't think we could find something that smelled worse than that big ape back there, but I was wrong."

"Your things are over there," Aliisza said, pointing.

Kael positioned Tauran near a wall where the angel could support himself. Then the knight reached for his sword. "Thank Torm," he murmured. "It feels good to have this in my hands again." After hefting the blade and feeling its familiar weight, he bent down and pulled Tauran's mace from the pile. "Here," he said, holding it out for the angel.

Tauran took the holy weapon. He slipped it into his belt, but the weight of the mace seemed to make him sag even more. "Thank you," he said, his voice barely above a whisper.

Kael turned back to Aliisza, who had guided Zasian to a relatively clean spot on the floor and had bid him to sit. "Now what?" he asked. "Tauran and the priest are in no condition to fight, and you and I cannot defeat the whole horde ourselves. Even after the battle with the devils, there's bound to be too many of them crawling through here. So what do we do?"

Aliisza bit her lip in thought. She turned to Tauran. "You can't move us?" she asked, fearing she already knew the answer.

The celestial shook his drooping head. "Even if I had the strength," he said, fighting back a coughing spell, "I am still cut off from Tyr. He has not seen fit to grant me his blessings yet."

"Then I'll just have to do it myself," Aliisza said uncertainly. "How hard can it be to make a doorway back out into the Astral Plane?"

"That may not make things any better," Kael said. "Who knows what is lurking out there? Especially considering how stirred up everything is after the destruction."

Aliisza gave her son a pointed look. "Do you have any better ideas?" When Kael shook his head, she said, "Then it's our only option. If we can get Tauran out of here, he might start healing."

Kael gave a sigh of uncertainty, but he nodded. "Give it a try," he said. "Staying here is certain death."

Aliisza sat and focused her concentration. She imagined a place in the Astral Plane, just beyond the reach of the chunk of world in which they were trapped. She closed her eyes and began to build up arcane energy.

If I survive this, she thought, it's going to hurt like the Nine Hells.

❖ ❖ ❖ ❖ ❖ ❖ ❖ ❖ ❖

Vhok's steps felt light and easy as he walked through the tunnels of the demonic stronghold. That was too easy, he thought. Tauran finally got a taste of his own rules, and he has found them wanting. The fool.

The only part that dismayed him was Aliisza. Even too feeble to draw on her magic, she had tried to stop him. She had made her choice. She's no longer the one I loved, he told himself. But I will miss her.

You will find another consort, Kaanyr Vhok. Right now, remember that you are free. You're free!

Vhok's stride was rather jaunty as he turned a corner and entered the great chamber where the marilith held court before, when he and Aliisza had come before her. She was there, surrounded by her minions. Two of the large, ram-headed fiends guarded the doorway, and when they spotted him approaching, they blocked his route with their wicked-looking polearms.

"I must speak with Vhissilka," Vhok said. "It concerns a means of returning us all to the Abyss."

"You will wait," one of the two guards said before he bounded off to inform the marilith. The other remained there, watching Vhok closely. He wondered if it was one of the survivors he had commanded earlier. He struck a pose of disdainful boredom and waited.

The guard returned, but the hyena-headed demon with the snake protruding from his neck, Grekzith by name, accompanied the lowly demon. The guard resumed its position on one side of the door, while Grekzith stood before Vhok and folded his arms across his chest, matching the cambion's haughty stare.

"My mistress is busy," he said. "Go away."

Vhok chuckled. "Vhissilka is not too busy to hear what I have to say. Go tell her I've found a way to get her back to her beloved Abyss. And tell her that circumstances have changed. She can have the angel. I have all the information I need from him."

The demon glared at Vhok. "I will also ask Vhissilka for permission to disembowel you for your impertinence," he said. He turned and stalked back to the marilith.

Vhok watched the exchange between demons carefully. As the molydeus whispered in her ear, the marilith's eyebrows shot up. She uttered some quick command and gestured for the other fiend to hurry away. By the molydeus's body language, Vhok could tell he was not happy.

Good, Vhok thought. The quicker he learns not to try me, the better.

The red-skinned demon stormed past Vhok with barely a glance. He exited the chamber and disappeared. Vhissilka gestured for Vhok to join her.

When the cambion reached the snake-bodied demon's side, she said, "You have found a way to return my army and me home?"

"Yes. I will set out immediately. I will locate a portal

leading back to the Abyss from the Astral Plane. Once I have found such a pathway, I will guide you and your army through it."

The marilith snorted. "You will simply depart and never return," she said, waving one of her several arms in dismissal. "I am no fool, cambion."

"The thought had crossed my mind," Vhok said, "but there is much more to be gained by returning with you." So much more, he thought.

"What do you gain?" Vhissilka asked, slithering around Vhok where he stood. "What is your advantage?"

Vhok drew a deep breath. "The angel that arrived with me has been the source of untold trouble for me. I want revenge."

"And how will you achieve such?" the demon asked, still winding herself around the cambion. Her coils held his ankles tightly together and she began to work her way up past his knees, closing in on him.

Swallowing back any concern he had for his own safety, he calmly replied, "The information I have gleaned at the angel's expense. I will sell it to the highest bidder when we arrive."

"No one will listen to you," Vhissilka scoffed. "You will be slain and cast into a pit the moment you set foot within in an archdemon's territory."

"Not if I am your ally," he replied. "Not if I allow you to claim much of the credit for the knowledge."

"Why would you do that?"

"Because it's the end result that matters to me," Vhok said. "I want a chance to make all the creatures of the House of the Triad regret they ever crossed me. You can help me make that happen."

"I accept," the demon said, coiling herself more tightly around Vhok, pinning his arms to his sides. "But with one change. You will remain here as my guest, along with the angel, the human, and the half-drow, which I know to be the alu's son. You will tell me everything you have gleaned from the angel, right here, right now. I will also torture the angel until he is completely broken, and compare what he reveals against your own claims. If I am satisfied, I might allow you to live. In the meantime, I will send the alu out to find a magic portal. She will be the one to lead us through it."

"But—" Vhok began, only to discover he had no air to finish his statement as the coils of the snake-demon suddenly constricted. He gasped and struggled, but her grip was absolute. Vhok felt himself growing faint. He could not get enough air. He opened his mouth to protest, to plead, but he had no voice.

Idiot! he fumed, fighting the panic that engulfed him. What have you done?

Just as he began to lose consciousness, he heard a deep voice from nearby. He recognized it as that of Grekzith the molydeus.

"Forgive me," the creature said, "but the others are not in the chamber where they were to be held. They have vanished."

"What?" the marilith screamed, tightening her grip on Vhok. He thought his ribs were going to crack. "Find them!"

"As you command," the red-skinned demon replied.

Vhissilka loosened her hold on Vhok the tiniest bit. It was not enough for him to move, but he was able to draw in a shallow breath. He spent a few thudding heartbeats panting as the spots faded from his vision.

"Where are they?" the marilith demanded. "What have you done with them?"

Vhok shook his head, cursing himself for leaving them to their own devices. "I don't know," he said. "But they can't be far. They're all weak, dying. Let me help you find them. The alu doesn't trust you, but she will come to me." It was a lie. One chance to slip away, he thought. That's all I need.

The marilith held him fast for a moment longer as she appeared to consider his request. Then she tightened the coils once more. "I think not," she said, crushing the air from him again. "You are much too valuable for me to allow you to escape. How else am I going to entice the alu to return?"

❖ ❖ ❖ ❖ ❖ ❖ ❖

Kael fought the urge to pace. He fingered the hilt of his sword as he watched Aliisza. The alu had been sitting very still, her eyes closed, for a long time. Though she seemed to be concentrating, her facial expression would occasionally ripple with frustration.

To pass the time, Kael would occasionally move to the exit of the chamber and peer out into the larger tunnel beyond. He stood there and tried to penetrate the silence, listening for some sign that there were threats nearby. He only detected something once, but whatever had made the noise, it never drew closer.

I cannot abide all this waiting, Kael thought, returning once more to stand by his mother's side. The longer we delay, the greater our chances of discovery. But he did not want to disturb his mother by voicing his concerns, so he instead turned his attention toward the other two refugees hiding with them.

Tauran seemed to be holding his own, though he was in poor shape. He sat with eyes closed, slumped against a wall of the fetid chamber, looking pale and drawn. Sweat trickled down his face and kept his once lustrous blond curls slicked down against his head. His wings drooped at his sides, and his breathing had turned raspy in his chest. Every time he suffered a coughing fit, Kael nearly went out of his mind with fear that they would be found and caught.

Zasian, on the other hand, did nothing. The priest had grown completely comatose, no longer responding to anything anyone said to him. Even touching him no longer drew his attention. He merely sat where Aliisza had led him, his eyes glazed. The glow he emanated had become strong and bright. It seemed to be the only thing about the man that exhibited any will to live.

Aliisza let out a growl of frustration. Kael turned to look at her and saw her open her eyes and frown. "I can't do it," she said, throwing her head in her hands and covering her face. "I just cannot get the magic to settle on a spot. Damn!"

Kael's spirits plummeted. They had no other options, unless they physically walked back to the surface of the cave complex and tried to reach the boundary of the strange mini-plane that way. He voiced the idea, but Aliisza shook her head.

"We'd never make it," she said. "There are too many fiends about, from both sides of the Blood War. And where we arrived, it's an ocean. We would have to swim for it, and it's too far."

"We've got to try," Kael said, kneeling down next to her. "We can't just sit here while you do this forever."

"I'm doing the best I can!" she snapped. Kael could tell she was close to breaking. "I never meant for it to come to this. I tried to stop you." Her voice cracked. "I tried to stop you."

Kael shook his head. He knew she referred to the fight within the rotunda. "It's in the past," he said, putting his hands on her shoulders. "You were doing what you thought was right." He gave her shoulders a squeeze to reassure her. It surprised him how fond he was growing of her. He had spent some of his childhood lamenting his fate at not having a mother, but he had not truly missed such a presence in his life in a long time. To suddenly embrace Aliisza as such was . . . unnerving and exciting all at the same time.

"We need a celestial," Tauran said weakly. "Someone with plane-traveling abilities. It's a shame Micus is lost to us. He could aid us."

Aliisza sat up. "Does it have to be an angel?" she asked, a strange hope in her voice. "Or just someone who can perform powerful planar-hopping magic?"

Tauran frowned and tried to focus his gaze in her direction. "Anyone could do it," he said. "An archon, a high priest, a—"

"A wizard," Aliisza added. A faint smile crossed her face. She moved closer to Tauran. Kael joined them both there. "Tell me," she said, "How does a Living Vessel work?"

"I told you," Tauran said, weariness filling his voice. "An angel can sacrifice—"

"No, no," Aliisza interrupted. "Not how it is created. How it is used. What do you do to fill it?"

Tauran frowned. "Usually, there is a ritual. The body of

the creature is brought near so that the soul can shift from it to the new vessel. Sometimes, in battle, it is less formal. So long as the two bodies touch, it can be done. But why?"

"Does the original body need to be alive?" she asked, pulling her sword free.

"No," the angel answered. "That is not necessary."

"Then maybe this will work," Aliisza said, turning the blade around so that the hilt faced her. Kael watched as she placed her fingers on a set of spots on the hilt and then pushed a certain way. The hilt twisted in her hand and the end slipped free, like a cap from a jug. A hollow chamber was revealed. Aliisza tipped the sword up so that something slid free into her hand. Kael recoiled slightly as he saw what the alu held.

There, in her palm, sat an ebony, desiccated finger, shriveled and delicate.

"How would you like to meet your father?" Aliisza asked, smiling up at Kael.

CHAPTER ELEVEN

Aliisza's hands trembled as she held Pharaun's finger. Her mind raced with a dozen thoughts, from wondering if her idea would really work to trying to guess what Kael and Tauran thought of her revelation. The idea of actually coming face-to-face with the drow mage sent shivers up her spine.

"My father?" Kael asked, his voice slightly timid. "That's his?"

"Yes," Aliisza said, "plucked from the Abyss after his death. I've kept it all this time, wondering if I would ever need to make use of it."

"He has no compunction to enter the Living Vessel," Tauran said. "It has been a long time for him. In some ways an eternity. And whatever has happened to him in those intervening stretches, he might not even recall you or your role in his life. His life itself might be nothing but a faint memory. Rarely is a Living Vessel used in this way."

Aliisza frowned. "But do you agree that it might work?" When the angel nodded, she said, "Then don't make me any more nervous than I already am."

Kael had risen to his feet and was pacing, his sword in his hand. "What makes you think that he will help us?" His tone had grown high-pitched, filled with nervous energy. "Or that he will want to know about me?"

Aliisza smiled. And so it comes full circle, she thought. "As a very wise person once explained it to me, in order to gain the benefit of caring about others, you have to be willing to surrender to the heartbreak that it might not work out as you expect . . . or hope." She cast a glance over at Tauran, who showed the faintest hint of a smile. "He's your father. At worst, your relationship with him will be nonexistent, just as it is now. At best . . ."

Kael blew a sigh that puffed his cheeks out. "Very well," he said. "It seems our only chance to escape this place, regardless. Let's do this."

Aliisza smiled and took the finger close to Zasian. She hesitated.

"What are the dangers?" she asked the angel. "What should we expect?"

Tauran shrugged. "None, that I know of," he said, his voice weak and raspy. "Just touch him with it."

"Will Zasian's mind return?" she asked, suddenly wary. "Am I dooming us instead of helping?"

"I cannot answer that," Tauran replied. "In all of this, there is great uncertainty. Nothing like this has ever occurred before." He broke into a coughing fit. When it finally subsided, he added, "But as Kael has pointed out, I see no other alternatives. Even if Zasian returns, you have not appreciably worsened our situation."

Grimacing, Aliisza turned back to the vacuous priest. That's debatable, she thought. Although I wouldn't mind the pleasure of gutting him, given the chance. She held the finger up to his gaze, watching to see if he would, at long last, react to something. He did not.

Do it, she told herself. Touch him.

Drawing a deep breath to bolster her courage, Aliisza tentatively reached out and placed the desiccated finger against Zasian's arm.

Nothing happened.

"It's not working," Aliisza said, sagging back. Disappointment sapped the energy from her.

"It may take a while for a connection to materialize," Tauran said. "Do not assume anything, yet."

Aliisza moved Pharaun's finger down to the priest's hand. She placed it into the man's palm and watched as Zasian's own fingers curled reflexively around it.

Aliisza sat back and watched. Please work. Maybe even the return of the Cyricist himself would be better. Please work!

Zasian sat passively in front of Aliisza, staring at nothing. She could detect no change in the Living Vessel.

Hope faded. Aliisza stared glumly at her own hands. Maybe Kael's right. We should make a break for the surface, try to get out to sea, find some way to escape. It might kill me, but I could do it. I could blow the demons away. Even Kaanyr. He doesn't know what kind of hell he unleashed, betraying me, she fumed. My last defiant act, obliterating him as the others slip away.

She shook her head and said, "Still nothing. I guess it was too much to hope—"

The illumination surrounding Zasian flickered.

Aliisza gasped and jerked her gaze back toward the man's face. Had there been a flutter of recognition there, in the eyes?

She held the priest's gaze with her own, watching it so intently that her eyes began to water. Another flicker rippled through the light, and it seemed to her to grow a tiny bit dimmer.

"Something's happening," Kael said, moving in closer. "I saw something."

"Pharaun?" Aliisza said softly, waving her hand in front of the priest's face. "Can you hear me?"

The return stare did not change, but the nimbus of light flickered and weakened.

"I think it's working!" Aliisza whispered. "He's coming!"

The thought of actually getting a chance to speak with the drow wizard gave Aliisza a little shiver. *What will he think?*

"Perhaps," Tauran said, struggling to sit up straighter and take a look himself. "But again, I must caution you. Do not expect him to react kindly to your summoning him. Indeed, he may not even know you anymore."

Aliisza ignored the angel's words. If Pharaun was being drawn into the vessel, he would remember her. She was certain. *He has to.*

Over several long moments, the emanation continued to flicker and fade. It had almost died out completely when Zasian jerked and gasped. He peered around, wide-eyed.

Then he screamed.

"By Torm, make him be quiet," Kael said in a strangled whisper. He reached out and clamped his hand over the suddenly frantic priest. The action caused Zasian to begin flailing violently. He slapped at Kael's arm and thrashed on the ground, kicking. All the while, he continued to try to scream.

Aliisza shoved Kael to the side and wrapped her arms around the wild priest. The thought that she was hugging a man she once hated passed briefly through the back of her mind, but she ignored it. She pressed her mouth close to Zasian's ear.

"Pharaun," she said softly. "Pharaun, it's me. It's Aliisza. Easy. I'm here. I'm with you."

Zasian screamed once more, a long, wailing, ragged sound, and then he crumpled, sobbing. He went completely limp in Aliisza's embrace.

"Get out in the hall and make sure nothing surprises us," Aliisza told Kael. "Hurry!"

Kael, his own red eyes wide, shook himself into action and got to his feet. He strode almost eagerly out of the hideaway and into the hall beyond. He disappeared, though Aliisza could hear him walking farther up the passage. She continued to console the human in her embrace, not certain to whom she was speaking.

"It's all right," she crooned. "I'm here. Aliisza is here."

Beside her, Tauran coughed. "It may take him too long to recover. Too long before he can offer any way out of here. The demons almost certainly heard that. They will be coming."

"Can you please try to find some hope?" Aliisza said. "I know you feel like . . . well, like hell, but your gloomy disposition is *not* helping."

Tauran began coughing again. When the fit subsided, he closed his eyes and slumped against the rock again. "Our time grows short," he murmured, "and I am slipping fast."

Aliisza turned her attention back to Zasian. She leaned back away from the man and peered into his face. The priest's eyes darted back and forth frantically, and he panted in fright. "Are you there?" she whispered. "Pharaun, is that you?"

"Why can't I see?" the man responded. "Why is it dark?"

Aliisza blinked in surprise. She realized the glow that had

accompanied Zasian since she had awakened in the rotunda had vanished entirely. They were engulfed in blackness. But *his eyes are now human eyes,* she realized, *and he cannot see as we can.*

She conjured a tiny magical light and placed it upon the hilt of her sword, after replacing the cap covering the secret compartment.

"It's all right," she said. "Do you know me?"

"Aliisza?" He looked at her face. Of course, it was Zasian's voice she heard.

"Yes," she answered. "Who are you? Do you know?"

"My lovely little minx, you wound me deeply. Despite being subjected to the most cruel and terrible torments for . . . for quite a long time, I do still know my own name. Pharaun Mizzrym, at your service."

Aliisza clenched her eyes shut in joy. She felt herself crying as she hugged her old companion and occasional lover tightly. "It *is* you," she said. "Thank the Abyss."

"I'd rather not," Pharaun replied. "It would be quite the good thing if I never heard mention of it again, in fact."

Aliisza almost laughed. *We did it,* she thought. *We managed to bring him back.* For a moment, she just sat there and hugged the man. *It's really him.*

Then a quiet cough from Tauran reminded her of the dire circumstances surrounding them. She pulled back once more. "Pharaun," she said, "we need your help."

"My help?" Pharaun replied. "How could I possibly help? I have no idea where we are"—he gazed down at the refuse at his feet—"though if I had to guess, I would say the sewer."

"Just about," Aliisza said. "But you're not quite away from the Abyss yet."

She spent the next few moments explaining the immediate situation. Pharaun tried to ask a few questions, but Aliisza rebuffed him. "We have no time for that right now," she said. "We need your magical expertise. We need to get free of here as soon as you can conjure a way."

The human face opposite her frowned. "That's quite the tall order," he said. "My magic is more than a bit rusty, and I have nothing with which to work."

"I know it's difficult, but you are our only chance. And not to put too fine a point on it, but if we are captured, you are too."

"Not quite the welcome I was looking forward to," Pharaun said. "But this isn't even my own body. If I were to attempt something of such magnitude right here, right now, I might just as likely deposit us in the scorching conflagrations of the Elemental Plane of Fire as someplace safe. I don't think—"

"Please!" Aliisza said, feeling her tightly wound emotions slipping again. "You've got to do something, or we're all dead. Be the Pharaun I remember." Aliisza found herself flinching from her own outburst. "I'm sorry. I am at my wit's end."

"Listen to you, apologizing," Pharaun said. Aliisza was still not used to hearing his words in Zasian's voice. She could only imagine how strange it must feel for him. "That's not the cunning little half-fiend I remember so well."

Aliisza grinned. "A lot has happened since we last parted ways. But we can reminisce later. We really do need to get out of here. Right now."

As if to punctuate her point, Kael called in a low whisper from the hallway, "Something is coming!"

"Wizard," Tauran said, scooting close so that Pharaun could hear him. "There is much you do not understand, but

I promise you that it is imperative that you spin some magic and conjure a way for us to flee. I cannot abide the thought of becoming the tortured plaything of a horde of demons."

Pharaun turned his head in the direction of the angel's voice. When he saw Tauran's angelic nature, he gasped. "It cannot be!" He let his eyes rove over the angel's wings, which were in sad shape at the moment. Tauran burst into another fit of coughing. Pharaun looked back at Aliisza. "You consort with strange friends, Aliisza. Where is your other half? You know, the cambion? What was his name again?"

"That's a long story," Aliisza said, trying not to wince. She took Pharaun's face and turned it back to her own again. "But it's a story for later. We have more pressing needs."

Pharaun glanced back at Tauran. "You do not look or sound well, my new friend. And let me assure you, I would rather not revisit that particular unpleasantness known as demon toy, either. I will do my best."

"What's happening?" Kael demanded from the hall.

"Shh," Aliisza answered. "He's thinking."

"Well, tell him to think faster!" Kael snarled back. "Whatever is coming is running now."

"Impetuous, whoever he is," Pharaun said, not looking up. "Another surprise for me?"

If you only knew, Aliisza thought, smiling again. Aloud she said, "What do you think? Any ideas?"

"It's strange . . ." Pharaun said, sounding distant. "Magic feels very . . . odd. Out of sync, if you will."

"It is," Tauran said. "Everything has suffered profound changes. Is it a hindrance?"

Pharaun shook his head. "No. On the contrary, I think I just might be able to conjure up a little trick. Normally this particular form of magic requires a focus, a small but elongated—"

"Later," Aliisza growled. "Just work the magic."

Pharaun snapped his mouth shut and pursed his lips in obvious aggravation. "Of course," he said in clipped tones. "Later." When he tried to rise he nearly fell over. "Goodness, I don't seem to have the strength I expected. Help me up."

Aliisza did as the wizard bid.

"Now the rest of you, link hands with me," Pharaun said.

Aliisza bent down and assisted Tauran to his feet. "Kael, it's time," she called.

The half-drow backed into the chamber, still watching the corridor. "They are at the far end of this passage," he said. "They can see the light." He spun around and took hands with the other three. "Do whatever you're going to do right now!"

Pharaun saw the knight for the first time, and his eyes grew wide. He stared first at Kael, then at Aliisza. His mouth gaped.

She knew he understood. "Hurry!" she yelled, yanking on his hand with her own to snap him out of it.

Pharaun shook his head to refocus and uttered a long string of arcane syllables. Some of them Aliisza recognized. Others were as alien to her as the strange tongues of the plainsmen of the Shaar in far southeastern Faerûn. The wizard finished his incantation with a commanding word.

The world shimmered, shifted.

A snarling face entered the chamber.

Everything rippled and faded from view.

❖ ❖ ❖ ❖ ❖ ❖ ❖ ❖

Eirwyn stepped back, evading the downward sword stroke of the undead knight before her. She batted his shield away with her mace and drew on her divine power. She gestured at the armored apparition and delivered the holy incantation in a clear, powerful voice. The blaze of light that infused the wraithlike warrior burst from the joints of his armor and radiated outward. It illuminated the deep gloom of the castle courtyard and revealed several other undead shuffling toward her and her two companions. The holy aura faded almost as quickly as it had appeared, and the knight crumpled to the ground with a metallic clank.

The angel shifted position in the snow and faced off against two more of the undead warriors. She brandished her mace, delivering a feint in the hopes of getting the two apparitions to become entangled, but they did not flinch. They seemed wholly unconcerned about their own well-being as they advanced toward Eirwyn.

"This is a fool's errand!" Garin said from nearby. He smashed the helm from atop another armored wraith and spun to attack a second. "There's no need for us to battle long-dead soldiers."

Eirwyn shattered a knight's shield before dispatching him with another blaze of holy might. "You don't need to stay," she said, leaping into the air to avoid three more coming at her. "I never asked you to suffer these trials and tribulations."

She landed next to the third member of her group, young Nilsa. The two devas positioned themselves back to back and continued to fend off the undead surrounding them.

"We stay as long as you do." Garin grunted from exertion. "Our orders are clear."

Eirwyn rolled her eyes and put a crushing dent into the breastplate of another foe. "Now who's running a fool's errand?" she asked. "Can Tyr really be so concerned with my business that he must send you to keep an eye on me?" She whirled and pummeled the shoulder of another armored ghost, sending the entire arm flying away to plop into the snow. "What could I possibly be up to that worries him so?"

"That's a very interesting question," Nilsa said, twisting around to hit an opponent that had managed to get very near the two angels' flank. "Considering you refuse to tell us."

Eirwyn made a disparaging sound and blasted two more knights with holy energy from a wave of her hand. "I told you, I don't know," she said. "Divinations aren't always so easy to interpret. I simply go where I'm needed and hope I figure it out in time."

The elder angel's companions did not answer her, so the three of them continued the fight in silence, save for the sound of metal crunching on metal and the occasional flare of holy power filling the gloom of the courtyard. When no more knights stood against them, the three celestials turned their gazes toward the periphery of their battlefield to make certain no reinforcements approached. Satisfied that they were safe for the moment, the angels made their way to an arched doorway set in one of the two towers guarding the front gate of the crystalline fortress. The trio did not fully enter the chamber beyond, but instead sought shelter in the alcove from the mysterious, greenish glowing snow that fell from the twilit sky.

To Eirwyn, the odd precipitation might have had a fey quality were it not for the incessant arrival of haunts trying to drive her from the place. She, Garin, and Nilsa had fought three engagements with the undead knights already, vying with the wraiths for control of the courtyard each time. She wasn't certain they were not the same spirits reanimating over and over.

"Can you at least give us some idea of why you are here?" Garin asked. "Some explanation that would satisfy our curiosity?"

"Yours, or those you serve?" Eirwyn countered. "You have made no secret of the fact that you are spying on me, to see what I might be up to. I say again: how could my business so interest the cohorts of Tyr?"

Garin sighed and said nothing more, but Nilsa, a younger, more impetuous angel, could not resist. "They do not trust you," she said. "They believe you are still in some way working against the Court, just as you did when you aided Tauran the Traitor."

Eirwyn tried to hide her smile as Garin made a soft noise. "Nilsa," he said, "she doesn't need to know our business. She is not a member of the Court."

"Precisely," Eirwyn said. "And by the same token, you do not need to know mine. My business does not concern the Court."

"I disagree," Garin said. "Tyr has a right to know when others plot against him."

"You overstep your bounds," Eirwyn warned. "When Helm was alive, I served both faithfully for longer than you have been alive. Do not presume to lecture me about plotting, child."

Garin did not respond, but Eirwyn felt him stiffen in anger next to her.

Eirwyn sighed softly, letting the tension she felt dissipate from her own body. "The truth is, I honestly don't know why I'm here," she said. "But something powerful and dire may befall the Court, indeed all of the House. And whatever it is, I have been drawn here to do my part to try and thwart it."

Eirwyn turned toward Garin and Nilsa, confronting them directly. "We do not labor on opposite sides of a conflict, except that which you choose to throw in our common path. I may yet need your aid, if you will give it, when the time comes. Mark me: This will affect every one of us before it's over. You cannot simply sit upon a fence and watch, waiting for me to slip up in some way. If you choose to do that, you will be forsaken."

"Weighty words for one who was, until recently, banished to a far corner of the House for transgressions against the Court," Nilsa said.

"Then is it your belief that all words spoken are tainted by the purity of the one who speaks them?" Eirwyn asked, her anger rising. "Am I to never again be trusted because I chose to keep my own counsel when your god slew mine? Because I refused to bend my knee to Tyr afterward?"

"Eirwyn, I—" Garin began, but the elder angel cut him off.

"Or is it, perhaps, a more base prejudice, born of the fact that I chose the wrong deity to follow in the first place? Am I guilty merely by association?"

Garin remained silent. Instead, his eyes widened as he peered at something over her shoulder, in the courtyard beyond their crude shelter.

Eirwyn spun, expecting to see more of the armored knights rising from the grave, ready to do battle with the intruders once more, defending their strange and wandering fortress adrift in the Astral for all eternity. What she saw instead made her heart thud in her chest.

A glow of light was just fading from around four figures who tumbled into the snow from nowhere.

❖ ❖ ❖ ❖ ❖ ❖ ❖ ❖ ❖

Tauran sensed everything change.

A great pressure ended, leaving the angel feeling light-headed. The overwhelming taint of evil that had pervaded everything around him faded, and he sighed in contentment. He would have liked to nestle down and sleep, but sudden and unexpected cold made him shiver. He opened his eyes to try to make sense of his new surroundings.

He found himself outside, lying upon snow-covered ground. A thousand tiny points of green light danced in his field of vision, drifting down from the gloom above.

This isn't right, he thought, perplexed and irritated. *Where are the others?*

Tauran caught the sound of voices arguing. He recognized them, but at the same time, they sounded muffled, distant. He tried to sit up and peer in the direction from whence they came, but his body did not want to cooperate. All the strength had been leeched from him in that horrible place, leaving nothing but the poisonous residue of raw, permeating evil.

He began to cough.

"See?" Tauran heard someone say, and he recognized Aliisza. "He's dying. We cannot stay here!"

"Nonetheless, our instructions are clear," said another voice, male, which sounded vaguely familiar to the angel, but he couldn't quite place it. "You are to remain here, bound to this place, until you agree to submit to the laws of Tyr. We cannot allow you to return, and we will not permit you to flee again."

So they have come hunting me still, Tauran realized. Tyr is not content to leave me to my doom. He has sent others to bring me to justice. So be it.

He tried to rise, to speak, but he still could not muster the energy to do either. He gasped at the ineffectual exertion and succumbed to the futility of it.

The cold grew worse, and Tauran felt his consciousness fading.

❖ ❖ ❖ ❖ ❖ ❖ ❖ ❖

"I do not understand," Pharaun said from behind Kael. "How did they find us here? None of us even knew where we would be until the moment we departed."

"I led them right to you," Eirwyn answered, sounding disgusted. She stood next to Kael, shoulder to shoulder with the knight. "I never would have imagined they would go to such lengths."

A figure loomed out of the darkness, walking slowly, inexorably, toward Kael, who stepped forward and swung his greatsword in an angular strike, cleaving the armored form from shoulder to hip. The mail parted like paper from the power of Kael's blow, and it collapsed to the snow, an empty shell.

Wielding his weapon felt so good to the knight, he grinned. Two more spirit warriors moved to fill in the space left by their fallen companion. He almost stepped forward to engage them, so eager was he to stretch too-long dormant muscles, but he stopped himself. Don't leave the circle, he chastised himself. Protect Tauran.

"They still blame all of us for what happened," Aliisza said, positioned at Kael's other shoulder. "As far as they're concerned, we precipitated the very downfall of the entire universe!" She sounded bitter to Kael as she slashed at something in front of her. The ring of steel on steel indicated that she had connected.

Eirwyn snorted. "I don't think even *they* believe we deserve *that* much credit," she said, "but with things in as much turmoil within the House as they are right now, we don't have much chance of clearing our names. They've already made up their minds, and we are left with two choices: surrender or perish."

Kael struck at another haunt in armor and watched it disintegrate. His body flowed from one stance to the next, his movement fluid. Three more figures moved just beyond the one he dropped, waiting for a chance to get at the half-drow and his companions. "And they did something to prevent you from just whisking us away?" he asked Eirwyn.

"Yes," the angel answered. "We have been dimensionally bound here until we submit to them. They caught me off guard, the moment you arrived."

Kael stepped back to avoid a lunging stab from one of the undead and nearly stepped on Tauran, who lay in the snow between them all. He still had not regained consciousness. "How many of these accursed things are there?" Kael asked, grunting as he swept his blade through one, then another in a single, powerful arc.

From behind him, a flash of light lit up the night sky.

Kael assumed that Pharaun had unleashed some bit of magic at the wraiths coming at them from that side. The thought that he stood in the middle of a strange keep adrift in the planar soup of the Astral, fighting side by side with both his mother and father, seemed ludicrous. After all these years, he thought, stabbing at another wraith, the whole family is together at last.

No, he thought, fighting a sudden sense of guilt. Tauran is my parent—mother and father—more than either of them could be. They may have sired me, but he gave me his care. Do not betray his dedication to you so quickly.

The number of ghostly warriors dwindled, and the companions made short work of the remaining few. When the battle was over, the four defenders stood their ground, catching their breath. Kael scanned the sky, looking for signs of the other two celestials who had approached them with Eirwyn, but there was no sign of them.

"They trapped us here and left," he said. Anger at finding himself trapped yet again filled him. His grip upon his sword hurt, he clenched it so hard. "That is not the way of Tyr. At least not the Tyr I thought I knew. Tauran was right. The Maimed One has strayed from the laws that defined him."

"They are not far," Eirwyn replied. "They know we must choose to surrender to them sooner rather than later. It's all very cunning, leaving us here, where we are constantly beset by these apparitions. They truly leave us no choice but to comply."

Not if I have anything to say about it, Kael thought. "If they were to be slain, would that break the binding?" he asked. A part of him regretted asking, but the rage he felt at their imposed impotence burned within him.

Eirwyn turned to the knight. "Do you truly mean to ask me that?" she asked. "Do you think Tauran would allow you to do such a thing?"

"How is that any different from their decision to condemn us to death here among these walking spirits?" he retorted. "It's as if they slew us by their own hands."

Eirwyn's expression softened a bit. "In their minds, we perish not through their cruelty, but through our own pride. We always have the option of accepting their offer."

"What, to be led back to the Court in chains?" Kael said. "To be paraded before the High Council and mocked? I think not."

"Even if you are innocent?" Eirwyn said, her voice gentle. "Even if doing so might mean saving your mentor's life?" She nodded in Tauran's direction.

Kael tried to release the anger building inside him. "I'm sorry," he said at last. "Nothing is simple and straightforward anymore. I always believed—Tauran always taught me—that if I followed the path of goodness and righteousness, no matter how hard that was, that justice would prevail." He looked down at the unconscious angel. "I don't know what to believe anymore."

Aliisza knelt beside Tauran, one hand upon his brow. She looked up at Kael and shook her head. "He's getting worse," she said. "Even now, getting him away from that awful place, he's so far gone he can't fight the taint. We have to."

Kael felt helpless. He turned his gaze on Pharaun. Though it was Zasian Menz's face he saw, Kael could see a twinkle of something kindred there, a flash of a knowing smile. The stranger shrugged at him.

Kael drew a deep breath, trying come to terms with the

decision. "Then we all agree?" he asked, looking from one face to another. "This is what we want to do? This is what we think is best for Tauran?"

Every head nodded.

"Fine," Kael said, casting his sword to the ground. He couldn't really blame them for their decision. He agreed with it, in fact. It just felt so dirty to him, giving up. It was not a feeling he much cared for.

"We surrender," he said.

CHAPTER TWELVE

Vhok couldn't stand the pain any more. He relieved the pressure on his arms by levitating his weight and grunted in relief. His ankles still ached, but he no longer felt as though he would be pulled in half. He cursed softly and heard the echo of his own voice within the shaft.

The half-fiend dangled in what he imagined was the inside of a tower or perhaps a round pit in the ground. Chains connected to shackles on his wrists rose into the darkness overhead, holding him in place. More chains on his ankles anchored a great weight hanging somewhere below him. Every shift, every tiny movement sent him swaying. When he held very still, faint howls or screams sometimes reached his ears, deeply muffled.

He had no idea where he was, or how long he had been there.

The ability to hold himself aloft with magic was his only saving grace. Without that, he would have already succumbed to the terrible strain. He certainly would have been screaming by then. His arms might even have been wrenched from their sockets.

Hot vapors wafted up from below, carrying an acrid odor that burned his nostrils and throat. Even with his natural affinity for heat, the air scorched. Sweat drenched him, ran down his naked skin in rivulets that tickled him maddeningly. The fight to resist twitching wore on him. The longer he remained still, the worse the tickling became, yet every time he flinched, trying to shake the trickles free, stabs of pain filled every strained joint.

Vhok cursed Aliisza for the hundredth time. He saw her face, that cunning, clever smile, mocking him, and he screamed insults at her. Somehow, she had found the strength to escape. He had underestimated her, perhaps. Though he was angry with himself for it, she still bore the brunt of his rage.

No, he realized. Zasian. Somehow, they must have coaxed the priest into healing her.

You cursed, guileful wench, he fumed. I should have killed you when you were down. You're too clever by half, always using those supple curves and that sultry smile to twist men's hearts. Tauran will get what he deserves. His pain will come, when you turn on him as you turned on me. I am a fool for ever having loved you.

The chance had been there to take her life, but he knew he had let his own fondness for her, his weakness, get the better of him. He had also made the mistake of playing his hand too early, revealing his intentions. That had been foolish; it would have been better to lie to them, tell them that he was off to seek help and then return with enough demons to corral the group. It had just felt too damned good to finally, *finally* be free of that awful, wretched compulsion.

Besides, it's still ultimately her fault, he reasoned. She was the one who changed, let her human side grow too dominant, allowed herself to develop weak, caring feelings. She is the traitor, guilty ten times over, and I hate her.

The rock that lined the shaft was not natural stone, as he had seen within Vhissilka's cave complex before. No, it had been built, crafted from great worked blocks, which was why he imagined he might be in a tower. He was in another's domain, but he did not remember arriving there. He simply woke from unconsciousness to find himself strung up like a piece of smoked meat, awaiting carving.

He had been fighting the cruel torture for time immemorial, it seemed. He alternated between countering his own weight in order to relieve the stress on his arms and supporting the weight below him to alleviate the punishment to his ankles. Sometimes, in between, when his magic gave out, he had to endure the full brunt of the torture.

At those times, it was all he could do not to scream.

I won't give them the satisfaction, he told himself. I'll let them pull me apart before I whimper like a child. And when I rip in half, I will find a way to return from the grave and track down that alu. Aliisza will regret her audacity. So help me, she *will*.

Vhok's mind drifted off into some pain-filled haze, so it was a moment before he realized that something had changed. Light shone down from above. Fiery red light. Flame.

He tried to peer up, but the glow was too bright, and he winced and blinked.

Vhok felt himself rise. He was being pulled up, and the chains jerked and bounced as whatever mechanism that controlled his ascent ratcheted. The jarring tugs sent new pain through him. For a moment, he truly did fear he might rip in half.

He ascended from the shaft into a dimly lit room—though it was more than bright enough for his light-starved eyes—dangling from a wooden derrick. He blinked, trying to get his eyes to adjust. He felt motion, sensed someone attaching something to the chains on his legs. Then there was blessed relief as the weight came off. He could not help the groan that escaped his lips.

The derrick swung wide of the pit. Vhok's arms were freed, and he fell to the stone floor like a rag doll. He lay there for long moments, writhing from the pins and needles in his joints as his blood flow returned. Screams echoed in the chamber. Some were still muffled, as though buried, but others were loud, harsh, as though someone very near him suffered immeasurably.

A wet splat accompanied an object tossed near his face. When he managed to focus his gaze, he saw a waterskin, though of what kind of skin, he did not want to speculate. He reached for the container and uncapped it. He drank greedily, letting the water spill down his chin. Before he had even half sated himself, the skin was taken from him and his own clothes were tossed down at his feet.

"Get up," a harsh voice commanded. "Dress yourself. Lord Axithar wishes to speak with you."

Vhok fumbled to put the clothes on, wondering who—or what—Lord Axithar was. They didn't return everything. Only his breeches, shirt, and boots. His armor, cape, and his equipment remained missing.

By the time Vhok was dressed and upright, his vision had returned to normal. He surveyed his surroundings.

One of the ram-headed demons watched over him, though Vhok was unsure if he had met this one before. The beast twirled its oversized spear-headed ranseur, waiting for him to finish. Other figures moved in the dimness of the chamber. He glanced at them and saw that he stood in the middle of a chamber of torture, built of the same stone blocks that had formed his pit—and that was, indeed, where he had been— and the cambion got the sense that he was in the bowels of some great fortress.

A bariaur thrashed within an iron frame nearby, its horned head and fists pinned within one set of stocks, all four of its hoofed feet similarly trapped at floor level. A group of demons, small imps with gray skin and oversized ears, poked and prodded the thing with sharpened iron rods. Dozens of trickles of blood seeped from puncture wounds, and the creature howled in anguish.

Against the closest wall, two dwarves with filth-matted dark hair crouched in cages too small for them. The first prison dangled from a length of chain perhaps two feet above a fire pit filled with glowing coals. The dwarf within panted as he pushed against the wall with his hands, trying to keep himself swaying and not lingering over the searing heat. The second one had his arms thrust through the top, clinging to the iron ring set into the stone ceiling where the chain was attached. He held both his own weight and that of the cage, which rested upon his stout shoulders, up away from a bed of coals. His arms shook from the strain of keeping himself aloft.

"Kill me," the one in the lower cage pleaded. "For the love of Moradin, do not let them roast me!"

Vhok smirked. He spied the waterskin clutched in his guard's free hand.

"May I?" he asked, pointing to the drink.

The demon grimaced but tossed Vhok the skin. The cambion made a show of uncapping the container and tipping his head back, letting the water pour into his mouth. A bit of it trickled down his chin. He swallowed and smiled at the dwarf. "You wouldn't happen to be from Sundabar, would you?" he asked.

The prisoner gaped at Vhok wide-eyed, forgetting for a moment to keep his swinging motion up. His blistered feet and buttocks began to smoke. He screamed in agony and fumbled to get himself moving again. In his panic, he could not get a good rhythm going, and his screaming increased.

The ram-demon yanked the empty waterskin out of Vhok's hands, turned, and led him out of the small room. "Come," it grumbled.

They ascended a large stone staircase, leaving behind the anguished cries of the prisoners. The ram-headed fiend led Vhok through a stout iron door and into a hall. The gloomy, smoke-filled passage led to another staircase, and then another. They climbed up and up, passing other demons along the way, some of them the lowly craven dretches that served as the bulk of the abyssal forces, others loftier, more cunning species. At one point, they passed three mariliths going the opposite direction, but none were Vhissilka.

The pair passed through another, larger door. A howling wind assaulted them, a hot, fetid gale that lashed at Vhok's clothes and hair. It carried upon it the stink of sulfur and death. A gray sky roiled above, and Vhok could not tell whether it was filled with low-hanging clouds or heavy black smoke. The underside of the seething haze glowed red-orange in places, and once, Vhok spotted a winged creature in silhouette against the burning light.

He and his guard came to a large balcony. The platform, made of lustrous black stone, clung to the side of a lofty tower. A narrow, arched walkway led from it to a similar porch ahead. Both spires rose from a massive sprawling castle, all of it constructed from the same glossy stone. The two crossed, and Vhok peered over the wall to the ground below.

The land, a broken surface of jutting, jagged rock interspersed with thick, thorny brambles and fields of gravel, was crisscrossed with deep crevasses. Orange light flared from within those trenches, and smoke poured from them, whisked away by the wind. In the flat spaces between the shards of protruding glasslike stone, swarms of creatures moved, shuffling together into groups. Larger demons herded the smaller ones, often with a slash of whip or weapon.

An army was assembling. A massive one. Vhok could see it happening as far as his vision would take him.

"Where are we?" he said to his escort. "Is this the Abyss?"

The ram-headed guard cast a glance back at Vhok and smirked. "Shut up and keep walking, cambion."

They reached the far side of the causeway and passed through another door. Once in the interior again, the roar of the wind vanished. Vhok's guard led him down one last, grand hallway. Prisoners lined it, creatures from every corner of the world and perhaps beyond. Each had been positioned within an alcove, impaled upon a slender shaft from back to front and angled slightly upward, so that the spike held the being aloft in a roughly standing position. Some dangled motionless, perhaps already dead, but others still squirmed and cried out for succor. None could slip free of their confinements.

Better them than me, Vhok thought. Unless . . .

A moment of panic passed through the cambion, and he was on the verge of turning and dashing away, back to the balcony outside, when the guard turned and faced a massive door of black. The guard pushed the portal open and led Vhok into a chamber that glowed with the fires of a dozen braziers. A roiling pit of magma bubbled in the center. Numerous other creatures moved through the large room, perhaps attending to some important business or other, but Vhok hardly noticed them. All of his attention was drawn to the lone, towering figure near the pit.

A great horned demon with a ferocious, almost bestial face and terrible gaze stood there, its black, batlike wings spread wide. Flames licked up and down its red skin and its fingers clutched a massive sword with a glowing, fiery blade. In its other hand, the towering demon idly flicked a whip that had tongues of flame snaking along it.

A balor.

❖ ❖ ❖ ❖ ❖ ❖ ❖ ❖

Consciousness returned to Kael. The faint tinkling of water splashed somewhere nearby. Confusion and disconcerting fear hit him as he opened his eyes. He did not remember where he was or how he had come to be there. Drawing on his military training, he took a deep, calming breath and examined his surroundings.

He lay upon a soft bed in a room filled with the faint glow of moonlight. He rose up on one elbow and saw that the pale lambency entered through a gauze-veiled archway.

It gleamed on white marble, casting a cool gray hue on the whole chamber. A writing desk sat against one wall along with a small shelf of books. On the near wall a sunken basin big enough to bathe within brimmed with water, and the bright sound of splashing he had first discerned came from there, where a steady stream poured from a fountain set into the wall. On the opposite end from the archway stood a darkened doorway.

We're home, he thought, letting his guard down at last. Then he grimaced. Tauran is safe, but we are at the mercy of the High Council. I hope it was worth it.

Kael sat up and stretched. He expected muscles to complain because of too many nights spent sleeping on hard stone in cold places, but he found that he felt fresh. He shook free of the covers and stood. He was naked, and he took a moment to examine his dark skin, seeking signs of injuries or poorly healed wounds or scars. In wonderment, he found none at all.

Am I dreaming? he thought. Are we truly home?

Yes, he thought. I remember the journey too clearly. The memory of surrendering, followed by the indignity of Garin and Nilsa binding all of them to comply before bringing them to the High Council chambers still left a bitter taste in his mouth. It had happened.

But then, what is this place?

His armor rested upon a stand at the foot of the bed, each piece laid carefully there, polished and gleaming in the lunar light, with fresh bindings, straps, and ties replacing old, worn ones. His greatsword stood there as well, oiled and sharpened.

They left me my weapons? Why would they trust me with

them now, after . . . ?

Nothing made sense anymore.

Kael turned to the archway and padded across the room. He pushed through the flimsy curtains and found himself standing upon a small balcony. The moon, hanging low in the sky, was round and pearly. Its glow illuminated the slopes of great Celestia, along with the clouds that ringed its hidden crown.

It is definitely the Court, Kael thought. *But it all feels too . . . peaceful.*

That thought surprised Kael. It wasn't that long ago that he could not have imagined expecting more tumult within the House.

But much has happened since those more carefree times, he mused. *Everything was . . . chaos when we returned. No High Council, and Garin and Nilsa behaving so oddly. Struggling to make decisions, as if they weren't quite sure. And then nothing. He could remember nothing after arriving.*

What did they do with me? With the others? Is Tauran alive?

Kael turned, walked back into the room, and passed beyond the darkened doorway into the interior area. He saw a cozy divan and more shelves filled with books. A plush rug had been tossed casually across the floor, and dark tendrils draped from bowls became potted plants and ferns when he stared at them fully. A door—shut tight—stood within the wall opposite where he had entered.

Kael crossed the rug and pulled the portal open a tiny bit, peering out. He saw a hall softly illuminated by round globes, glowing a warm, yellow-orange color, spaced periodically down its length. He spotted no one else, nor did he hear any other sounds.

I must be dreaming, he thought. This definitely looks like the Court, but where is everyone?

Shaking his head, not sure what to make of his own solitude, Kael turned back inside and went to his armor. He donned his clothing and took up his sword. He cast one last look around the room and, satisfied that he was leaving nothing behind, the knight headed out into the hall, pulling the door shut behind him.

In one direction, the passage simply led to more doors like his own, and then it ended at a window. In the other, he could hear a faint breeze stirring wind chimes around a corner. He headed that direction.

He found a courtyard at the end of the hall, a pleasant, inviting place filled with meandering paths, cozy benches, and carefully cultured vegetation. He noted the trees in particular, the leaves of which captured the light of the moon and reflected it.

Or perhaps they glow from within, Kael mused.

The wind chimes he had heard hung from the branches, and the breezes that blew through the leaves carried the fragrance of blossoms. Near the center of the open area, Kael spied a shallow pool. In the midpoint, a statue of an angel rose up, wings spread wide, paying homage to the heavens overhead.

I know this place, Kael realized, moving to stand beside the pool. I have been here before, on a night just like this. Tauran brought me here. To meet my mother. Tauran said I should give her a chance, but I wasn't interested. I did not know her then. How strange that I would end up back here now, wishing to spend a moment longer with her.

Kael gazed down into the water and caught the reflection of overhanging branches in its gently rippling surface. Memories of the strange, disorienting encounter, when Aliisza had changed places with him, stolen his body, and escaped, came flooding back into his mind. He remembered waiting in the shadows, listening to her reveal her fears and doubts.

Kael turned to look in that same spot.

A figure sat there, cloaked in those same shadows, watching him. "It's not real, you know," his mother said.

Kael smiled. Aliisza rose, stepped out from the gloom, and crossed the grass to stand before him. She took both his hands in her own and peered into his eyes.

"It's all just an illusion," she said, her smile sad.

Kael tilted his head to one side, puzzled.

"This," Aliisza said, gesturing around them. "The garden, the Court, all of it. We're not really here."

Kael frowned. "Somehow, I already knew that. But what is it, then? And if it's not real, then am I really talking to you?"

Aliisza's smile widened the tiniest bit. "I would ask the same thing, but for some reason, I know we're both really here."

Kael nodded, but her explanation didn't make him feel any better. "What is this place?" he asked.

She dropped his hands and strolled toward a bench. She took a seat on it and tilted her head to one side as she stared up at her son. Her eyes were intense, watching him. "This was my prison," she said quietly, "when I first came here."

"Ah, yes," Kael said, remembering hearing descriptions of the mirror-place whenever he asked about his mother. "Tauran spoke of it when I was young. They said you were happy here."

Aliisza snorted. "They lied." She peered into Kael's eyes again, and the sensation it created, as if she were trying to see deep inside him, was growing unnerving. "Most of the time, I didn't even realize I was here. I was trapped in fictions, forced to learn about the more caring, considerate side of myself."

"You sound wounded," Kael said, turning to sit beside her so that she would stop staring at his face so intently. "Like you still resent it."

Beside him, his mother shrugged. "I do," she said. "Tauran was doing what he thought was right. But the decisions the angels make are every bit as conniving and selfish as any demon's choices. They just cloak it in words like 'honor' and 'justice,' and they codify the machinations into a set of laws so that everyone gets manipulated evenly. Then they can point to it and say, 'See? We're in the right because it's all equal; everyone has to abide by the same rules.' "

Kael frowned. "And that's not good enough? Do the laws not treat everyone fairly?"

Aliisza shook her head. "That's not the point." She turned to face him. "Do you think we did the right thing, surrendering to Garin and Nilsa so they would bring Tauran back? To save his life, did we do what had to be done?"

Kael cocked his head to one side. "I don't know."

"Why do you doubt it?"

He sighed. "Because it felt wrong. Because it felt like we should fight harder to prove that we were right." He clenched his fists in anger. "Because Garin and Nilsa infuriated me with their absolutism."

"I think there's another reason," Aliisza said. "When it came time to free Kaanyr, Tauran claimed he couldn't break his word. Even though it probably meant the death of us all, he wouldn't do it."

"It was the just, honorable thing to do," Kael said, feeling a bit indignant. "He gave his word."

"You argued with him at the time," Aliisza pointed out. "So did I."

Kael nodded. The guilt of his lapse made him stare at his hands again in shame. "That was wrong of me," he said. "It was a moment of weakness."

"Nonsense," Aliisza said. "Tauran was willing to defy the High Council and his own god to go after Zasian. He was even willing to drag you along with him, and you didn't protest then. You went along with it, because you knew it was right. So what was different about freeing Kaanyr?"

Kael shrugged. "I don't know. I don't know what's right or wrong anymore."

"The reason we both became so upset with him is because we could see what he was really doing. He was giving up."

Kael cringed at his mother's words. "Don't," he pleaded. But he knew she was right.

"Look at me," Aliisza said. "He was ready to die. He had accepted it, even remarked that death would have been preferable to . . . what else he faced. He freed Kaanyr because he had accepted his fate."

"And we weren't ready for that," Kael said, understanding at last. "We wanted him to keep on fighting, so we could return and see his honor restored."

"Yes," Aliisza said. "He was trying to set us free. I even think, in a strange, weird way, he wanted you to see, one last time, the folly of slavishly adhering to the law. Releasing Kaanyr from the compulsion was the means to do both."

"But that put us in greater danger from Vhok. I don't

think Tauran intended for that to happen."

"Neither do I. That was just a miscalculation on Tauran's part. I think he believed that Kaanyr would take me with him and flee, and then he would convince you to go, too. In his mind, getting left behind was a just end for his crimes against Tyr. I think that he at last had come to understand just how absolute his own self-destruction was and was trying to avoid reconciling it within himself."

Kael considered everything Aliisza said. It hurt to think that Tauran would do that, but he couldn't deny that he had sensed it in the angel, too. "So now you're asking me if we should have brought him back here," he asked, "when maybe he didn't want to return?"

"Something like that," Aliisza said, and she smiled faintly. "We didn't want for him what he wanted for himself. He perhaps didn't think he could face up to his own flaws. Did we do him any favors? I don't know. But I do know this. You asked me if the law didn't treat everyone fairly. I can't answer that, but I can say, having watched the toll it took on Tauran—and you—trying and failing to stay within the strictures of a set of laws, that nothing should dictate our lives in such an absolute way."

"Oh, well said," a voice from behind them said. "I couldn't agree more."

Kael rose to his feet with his blade free and spun to see who had intruded on his conversation with his mother. A drow stood there, a little way back, on a flagstone path. Even in the soft light of the moon, leaves, and faint globes, it wasn't hard for Kael to see his own features in the midnight face. His own garnet eyes stared back at him, surrounded by a tousled mane of white hair. The dark elf was slender of build, and his clothing bespoke wealth and perhaps even a little self-importance.

"Pharaun!" Aliisza said, rising and moving quickly toward the drow. "I wondered if you would show up."

Aliisza hugged the drow, then leaned in and gave him a gentle kiss on the cheek. "I'm glad you're here," she said.

"Yes, well," the drow answered, examining his own body as he spoke, "I have to tell you, I'm more than a little surprised myself. So much to figure out in such a short time. The matron mothers never even kept me guessing *this* much."

Aliisza tilted her head, considering. "I wonder, though, why we all managed to be here together. Maybe they wanted a chance for us to talk."

"More likely they want to listen in," Pharaun replied dryly. "See what we'll reveal."

"We've got nothing to hide," Aliisza said, sniffing.

"Speak for yourself," Pharaun answered with a wry chuckle. "I'd prefer that my life not be an open book for angels."

Kael found it hard to keep from squirming. That was his father standing there, his blood sire, and he wasn't sure how he felt about it.

Tauran is my father, he told himself. He's the one who raised me.

"Well met, Kael," Pharaun said as Aliisza led him back over to the bench. Kael didn't say anything as the drow sized him up. "You are quite the impressive specimen, lad. I guess we can really cook, eh, Aliisza?"

Aliisza giggled, but there was a nervousness to it.

Kael scowled. "So, you're my father," he said at last, unsure how to proceed. A part of him was thankful for the chance to visit with the drow while not under constant duress, but having the opportunity suddenly didn't seem quite so . . . beneficial. "Not what I expected. Or imagined."

"I would hope not," Pharaun replied with a self-satisfied grin. "I doubt dear Aliisza here could really do me justice. Even for one as glib-tongued as she, it would be hard to truly explain a Master of Sorcere. You must actually meet one to understand. And now you have! Consider yourself fortunate. It is not every day one has the privilege of doing so."

Kael's frown turned into a smirk. "Was he always this vain?" he asked Aliisza, put off by the drow.

Aliisza laughed, and it was genuine. Pharaun, Kael noted, was decidedly less amused. "Actually, yes," she said. "He was. Is. But don't hold it against him, Kael. If you had ever seen Menzoberranzan or met a matron mother, you'd understand."

Pharaun turned to Aliisza, feigning a pout, and said, "Just what have you been teaching our son, you troublesome tart?" he asked. "Clearly not any of the important things, that's plain to see. And will someone please explain to me why he's dedicated his life to the likes of such a stuffy, overblown cad as Torm?"

Incensed, Kael took a step toward the drow, his grip on his sword tightening.

Pharaun, his eyebrows raised in surprise, retreated a step, his hand slipping inside his tunic.

"Stop it, both of you!" Aliisza said, stepping between the two and planting her hands against their chests.

Rage still burned within Kael at the insult, but he grudgingly relaxed, and when his counterpart did likewise, Aliisza sighed and dropped her hands.

"Men," she grumbled, returning to the bench. "Come, sit with me, both of you. I don't know how much time we have, and I don't want to waste it watching your egos clash."

Kael grimaced, but he took a seat next to his mother. Pharaun positioned himself on her other side. The three of them sat in silence, staring at the water before them.

Finally, Aliisza spoke again.

"I'm going to tell you both a story. Each of you has heard some of it before. Neither of you has heard it all. When I'm finished, maybe each of you'll understand the other a bit more." She paused, drew a deep breath, and began.

The alu spoke of her time in the deep halls far below the surface of Faerûn, when she and Vhok had been together. She told the tale of how she'd met Pharaun, and of following him through what seemed like the entirety of the Underdark.

"Why?" Kael asked at one point. He couldn't wrap his mind around the idea that the alu would care that much about the drow. *What could she possibly see in him?* he thought.

Aliisza shrugged. "He made me laugh," she said, as though hearing his thoughts. "He was witty, and when we were together, even though he knew I was fishing for knowledge, he didn't care." She sighed. "I think, looking back on it, that I liked the fact that he enjoyed my company so . . . honestly. I had never felt that from . . ." She trailed off, and there was a hint of wistfulness in her tone.

"Not even a little bit because I'm so irresistible?" Pharaun interjected. "You certainly seemed to act that way at the time."

Aliisza giggled, and she sounded like a giddy girl to Kael. He cringed. *I don't want to know about that,* he realized.

The alu continued, explaining all the way to how the two

of them had wound up trapped within the dark recesses of a cave in a chunk of what had once been the Blood Rift. Her voice grew hoarse briefly as she spoke of Vhok's trickery and ultimate betrayal.

When she finished, the three of them sat quite still for a long time. "What a strange, mixed-up life this has become," she murmured. "How did things turn out so . . . convoluted?"

"Life just has a way of performing such tricks, Aliisza," Pharaun answered. "Whether because of the capriciousness of gods or the ambitions of others, you often find yourself tangled in a web of complicated design, wondering how you managed to get there. Look at me. I thought I was destined to rule Sorcere, but I wound up here, sitting in a make-believe enchanted garden, a prisoner of Tyr's servants, all because you decided to save my finger.

"Speaking of which," the drow said, changing the subject, "Just what do we expect to happen next? While this is a much improved prison compared to the one I enjoyed as a guest of the Spider Queen, I do not think they intend to leave us here. One of our captors made mention of a trial, I believe?"

"Yes," Aliisza said. "We will be called before the High Council, a collection of angels with Tyr's direct ear, to answer for our crimes."

"Oh, well, that shouldn't adversely affect me much," Pharaun said. "I have little to do with this whole affair."

The drow rose to his feet and looked at Kael. "I had what could perhaps be called a friend—if drow were inclined to consider such things—back in Menzoberranzan. A blademaster, one with his weapon and all that. You remind me a bit of Ryld. He saved my life a time or two, and I'm afraid I didn't always do my best to return the favor." Pharaun shrugged.

"Such is the way of my people, you see. But seeing as how you remind me of him, I'll perform the highly unusual act of honoring his memory by giving you some advice I probably should have passed on to him."

Kael wanted to chuckle. *Advice from a father I hardly know? Should I be grateful?*

Yet a part of him craved some deeper understanding of his sire. He wanted to see how much of himself might be hidden within the drow.

"Never get caught up too much in duty, honor, and sacrifice," Pharaun said. "Not because they're not worth it or because they leave you hollow and wanting in old age." He drew a deep breath. "No, it's because those things are inevitably tied to someone else's agenda, my dear boy. And by the time you discover their agenda and yours are no longer compatible, it's usually too late."

Kael considered the drow's words. "Are you speaking from experience?" he asked.

Pharaun chuckled. "Bright lad we've got there, Aliisza. Takes after his father." He turned to Kael. "You would think so, based on my sad tale, yes? But no, my woes came about purely because of my own selfish agenda. I got greedy. A far more laudable goal, in my esteemed opinion, but one equally as likely to get you into just as much trouble as duty, honor, and the rest."

Kael did smile, then.

"Listen, my boy," the drow said, drawing Kael out of his thoughts. "I can see you sitting there, trying to decide how much of me is in you, how much of your mother is tucked away in there, and how much of this angel, Tauran, who raised you, truly shaped you. Based on what I've heard tonight, my guess is, you're not certain how you will feel about the answer."

Kael gave the drow a steady look. "Very astute," he said, but inside, his emotions were churning. Who am I? he wondered. What parts of me are really *me*?

"The truth is, the answer doesn't matter," Pharaun said. "At the end of the day, when the tale has been told and your reckoning is at hand, you've still made all the choices. At the end, you've only got one person, and one person only, to answer to. Yourself." His tone grew a bit wistful. "I learned that the hard way, standing on that Abyssal Plane as the spiders kept coming." He blinked and returned his gaze to Kael. "It's not me, it's not her"—he pointed to Aliisza—"it's not that angel who raised you. It's not even your god. Unless you're satisfied with the choices you've made regarding them and how you choose to deal with them, none of the rest matters."

Kael spent a long time thinking on what both his father and mother told him, and it was brightening into dawn when he felt himself being drawn away from that illusory place and back into his own body.

CHAPTER THIRTEEN

Tauran opened his eyes.

The angel was home. Or at least, in a place that felt very much like home. He found himself in a bed in a chamber of white marble and warm sunlight. The scent of fresh flowers wafted through the room, and he spied several hanging baskets overflowing with green and blossoms. The sound of chirping birds and lazy breezes through wind chimes reached his ears from somewhere beyond the room.

I live, he thought. I don't deserve it, but I live. He pushed the thought that perhaps he didn't wish to remain living out of his mind and sat up.

Tauran drew a deep breath and sighed. His body felt tired but comfortable. He felt no taint of the evil that had pervaded him. Any residual aftereffects of his ordeal within the confines of that black, wicked cave seemed to have vanished.

The physical scars are gone, he thought. Would that it were so easy to heal the mental ones.

He thought of Kael and Aliisza. Did they survive? he

wondered. They must have. They were there, with me, in the cold. And . . . others.

Dissatisfied that he could not remember more of how he had returned to the Court, Tauran rose from the bed, found his clothing—but not his mace—and dressed. Though he missed it, it felt somehow fitting that his badge of honor had been taken from him. Still he felt anxiety. What will they do? What will Tyr decree? There is but one way to find out.

The angel headed for the door. He reached for it, but for some reason, he could not make himself touch the thing. Frowning, he tried again.

They have compelled me, he thought, a flicker of panic rising up inside him.

Tauran turned and moved toward the balcony and the sunlight. He passed through the doorway and out into the warmth. The breezes ruffled his hair. Celestia loomed before him, its high peak hidden in a ring of clouds. Suddenly, he wanted more than anything to go there, to glide along its vast surface, to sail over its valleys and ridges. He willed himself to spread his wings and fly out into the blue skies, to soar high above the clouds, but he simply could not.

I have been reduced to a common prisoner, he thought. Shame filled him. I brought it on myself.

Because I was doing what I thought was right! He wanted to rail against his predicament, to scream that he deserved better, but he recalled his vow to accept the consequences. Now the reckoning is at hand, he told himself. Can you no longer face it?

No. Tyr, please forgive me! I was trying to help!

Suddenly, the angel remembered Aliisza, standing in the

rotunda, next to Micus, crying out very similar words. I was trying to help, she had said.

She deserves better than this, even if I do not, he insisted.

The angel stormed back to the door and called loudly through it. "I must have an audience with the High Council at once!" When no one opened the door or even answered, he yelled even louder. "I demand to be heard! I am no forsaken fiend to be broken and remade. I accept my guilt, but the others do not deserve this punishment! Answer me!"

Nothing.

The exertion of shouting made Tauran feel unsteady on his feet. Breathing hard, he sought the bed and sat upon it.

You've been sick, he reminded himself. And you no longer enjoy the beneficence of Tyr's healing presence.

That thought dug into him hard, made his throat constrict.

After a while, when he felt his strength return to him and impatience set in again, Tauran navigated the entirety of the room, examining every detail, seeking some sign of his fate. He followed every wall, studied every piece of furniture. As he walked, the chamber began to feel constricted, too small for him.

This is terrifying, he realized. How could anyone stand this for days on end? He thought of Aliisza, trapped in her own room, desperate to flee, to escape her fate. I did that to her. To all of those I brought here. It was done with a thought to kindness, but now I see how it is but a thin veil. The illusion against the truth cannot hold.

We are not so noble as we like to imagine.

With that thought came realization and acceptance that

he had done everything, that he had defied the High Council and Tyr himself, because somehow, he had come to realize this truth long before then. Even as noble as their purposes might be, angels were imperfect, not without blame.

Their punishment of me—and of my companions—will be imperfect too, he lamented.

When a knock came at Tauran's door, it was much later in the day. The sound startled the angel out of his brooding. "I cannot touch the portal," he called, standing.

The door opened and Garin peered in. "I am glad to see you up," he said. "May I enter?"

"Do I have a choice?" Tauran asked evenly. He was suddenly angry, indignant. You are no better than me, he thought, staring at the visitor. At the same time, he felt self-conscious, unsure of where to put his hands. "Could I keep you out if I wished it?"

Garin's frown was fleeting. "No, but I am no boor, Tauran. It is your room, and I am a visitor at the moment. Now, may I come in?"

Tauran motioned for the other angel to enter. He did so, shutting the door behind him. Tauran turned and sat on the bed once more.

"Now that you have recovered sufficiently, I will let the High Council know to summon you," Garin said, turning and pacing. "Or at least, what's left of it."

"What does that mean?" Tauran asked, watching his guest. "What has happened?"

"There was a schism," Garin explained. "The High Councilor and two others divorced themselves from it over the decision to pardon Eirwyn. Another councilor has vanished, thought to have lost her faith in the aftermath of Mystra's death. They are down to five, and they bicker constantly."

"Over what?" Tauran did not like what he was hearing. Too much instability. Tyr had not yet found his footing again, the angel feared.

"Over how to deal with the waves of wild, uncontrollable magical backlash, over what to do about the demon incursions, over why Tyr seems uninterested in—" Garin snapped his mouth shut. "Enough. I shouldn't be telling you this."

"Why not?" Tauran asked, rising to his feet, feeling the old sense of duty and responsibility fill him once more. "It's still me. I still care. Let me help."

Garin stopped and stared at him. "Why would you even suggest such a thing? You must account for your crimes against Tyr."

"I know," Tauran said, trying to keep his voice calm. Inside, he felt his heart flutter. Perhaps, he realized, a part of me hoped they might follow through with it. Foolish. "But there is still much I could offer. Information, freely given. Not as part a pardon"—to dream of such is too much, he thought—"but because it's the right thing to do."

Garin shook his head. "That is not for me to decide," he said. "You must offer that to the High Council. I wouldn't hold out much hope, though. Opinion against you has hardened considerably. Everyone sees you as a traitor, Tauran."

"And what of my companions?" Tauran asked. "They are not bound by the same laws that I am."

"True," Garin replied. "Though in this instance, it might be better for them if they were. They are all in similar circumstances, likely to be found guilty of conspiracy against the House. Only you and Kael stand much of a chance of light sentences, perhaps only banishment. For the half-fiend and the priest, the outcome is—"

"He is no priest," Tauran said. "The soul of Pharaun Mizzrym, drow wizard of Menzoberranzan, occupies that body." I've got to make them understand! "He did nothing against this House. They must set him free."

"So he has claimed," Garin replied. "But the truth of it will come out at the hearing. For now, we must assume the worst."

The worst, Tauran thought, despair filling him. I've brought this on all of them. It turns my stomach to think of facing my fate, but they do not deserve this. He let his gaze drop to the floor. "So much pain I've caused," he murmured.

The other angel took two steps until he was right before Tauran. "These are grave times, my friend. You are in deep trouble. The entire House is in danger of dissolving. Tell me what happened. Maybe I can help. Where is Micus? What part did you play in Mystra's death? Help me help you."

Tauran looked at the other angel. He understood all too well the celestial's perspective. In another time, that might have been him standing there, in Garin's place, pleading with someone—perhaps Aliisza—to work with him, to cooperate. But it felt so different to be on the other side, facing the recriminations. He chose his next words very carefully. "I will answer your questions, though it will make no difference. I do not regret my actions"—I don't!—"nor those of my companions. Not because I desired any devastating outcome, not because I wished ill upon the House, but because I do believe, in my heart, that we were trying our best.

"Everyone is fallible, Garin. Even gods. Unfortunately, too many of us can't see that until it's too late. So I suspect will be the case this time. If the House suffers as you describe, then punishing my guilt will not assuage that. The trouble runs much deeper, my friend. I understood that, even from the beginning, but no one—least of all Tyr—would listen. I fear that it is happening still. None of you will see the rightness of my actions until it is too late."

"Such words will not help you when it comes time to face the High Council, Tauran."

Tauran sighed. "I never said I expected it to. I merely want to make you understand that I am content with my fate in this matter. I don't need you to save me. I stand by my decisions to defy the council."

Garin's shoulders slumped. "So be it," he said. He turned away, toward the door. When he reached it, he stopped and turned back. "You know, Micus always told me that he considered you one of the wisest, most dedicated friends he had. That was before, of course, but he said it often. I'm struggling now to see in you what he did. I want to, I really do. But it's difficult."

With that, Garin pulled the door open and departed.

Tauran sat for a long time, staring at where Garin had been. He turned his many thoughts over and over in his mind.

It was dark when they came to get him.

❖ ❖ ❖ ❖ ❖ ❖ ❖ ❖

A rush of fear crashed into Vhok. His knees went weak enough to buckle, and he sagged. He stared at the glossy black floor before him, feeling the intense heat rising from it. He was certain the baleful creature across the room intended his death, had only to realize Vhok was there before giving the command. Or striding across the floor and delivering the death blow himself.

Stand up, you fool, he thought. Do not cower. He is just another demon.

But a balor was *not* just another demon, and despite the many long years the cambion had spent in the company of lesser fiends, palpable terror drained the power from his limbs as he gazed upon the fearsome being looming before him.

"Get up!" snapped his guard, yanking Vhok by the shoulder to his feet. "Do not make Lord Axithar come to you!"

The thought of displeasing the balor made Vhok convulse in fear and delivered a sudden, hidden reserve of strength into his body. The cambion scrambled up again and stumbled along, following his jailer deeper into the chamber.

As Vhok and his escort drew close, the balor turned its eyes toward him. "You," he said. His deep voice rumbled through the chamber, making the very air vibrate with its power. "You are the one that traveled with the angel."

Vhok swallowed once, afraid of admitting the truth, terrified of lying. He didn't trust his voice, so he nodded.

The balor frowned. "And you have been to their plane? To the stinking heavens known as the House of the Triad?"

Vhok nodded again. "Yes," he gasped. "I went there to deceive and steal from them." And it was a big mistake, he thought, thinking of what he would look like, impaled within an alcove.

Lord Axithar smiled. "Good," he said. "Tyr's 'glorious' domain is in chaos. I wish to take advantage of his vulnerabilities. You will tell me all you know of the place."

Vhok swallowed as the guard backed away and left him there to face the powerful demon alone. "Of course," he said, struggling to regain some composure. He clasped his hands behind his back as if he were about to begin a lecture. "On what subject do you wish to know more?"

"The House," the balor replied, snapping his whip. "The land, the fortress. I wish to know everything. You will describe it all in exacting detail."

Ah, Vhok thought, warming to his task. Perhaps . . . "I know much, great lord," he said, "as I explored much of the House personally."

"If you are lying, I will flay every inch of your skin from your body," Lord Axithar growled. He took one step toward Vhok, making the floor of the chamber bounce.

Despite himself, Vhok dropped to one knee. "I would never consider crossing one of your stature, great lord," he said, staring at the balor's black, cloven hooves. "I wish to curry your favor in whatever way I can so that I might receive something in return. I will offer you what information I have, and I vow that it is the truth."

The balor chuckled, and it sounded more like a deep-throated growl than anything to Vhok. He risked another glimpse up at Lord Axithar. "Already vying for power," Axithar said. "At least you are an honest fool."

Kaanyr winced, fearful that he had angered the beast.

The demon stroked his chin with his coiled whip and began to stroll around the chamber, pondering. The other demons in his presence scurried to keep out of the way. A dretch that did not move fast enough wound up skewered on the point of the balor's sword. The wretched creature screamed and wriggled for a moment.

Kaanyr winced again. Sending a message? he wondered. No, he admonished. You are worth more to him alive. You can be valuable. Prove it to him.

The demon lord flicked the dretch away and turned back toward Vhok. "If I find your information to my liking, I might give you great boons," he said. "Then again, I might choose to rip the information from your mind and not give you another thought."

"True," Vhok said, choosing his words carefully, "but I could prove to be such a valuable resource in other ways. It would be a waste to expend my talents so quickly."

"A waste?" The balor growled, a sound that made Vhok's midsection buzz. "Do you accuse me of frivolity?"

Vhok shook his head vehemently. "No, Lord Axithar. I only wish to make you aware of how useful I can be."

"You think highly of yourself, cambion. You are dangerous."

Vhok felt his breath grow short. He was ruining it.

Prove it to him.

With every bit of his willpower fighting to keep from turning and fleeing, Vhok gave the balor his full gaze. "Make me dangerous to your enemies, Lord," he said. He hated how much pleading there was in the tone of his voice, but he pressed on. "Let me serve you in myriad ways."

"What exactly is it you want for this magnanimous service?" the balor asked, turning to stroll across the chamber again. The flames writhing upon its body glowed brighter. "Tell me quickly. I grow tired of you and your game."

"A command," Vhok replied, hoping against hope that he was not pressing his luck too far. "Give me a command of my own and let me use it to pursue your enemies. Not just during the attack on the House, but across the multiverse."

The balor laughed again. "Are you a general?" he asked. "You do not look like a general."

"Where I once dwelled, I was," Vhok said, trying to hold himself a bit straighter, even though he still knelt. "I commanded an army. I could serve you well in this way."

The balor continued to pace, circling Vhok. The cambion could feel the fire radiating from the towering demon as he drew close. The fiend leaned his head down so that it was right next to Vhok.

"We shall see, cambion," Axithar said in a low rumble. "For now, tell me what you know."

Vhok began reciting anything and everything he could remember about the House of the Triad. He described the lands, the floating islands, and the Court. Lord Axithar listened attentively and asked many questions, and when the cambion did not know an answer, he admitted it. Vhok gave more than just facts, though. He offered his opinions on the weaknesses of the realm's defenses. He described how he might attack the Court, how he would divide his forces, and what he would expect the angels to do in reaction to such an attack.

The description became a discussion. Lord Axithar debated details with Vhok, nodded when he liked what the cambion offered in the way of strategy and tactics, grimaced and stomped around the room when he did not. Vhok was careful to remain deferential, but as the hours stretched on and he grew more comfortable that the balor believed him knowledgeable, the half-fiend relaxed, became more assertive with his theories.

When he was finished, Vhok's throat was parched, but he was certain he had satisfied Lord Axithar's demands to prove himself worthy.

"Go," the balor commanded at last.

Lord Axithar motioned for the ram-headed demon that had brought Vhok to come forward. "Give him guest quarters," the balor instructed. "See that he has every comfort. Food, wine, female companionship. Do not leave him wanting for anything." He looked at Vhok then, who was trying very hard not to grin. "Rest, prepare. You will have your command."

Vhok bowed deeply before Lord Axithar. "I am most grateful, my lord. You will reap the rewards of this wise decision."

The balor waved him away, and Vhok left the searing throne room, following the ram-headed demon back down the wide hallway. This time, the cambion hardly noticed the tormented beings writhing in the alcoves.

❖ ❖ ❖ ❖ ❖ ❖ ❖

Aliisza stood, as her companions did, in the center of the semicircular chamber of the High Council. She wore a simple robe of white cloth. Though she had already been compelled through Garin and Nilsa's divine magic to cooperate, she had been restrained with manacles that she could sense would prevent her from doing any sort of magical travel.

They remembered my trick with Kaanyr before, she thought, feeling morose.

Beside her, Kael, Pharaun, and Eirwyn stood similarly attired and restrained. The drow appeared in his true form, as he had the night before, in the enchanted garden. Aliisza had blinked when he arrived in such a state and had given him a quizzical look.

"A bit of divine intervention," he explained with a mock whisper, "the granting of a small request."

The only one they were waiting for was Tauran.

The chamber felt different to Aliisza. She could sense an undercurrent of chaos mingled with the officious, business-like manner of those in attendance. Much had happened since she and her companions had departed, and little of it appeared good.

Nothing was more evident of that chaos than the absence of four of the High Council members, including the High Councilor. The bench upon the dais sat half empty. The group of solars who were in attendance looked concerned, agi-tated. Their behavior was much more animated than Aliisza remembered, and their pearly white faces and golden eyes wore expressions of disquiet. They constantly leaned close to one another, whispering and gesturing.

The collection of hound archons hovering around the defendants only added to the air of perturbation. Indeed, the sheer number of guards amazed Aliisza. The celestials had assigned no fewer than three guards per prisoner.

They are taking no chances, Aliisza realized. *We really must have put a scare into them.*

For a moment, she felt a swell of pride at having flustered the haughty angels. It was a fleeting emotion, though, overwhelmed by despair. And anger. Her sense of betrayal at the hands of the celestials had grown since her discussion with Kael and Pharaun in the garden, and she was finding that her sense of helplessness to do anything to convince the angels of their good intentions was begin-ning to enrage her.

Why do they have to be so damned disciplined? she

lamented. Their rigid code is going to be their downfall, and they're taking us with them.

It didn't help Aliisza's mood, imagining Kaanyr somewhere distant, laughing at her.

Why did I come back? she asked herself yet again. *Why did I talk myself into thinking this was a good idea?*

It wasn't a good idea, it was the only option, she told herself. *It was this or die. You made your choice. Even back when you agreed to follow Tauran. You could have left all this long ago, when you first woke up in the storm dragon's lair. So too late for regrets now, fool girl.*

She heard that final comment in Kaanyr's voice. It made her wince. *Fool girl, indeed,* she thought. *Kaanyr was right. This place did change you.*

Aliisza cast a quick, furtive glance at Kael, who stood next to her. He stared at the floor, apparently deep in thought. A frown filled his mien, and she could see his hands clench and unclench. Her heart went to him.

He's watched so much of what he believed in crumble. He struggled so hard to embrace this life, this world. He would have done anything to serve the angels. Tried to impress them with his loyalty. Some thanks he's received. But why does it hurt me so much? she wondered. *Because they disillusioned my son.*

Bastards, all of them.

On the knight's other side, Pharaun gazed around in fascination. The drow seemed almost delighted to be there, witnessing such events.

Aliisza felt a hint of a smile cross her face, watching the wizard. *So typical,* she thought. *No matter how dire the circumstances, he never sheds that clever glee. Does he ever feel* regret? He may today. At least this time, we had the chance to—

The doors opened and Tauran entered, escorted by his own trio of archon guards. He had his hands manacled too. His face was furrowed with lines of sorrow and regret. It made Aliisza's heart weep to see the angel so run-down, so trampled by events. He never looked up at the rest of them standing there, waiting for him.

She remembered what she'd said to Kael. He doesn't want to be here, she realized. He can't bear to face this. Not what's coming for himself, but for us. Gods and devils, this isn't fair. He deserves better. We all do!

The acting High Councilor brought the court to order. "It is this court's intention to determine what, if any, acts of conspiracy have been committed against the House of the Triad and the Court of Tyr by those standing before us this day. We will begin with each defendant providing what testimony he or she wishes. Afterward, sentencing will be carried out."

Tauran began, offering in exacting detail everything that had happened to him in the time since Aliisza had first come into his care. Eirwyn followed, providing her own perspective, and then each of the others, in turn, were able to testify. By the time Aliisza had finished, her legs ached and she wanted to sit and rest. But she couldn't think of another thing to add. The councilors asked a few questions, mostly as points of clarification. When they were finished, the acting High Councilor addressed the group.

"We will adjourn for a time so that the council can deliberate. Guards, separate the prisoners."

The archons guided each of the defendants to a separate place within the chamber as the solars vanished.

Aliisza asked if she could sit, and the archons led her to a bench. She sank onto it gratefully as the three celestial hounds surrounded her. She looked across the room to where each of her companions also waited, each one permitted to sit, none allowed to speak. She tried to meet the gaze of each one in turn, to smile hopefully at them, wanting so badly for the council to find them faultless and at last recognize the service they had done for the Court.

Only Tauran never looked up to meet her stare.

It did not take long for the councilors to come to a consensus. They reappeared and instructed the guards to bring the defendants before them once more.

The acting High Councilor addressed the group. "Through these hearings, it has become apparent to this court that you stand before us not as conspirators, nor as allies. You simply acted in accordance with your own beliefs and did what you thought at the time to be right. Some of your choices seem questionable in hindsight. Some might have turned out better had others listened to you more closely. Your hearts may have been in the right place, but you failed to uphold the laws of the Court and the House, and sentence must, by law, be meted out."

Aliisza closed her eyes. They're really going to go through with it, she thought. Even after all that's happened, they can't get out of their own way enough to see the folly. Damn them!

The High Councilor continued. "It is therefore the decision of this body that each of you be sentenced, according to your role in this fiasco, as follows:

"Eirwyn, in accordance with your previous pardon, you are free to pursue your personal agendas and keep your own counsel, provided you make no further effort to aid and abet any of your co-defendants."

Aliisza looked at the angel and saw her shaking her head, frowning.

"Kael, you will be remanded into the care and custody of a suitable representative of Torm, where you will continue your studies under a new tutor."

Kael flinched and closed his eyes, and Aliisza's heart broke for him.

"Pharaun Mizzrym, you occupy a body given to you by those who had no right to offer it. Furthermore, as has already been discussed with you, we have determined that the Vessel into which you entered was imperfectly formed and is deteriorating. You cannot survive in such a fashion for long, and based on your life's achievements, we do not see fit to grant you succor here. Therefore, this court sees no alternative but to banish you from this Vessel and send you back from where you came."

Aliisza saw Pharaun grimace the slightest bit, but that smug smile soon replaced it. "I think we can all agree that I should have seen that coming," he said. His voice was unusually soft.

Damn you all, she thought. *There's more compassion in him than in the lot of you put together.*

"Aliisza," the High Councilor continued.

The alu swallowed hard and braced herself. *Do it,* she thought, directing all her anger at the speaker. *I don't care anymore. May you all rot in the Abyss!*

"Your time spent with us in the Court has proven to be . . . chaotic. While we cannot in good conscience find fault in your actions these last days"—*How noble of you,* the alu thought, feeling no pride in such a revelation—"we also cannot comfortably justify permitting you to remain within the Court or the House. Therefore, we are banishing you from this plane forevermore. You will be returned to your homeland immediately."

Aliisza felt numb. She supposed it was the best that she could have expected, but they had still punished her more cruelly than imprisoning her forever could have. Her friends, her family, had been stripped away from her. Forever. And she had nothing to return to. She felt like a vagabond.

Finally, the acting High Councilor turned to Tauran. "Your exemplary record is long and storied," she said. "And your heart, as it has been revealed to us, is true. Your actions were indeed those of one who believed he was working in the best interests of the Court, and of the House. However, your judgment is now what is under question. You deliberately chose to disobey this council on several occasions, you attacked your fellow devas in order to thwart them in their own duties, and you have repeatedly called into question the rightness and righteousness of Tyr and his decisions. Most importantly, you seem unrepentant. Do you deny this?"

Tauran drew a deep breath before answering. "I do not," he said, his voice clear. "I stand by my judgment."

Aliisza could see, though, that the accused angel's hands shook. She clenched her own into fists to keep them from doing the same.

The High Councilor frowned. "I see. You leave us no choice, then."

What? Aliisza thought. There might have been a choice? Tauran, repent! she silently screamed at him. Beg Tyr's forgiveness! He will embrace you again!

But the alu knew what was in Tauran's heart.

The High Councilor continued. "I therefore sentence you to be stripped of your divinity and your immortality forever. You are banned from the House of the Triad."

Tauran bowed his head and said nothing.

The only sound filling the chamber was Aliisza's sobbing.

Chapter Fourteen

Vhok's foul mood soured any enjoyment he might have gotten out of inspecting his troops. The demons that stood before him, shuffling about in uneven lines, with their mismatched weapons and undisciplined demeanors, only infuriated him more. They stank, scuffled, and didn't seem to care one whit that they were supposed to be standing at attention.

"These wretches aren't fit to slop latrines," he snapped at Vhissilka, who slithered along beside the cambion.

"I'll be certain to inform Lord Axithar you said so," the marilith replied.

Vhok grimaced but said nothing further as he continued down the line. Finding out that morning that he would answer to Vhissilka during the coming battle had not improved his mood.

All the women in my life have brought me nothing but misery, he fumed. Mariliths in particular find such creative ways to spoil my fun. But it was Aliisza's face that would not leave his mind's eye.

He had retired to his opulent quarters as Lord Axithar's guest the night before, eager to partake of the luxuries the balor had provided him. The feast was delectable enough, more food than he could have eaten in ten meals, and enough wine to pickle a dragon. In truth, it wasn't the best Vhok had ever enjoyed, but he could hardly complain after the trail fare he had dined on for far too long previously.

Then musicians, entertainers, even willing concubines had come to his chambers, all desperately eager to please him. Vhok tried to ignore the haunted looks in most of their eyes as he partook of the sights and sounds.

But in the end, it had been Aliisza that had dominated his thoughts. The harder he tried to dismiss her from his mind, the more she lingered there, taunting him. She would never leave him be.

I should have killed you when I had the chance, he thought. *But you'll be dead soon enough. If magic doesn't kill you, an enemy will. Now get out of my head!*

"Your heart doesn't seem to be in this," Vhissilka said. "Perhaps I should request a different captain for my banner guard."

Vhok forced himself to return to the moment. "Staring at them for hours won't make them better soldiers," he grumbled. "I have no more use for this."

"I agree," the marilith said. "Instead, let's return to Lord Axithar's keep. I have a surprise for you there."

Vhok gave the demon a sidelong glance. *Any time a demon speaks of surprises, it's usually unpleasant. What is she conspiring to do to me?* But she had already turned away and was gliding toward the towering fortress. Shrugging, the cambion followed her.

Once inside the massive keep, Vhissilka led Vhok to a large courtyard with a parapet that overlooked the assembled hordes under Axithar's command. The gathering of demons stretched as far as the smoke drifting across the broken plain would allow him to see. It was an impressive army.

We'll need every bit of it to overthrow the angels.

Vhissilka drew Vhok's attention toward a small side area. A swarm of demons moved around something large, but the cambion could not get a clear look at it. Then, as they drew closer, a great, howling cry rose up and some of the demons scattered.

Enclosed within a stout iron cage, slamming against his prison in a rage, stood the abomination that had once been Micus and Myshik. He issued a piercing scream and lunged at one end of his prison, trying catch a dretch that had drawn too close. The abomination caught hold of the demon's arm and ripped it completely off the hapless creature's body.

The dretch jabbered in pain and staggered away, spouting black blood everywhere. Two other demons pounced and rended it, feasting on its flesh. Others swarmed over it too, until Vhok could no longer even see the carcass.

"You!" Micus screamed upon spotting the cambion. "Traitor!" He threw his misshapen body against the bars of his prison frantically, over and over again, trying to get at Vhok.

The half-fiend stepped closer to get a good look at the captured thing. Time, torment, or both had warped Micus further. He no longer bore any resemblance to an angel. If Vhok had not seen Micus before his transformation, he would not have guessed at his celestial origin.

Micus's skin had turned a mottled purple color and had begun to fleck off in places, leaving gaping wounds that festered a yellowish green color. His face bulged in odd places, and his eyes, once such an intense black color, gleamed red in the shadows of the cage. His dark hair had grown long and unruly and dripped with sweat as he thrashed around inside his cage.

At the level of his gut, Myshik's beady gaze still fixated on him, with its maw opening and snapping shut eagerly over and over again. Vhok saw no sign of anything greater than animal instinct in that stare. For a moment, he imagined what it must have been like for the angel to discover he had been fused with the half-dragon. He suppressed a shudder.

"We caught him shortly after you and your companions became my guests," Vhissilka said. "He has gone mad with rage. He shouts your name from time to time, even though this is the first moment he's set eyes on you since we seized him."

"He blames us—me, in particular—for his condition. He thinks I led him into a trap just so he could be transformed into such a thing."

"His mind is nearly gone," the marilith said. "We have made much sport with him and broken whatever celestial part of him might have remained. Now he only wants to kill."

Vhok had a sudden, titillating thought. "It is unfortunate that he appears so uncontrollable. What a nice, ironic surprise it would be to spring him on our foes today."

"That's precisely why I brought you here," Vhissilka said. "You knew him before. Could he lead us to where the angels' defenses will be weakest today?"

Oh, you clever girl, Vhok thought. "If his memory of the place is intact," he said. "But the question of control remains. How could we possibly force him to attack the celestials instead of our own troops?"

Vhissilka smiled. "If you look closely, you will see that the creature now bears a steel collar."

Vhok tilted his head down and spied the circlet of metal surrounding Micus's throat.

"This," the marilith said, holding up a bracelet that matched the collar, "is the means to dominate the creature before you. However," she added with caution, "once I place it on your arm, you cannot remove it save severing the limb, unless the abomination dies."

Vhok took the bracelet from Vhissilka and examined it. It was a simple length of metal that appeared to have been crudely hammered into a rounded shape. The ends did not quite meet, providing just enough room for someone to slip the item over a hand. He held it up to the angry red light of the sky and considered.

"Are you offering this to me?" he asked. "A secret weapon in addition to leading your honor guard?"

The marilith smirked. "It is Lord Axithar's wish that you command the creature. He thought it fitting, given how much the creature hates you and how the very heavens from which he came will find him anathema."

Vhok chuckled. He already had another idea, an even better way to make use of Micus. "I accept," he said, and he slipped the bracelet over his arm.

The band of metal closed, tightening itself and reforming its shape until it gripped the cambion's wrist snugly. When it stopped altering, it was tight but not uncomfortable.

Vhok could feel the link between himself and Micus that had formed. He felt the hostility from the ruined angel, the rage and despair battering against his mind, but the link held the forces at bay. The cambion sent a mental command to

Micus to quiet down and, even though he felt the resentment, the abomination stopped outwardly raging, standing still and easy within the confines of his cage.

"Oh, this will serve nicely," Vhok said, delighted. "I can think of many things to do with him."

"Your orders are to command him to lead us to the House's weakest points. He will know how they will attempt to defend against us. You will force him to thwart that defense."

Vhok bowed at the marilith and said, "As you command." Silently, he added, *he's going to do more than that for me. I have a Lifespring to visit.*

❖ ❖ ❖ ❖ ❖ ❖ ❖ ❖

Kael watched from the edge of the common as groups of soldiers assembled. Angels and archons, warriors all, gathered and milled upon the green, waiting. Kael waited with them, and he could sense the anticipation emanating from them. From time to time, he cast a glance up, toward the top of the mountain, to the highest tier of the fortress-city of Trueheart. There, beyond ring after ring of stout defensive walls constructed of huge stone blocks that ascended the sides of the mountain, stood the palace of Torm.

The knight's heart was glad to be there. He felt an old kinship with the fortress-city and its inhabitants that he had never quite mustered for the Court of Tyr.

I am a warrior, a servant of Torm. This is where I belong.

Thinking it made Kael feel a little better, but he knew that only time would heal the wounds he felt. He was content to move on, to turn the page to a new chapter of his life. But he mourned the decisions of the High Council, the severing of his relationship with Tauran.

If they had sentenced Tauran to death, that might have been better than this, he thought. Knowing he's out there, somewhere, wandering, lonely, without a deity or a cause to serve. That hurts more.

You were a good mentor, my friend. I will miss you. What the High Council decreed was shameful. You deserved better. You were a wise and noble servant, and they should have listened to you.

Kael caught himself growing angry all over again and reminded himself of his vow to leave it in the past.

Time to move on. Let it go.

He had tried repeatedly to tell himself that the anger and resentment was just another example of how much he had let himself become too involved in the affairs of the Tyrrans. Tauran had mentored him well, perhaps, but Tauran had also wandered from his path, and Kael had been dragged—albeit willingly—along, too.

It wasn't your fight. Don't continue to make it your problem.

Kael sighed and thought of his mother. In a way, he was thankful that she was gone from his life too. He understood her much better after the night they had spent talking, by the pool in the enchanted garden. He accepted that she had become much more than her heritage, just as he had always strived to overcome both the fiendish and drow blood in him. He no longer blamed her for what had gone wrong with Tauran's efforts. She had been, in many ways, just as loyal as Kael himself.

But at the same time, Kael saw her as turmoil incarnate. Everywhere she became involved, chaos followed.

It's her nature, he reminded himself. She is what she is in that regard, even when she tries not to be.

For that matter, the same could be said about Pharaun. A product of his society, all wrapped up in his strange games of intrigue, noble house battling noble house. Kael couldn't imagine playing such games, constantly awaiting some espionage or double cross to ruin his plans. He could never be a drow.

But the son of a drow . . . if they are creatures of their own nature, what does that make me?

They only sired and bore you, he argued. Nothing more. You are more than just the product of your parents. You are what you make of yourself. Be different. Stay true to your beliefs! Aliisza proved that it can be done. Honor her in that way.

Kael blinked and shook his head slightly to rid himself of the conflicting thoughts. Move on, he thought again. Remembering Pharaun's advice, he added, be true to who you are so you can answer to yourself at the end of your time.

Shaking off the morose thoughts, the knight turned his attention back to the gathering of soldiers. He scanned the pennants flapping in the warm breezes, seeking the one with the white hammer within a circle on a purple field. He suspected it would not be hard to spot, but thus far, it was not there. His new commander had not arrived, yet.

Come soon, Kael urged. This idleness gives me too much time to think.

A group of hound archons outfitted for battle strolled past the half-drow, deep in conversation. Their discussion was animated and loud, and he could not help but overhear parts of it.

"I don't understand why he waited as long as he did," one of the dog-headed creatures said. "It seems like his indecision has cost the House precious time and resources."

"Why resources?" one of the archon's companions asked.

"Because so many deserted him already, and not all of them have come over to join us. If he had been more willing to—"

"You tread on dangerous footing," another warned. "Tyr has his own reasons for surrendering his power, and only he could comprehend when the right time was to do so. You should not be so quick to—"

"Excuse me," Kael said, his voice shaking. The words he was hearing sent a shiver of cold fear through him. "What did you just say? What did Tyr do?"

The archons slowed and turned to the knight. They looked puzzled at his question. "You have not heard?" one of them asked.

Kael shook his head. "No. I only just arrived. But I came from there, and I did not hear any news."

"Indeed, it only happened this morning," the hound warrior said. "Tyr is abdicating his godhood. He has granted Torm his deific power and counseled his followers to offer their allegiances to the True One. Illmater has returned to the House to aid him in this transfer."

Kael swallowed, trying to absorb what he was hearing. "Why?" *Did our actions lead to all this? Did Tauran's wavering faith cause this crisis? No. That is not possible. We were trying to help!*

The archon shrugged. "They say it's because he has lost faith in himself, in his own ability to lead and judge," he said. "All the turmoil within the Court just took its toll, I suppose."

Kael put his hands to his head. What have we caused? No! Zasian and Cyric did it! Not us!

The archon was still speaking. "And now, with the invasion, maybe he felt it would serve everyone better. I do not pretend to understand the wisdom of the gods."

Kael's head snapped up again, a surge of shock hitting him anew. "Invasion?" he asked. "What invasion?"

"Where have you been hiding, soldier?" the archon asked. "Demons. Hordes of them are coming. The Abyss is disgorging them faster than our spies can count, and they march toward us. Haven't you seen the mustering?" The creature gestured at the gathering army on the green. "What did you think all of this was for? We prepare to march to war, soldier. You'd better get to your unit."

"Oh, by Torm," Kael breathed. It was happening. What Vhok had suggested, half in a bluff, was coming to pass. The cambion had vowed to reveal what he knew, expose the weaknesses of the House, to the abyssal lords. Had he done it? Had he somehow reached them and convinced them to muster their armies?

That must be it. I have to find Tauran.

"Thank you," Kael said, but his mind was already whirling with possibilities. He turned to the green and sought the standard of his new commander once more. He finally spotted it on the far side of the common. The officers had arrived. Kael sprinted for the flapping pennant, leaving the archons staring at him in puzzlement.

When Kael reached the point where his commander's staff officers had gathered, he gave the closest one a salute and said, "I am Kael, Knight of the Order of the Vigilant and recently returned from the Court of Tyr. I am reporting for duty, but

I beg leave to return to the Court. I just heard about Tyr's abdication, and I have urgent business there."

The angel returned the salute and gave him a puzzled look. "Of what do you speak?" he asked. "We march soon, knight, and we will need every able blade we can muster."

"I know, but I believe I am more needed there, where I can halt a great travesty from occurring."

The angel shook his head. "I'm sorry, soldier, but I can't grant you that leave. Everything is chaos over there right now, and whatever good you think you can do, you will be needed here more. Now, get ready to march."

With that, the angel turned away and left Kael standing there. The half-drow clenched both his teeth and his fists. He wanted to argue with the angel, make the celestial understand how important it was to reach Tauran and the others.

He's still trying to reach the Lifespring, even after all this time. It's just the kind of thing he'd do, to spite all of us. And if he gets there and gains its power and energy—or worse yet, brings a company, a regiment . . .

We must stop him from doing that. It could turn the tide of battle against us!

But Kael's thought was a hunch, nothing more, and he knew no one would listen.

Grimacing in defeat, he turned away and made his way toward the gathering troops who were collecting their gear, donning tabards with the same hammer-and-circle symbol on them, and readying to go to war.

If Tauran were here, Kael thought, *he would go anyway.*

Yes, and that's why he is no longer a member of the Court. You must not abandon your own duty. You are a knight of Torm.

No, the half-drow decided, stopping in midstride. This is too important. You know it is. And you're terrible at following orders, soldier. Tauran spoiled you. Go find them!

Remembering Pharaun's words about answering to himself, Kael turned to see if any of the officers were nearby and watching. Satisfied that he would not be noticed, his mind made up, he moved away from the milling mass of soldiers and hurried for the front gates of the city.

He hoped he was not too late.

❖ ❖ ❖ ❖ ❖ ❖ ❖ ❖

"It's time," Nilsa said, framed in the doorway of Aliisza's chambers.

The alu turned from where she was standing in the middle of the room, gazing around at the familiar white marble and baskets of vines and flowers. She looked at the angel. "I know," she said. "Give me one more moment. Please."

The slightest hint of exasperation clouded Nilsa's expression, but she nodded and stepped back out of the chamber, leaving Aliisza to herself.

Aliisza drew a deep breath and inhaled the fragrance of blossoms. She listened to the breeze ruffling the wind chimes on her balcony. She strolled to the railing and looked out, staring at the brassy blue sky and the array of clouds surrounding the great mountain of Celestia, which disappeared into more of them high above.

I can't believe I'm thinking this, but I'm going to miss this place.

The alu remembered the very first time she had gazed upon the great mountain. It had been the day Tauran had brought her to the House. They had appeared on an island of sweet-smelling grass. His angelic brilliance had dazzled her. How long ago that seemed.

She had tried to fly up into the heavens surrounding that mountain, tried to penetrate the clouds and find escape beyond them. *I was a fool. Often.*

Aliisza wondered if Eirwyn was already there, on Celestia. The angel had claimed she would travel back to Venya, to serve Erathaol as a seer.

Leaving this place behind, the alu thought. *I suppose Garin has already taken Tauran away too,* she mused.

She imagined the celestial magically transported her friend to some other realm in the cosmos, just as Nilsa was about to do to her. *Just whisk us all away, like sweeping dust under a rug. Out of sight, out of mind. That's the way to deal with your problems, Tyr.*

Aliisza felt another sudden pang of sorrow. She wanted to see Tauran again. She wanted to say goodbye. Then inspiration hit.

Why don't you go with him?

She wondered if it was even possible. Aliisza had planned to return to Faerûn, most likely Sundabar, although she hadn't truly made up her mind yet. It seemed like the natural choice, but then, she had never been anything more than an interloper there.

Or anywhere, Aliisza thought. *You are an outcast, an orphan. Like your son.*

More sorrow washed over her. *I'm losing them all. Kael, Pharaun, Eirwyn. Even Kaanyr. Everyone who became part of my life, yanked from me by—what was it Pharaun said?—the capricious whims of gods.*

But it doesn't have to be this way.

Aliisza turned her back to the room and crossed it. She reached the door and pulled it open, stepping out into the hallway. Nilsa still stood there, waiting.

"I want to travel with Tauran," Aliisza announced. "Where is he going?"

The angel shook her head. "That's not possible," she replied. "You must return to the place from which you came. I am to take you to the city of Sundabar."

Anger boiled in Aliisza. "Why? You could take me anywhere, so long as I never bothered you or your kind again. Why does it have to be there?"

Nilsa sighed. "You're right, so far as that goes. But I have been given specific instructions. It's not up for debate."

Aliisza cocked her hip to one side and folded her arms across her chest. "That's not good enough," she said, giving the angel a pointed look. "It shouldn't matter, and I want to know why."

Nilsa stared right back. "You don't want to have this argument with me."

Aliisza snorted. "Why, because I'll lose?"

"No, because I don't need to debate you. I have a duty to perform. I'm not going to let you change my mind, no matter what you say. If you persist in trying, if you make it difficult for me, I will simply knock you silly and dump you in an alley somewhere in your city. So make your choice."

Aliisza fumed. She knew the angel could do it, simply by drawing on her divine power to stun the alu. But that didn't make it right.

For a moment, she fought the urge to punch the angel in the nose. Finally, as the rage subsided enough for her to control herself, she said, "Can you at least tell me where he's going so I can find him?"

"No."

"Gods and devils, why are you being so difficult?" Aliisza yelled, tears of helplessness welling up. "He's my friend. Can't you set aside your edicts long enough to give me some small thing?"

A momentary look of compassion crossed Nilsa's face, but she smoothed her expression quickly. "It was decided that you should be separated, never to see one another again," the angel explained. "There can be no risk of you coming together to cause further trouble for the House. I'm sorry, but that's the way it must be."

"I hate you all," Aliisza whispered, choking back sobs. She crumpled to the floor. "I hope you and your stony god wither and die."

Nilsa pursed her lips and reached for Aliisza. "Enough of this," she muttered, grabbing hold of the alu. "We're leaving now."

Aliisza started to jerk free of the angel's grip. She wanted the fight, wanted to force the cold, heartless celestial to follow through on her threat. It would prove that Aliisza was right in her assessment of how unkind and unfair Nilsa truly was.

Nilsa opened her mouth to say something, perhaps even to utter a word of power and knock Aliisza silly as she had promised, but a voice from down the hall interrupted her.

"Hold, Nilsa." It was Tauran. He and Kael approached together, Garin right behind them. Aliisza's heart leaped at the sight of them both. A foolish grin spread across her face.

"What are you doing here?" Nilsa asked in surprise, frowning. "Garin, our instructions were clear."

Aliisza yanked herself free of the angel's grip, jumped up, and ran to Tauran and Kael. She wrapped an arm around the fallen angel and the knight and hugged them both tightly. Warm feelings of hope and possibility coursed through her, where only despair and defeat had dwelt before. "I thought I'd never see you again," she said, her face buried in their shoulders. She felt Kael chuckle softly as the two of them returned her embrace.

Behind them, she heard Garin say, "It's changed, Nilsa. Everything's changed." The weary sound of his voice made Aliisza wince.

"What are you talking about?" Nilsa asked, walking up behind the alu.

"Tyr is surrendering his godhood," Garin answered.

Aliisza pulled back with a start and looked at Tauran and Kael. "What?" she asked. "Truly?"

Kael nodded and Tauran said softly, "He has already done it." His face held a grim expression, a visage that Aliisza had come to think of as a scar, every bit as permanent a fixture as a sword wound.

Aliisza turned to look at Nilsa. The angel had a stricken look on her face. She stared at nothing, her mouth opening and closing. Compassion welled up in the alu. She didn't know what to do. She took the angel's hand in her own and said, "I'm sorry."

Nilsa stared back at her. "It's true. I can't feel him with me anymore. I've lost Tyr." Her hand shook in Aliisza's grasp.

"He's sending all of us to serve Torm, and he's marching to war under Torm's banner," Garin said. When Aliisza turned to gaze at him, his wide eyes, usually so keen and piercing, looked lost.

Tauran said, "We have all been asked to aid in the fight. The demons are coming."

Aliisza gasped. "Demons," she said. "Does that mean—?" Kaanyr. It's just what you would do, isn't it?

"Yes," Kael replied. "Tauran and I agree. If Kaanyr is with them, he will try to reach the Lifespring."

"It would be the final insult hurled at us," Tauran said. "Invade the blessed House, find and bathe in the Lifespring. The one thing he sought in all this and was ultimately denied."

"He shouldn't be allowed anywhere near it," Aliisza said.

"No, he shouldn't," Tauran agreed. "Even on principle alone, I would deny him that which he desires most. But beyond that, with the power of the Lifespring at his disposal, he could become a dangerous force for the abyssal lords."

Aliisza bit her lip. The pain of his betrayal was still fresh. She wanted to hide away, wanted to avoid seeing the cambion again. But too much was a stake.

"We must stop him," she said.

CHAPTER FIFTEEN

"Are you sure?" Garin asked, offering a sincere yet hopeful smile. "We could really use you with us."

Nilsa, whose haunted expression bespoke her struggle to come to grips with Tyr's abdication, added, "It's going to get rough today."

Eirwyn nodded and offered her own apologetic smile. "Yes," she said. "Though I know the importance of getting every possible soldier on the battlefield, I sense that I am needed elsewhere."

As if to reinforce the grimness of the moment, a band of high clouds drifted across the sun, bringing a hint of gloom. They stood on a small, high plaza, near the very top of the tallest buildings of the Court, where the breezes were fresher and unimpeded. The wind ruffled the angel's hair and carried the barest hint of an odor of smoke upon it.

Most of the angels of the Court and Trueheart had already headed toward the front, preparing for the impending onslaught of demons headed toward the House. The great hall of Tyr stood nearly empty below the trio.

"What have we come to?" Garin said softly. "The end of an age? Is this how even the gods pass?"

"Don't say that," Nilsa admonished, her sorrowful look deepening. "Tyr has chosen to walk among his people as a warrior once more. When this unpleasant business is finished, and he has cleared his head of whatever troubles him, all will be set right."

"I hope, for both your sakes, that it is so," Eirwyn said. She reached out and clasped both Garin and Nilsa on the shoulder. "I understand the pain you are feeling. I pray that your sadness, unlike mine when Helm fell, is brief and supplanted by joy again very soon." She paused and cast her gaze down at the stones between their feet. The next part was harder to say. "I want both of you to know that I bear neither of you any ill will. You have been loyal servants of Tyr, and now Torm, and none can fault you for fulfilling your duties."

"Thank you," Garin said, and he sounded genuinely relieved. "I'm sorry it came to all this."

Nilsa didn't say anything, but she came toward Eirwyn and hugged her tightly.

When Eirwyn pulled back at last, she said, "We all still fight the fight of law and goodness. I am with you in spirit. But I must do this. I sense its importance."

Nilsa looked doubtful, but Garin gave one knowing nod in return. "Very well, then," he said, "You do what you must. We will miss you."

"May the blessings of Ty—of Torm be with you," Eirwyn said. "Drive them from our holy lands."

"We will," Garin said. He and Nilsa turned to go. They leaped into the air together and swooped out over the railing, leaving Eirwyn standing upon the balcony of the Court by herself. Her eyes followed them as they soared down and away from her, until they were nothing more than tiny specks upon the horizon.

Eirwyn fought a brief pang of guilt for not going with them to Deepbark Hollow to face the invading demons. The angels and archons there were in for a terrible fight. They would need every last able body they could muster.

You have other matters to attend to, she reminded herself. They will prevail without you.

Eirwyn fanned her wings and leaped into the sky, soaring aloft into the gray afternoon. Despite its emptiness, she felt a pall on the House, a grim foreboding of what was to come. She wondered whether Tyr still dwelt within, if the melancholy she felt emanated from the former god, radiating his sorrow.

He still commands an impressive presence, Eirwyn realized. He knows much blood will be spilled before the day is through. He laments how many celestial creatures will die today.

Many more demons will perish, she thought. The House of the Triad will stand against all evil.

With that resolute thought firmly in her mind, Eirwyn winged her way in the opposite direction of Garin and Nilsa, heading toward another part of the plane, on the far side of the great mountain of Celestia. The fresh wind blew at her back, and she quickly left the gleaming white of the Court behind her.

She couldn't say with certainty what led her in the direction she had chosen, only a divine sense, a calling that her presence was needed. That was the way of things with her divinations. She could not always explain why she felt what she did, only that the urges were invariably accurate. She felt a familiar comfort in it all.

As she flew beneath the darkening clouds, she tried to gauge where she ought to seek. She followed her instincts, altering direction more than once as she felt herself getting off course. Before long, she realized where she was headed.

The Lifespring.

That was odd. She would not expect anyone to be there, not on that day. Everyone would be at the front, fighting to hold back the tide of demons who were trying to break through the weak point of the plane. Then a glimmer of an idea occurred to her.

I wonder . . . Tauran, I feel your hand in this once more.

Suspicious that she was on a collision course with old friends and enemies alike, she surged ahead with renewed determination.

When Eirwyn reached the great floating mountain hovering among the clouds, the beach appeared deserted. The golden waters churned within the great basin, tossed about by the brisk winds that blew across them. She was tempted for a moment to take a quick dip, to allow the healing touch of the magical forces there to soothe her weary body and mind, but she resisted. A sense of urgency buzzed in the back of her mind. Whatever had drawn her here, it demanded her immediate attention.

She descended to a point along the narrow beach near where the flowing waters spilled over the side and disappeared into endless white below. She settled onto the sand there and looked around, trying to find some sign of what she was meant to do. Nothing caught her attention.

Eirwyn frowned. If Tauran has need of me here . . .

She could not shake the feeling that she was not alone.

"Eirwyn!" a voice called from high above.

. . . he would be in his favorite spot, Eirwyn finished, grinning.

The angel turned and craned her neck, seeking Tauran. She spotted him easily, standing near the apex of the highest, sharpest pinnacle of rock, where the waters flowed out of the mountain to splash into the pool below.

Tauran waved to her and motioned to her to join him. She could see that others were there as well.

Eirwyn took flight again and headed to the top. When she settled upon the stone outcropping of rock, she found Kael, Aliisza, and the drow wizard with Tauran.

Tauran stood before her, and she was struck by how weary he appeared. His hair, always so golden in the sun, had become a muted brassy shade and didn't retain its luster of before. His face was gaunt. His eyes had sunken a bit into his skull.

She embraced Tauran and held him tightly for a long moment. She could feel the tension in him, but she refused to let go until some of it drained away, and then she was practically holding him upright.

"The road has been long, my friend," she whispered to him. "But I still feel the strength of righteousness within you. And I am here to share your burden, as I know you would share mine."

Tauran clenched her more tightly, then released her and stepped back. A small glimmer of gratitude shone in his eyes. "Thank you," he said, his voice thick.

Eirwyn turned and greeted each of the others with smiles and hugs. "I should have known I would find you all here," she said at last. "Banded together to the end, following your own course, listening to your own wise counsel before accepting the edicts of any other."

"We believe Kaanyr will come here," Aliisza said. "We think he still intends to bathe in these waters."

"We all came to the same conclusion when we heard that war was brewing," Kael said.

"It's what he would do," Tauran said, "just to spite all of us and fulfill what he probably insists is his rightful destiny or some such nonsense. We intend to stop him."

Eirwyn looked over at the drow. "You agree with them?" she asked.

Pharaun shrugged. "I haven't the barest glimmer of an opinion about the cambion's motivations," he said with a chuckle. "But seeing how my prospects are decidedly non-existent, I gave in to whims of fancy and decided to join the fray."

"Sounds good to me," Eirwyn said. "How can I help?"

"You don't need to aid us," Tauran said. "You've already given up too much for me as it is. I cannot ask for more from you."

Eirwyn rolled her eyes and grinned. "Oh, don't be so melodramatic, Tauran. You should know me better than that by now. You think I just happened to stumble upon you four here while out randomly flying around? I knew I was needed, and I came. Besides, my only other option was killing demons, so it sounds like a wash, to me."

Tauran laughed. It was the first time in a long time that Eirwyn remembered him doing so. "Fair enough, my friend," he said.

"Now, what's the plan?" Eirwyn asked.

"No plan," Kael said. "We simply wait and watch."

"We aren't sure how Kaanyr intends to get here," Aliisza said. "He might come alone, hoping to slip past the House's army, or he might attempt to bull his way here with a horde of his own. I'm betting on the latter. He was never one for subtlety."

"Whatever he does," Tauran said, "from up here, we'll know when he arrives."

Eirwyn hefted her mace. "When he does, let's make sure he regrets it."

❖ ❖ ❖ ❖ ❖ ❖ ❖ ❖ ❖

A long, ragged line of celestials ran through the woods, angels and archons forming a defense against invasion. They waited and watched the barrier between their own world and the void beyond. The forested land felt calm and pure, towering trees interspersed with green thicket upon the leaf-covered ground, right up to the point where magic altered the fabric of reality. There, the land stopped, and the shapeless clouds of elsewhere crackled with blue lightning.

Every celestial stared at that seething maelstrom, waiting.

Garin and Nilsa stood on the edge of a large clearing, a wide glade that spread out for perhaps three hundred paces and abutted the preternatural storm. The pair of devas commanded a company of archons, the hound warriors milling on either side of them. Their responsibility was the clearing. Nothing was to be allowed past them.

"Garin, I don't think I can do this," Nilsa said, standing next to him.

The deva pulled his gaze away from the roiling, purplish

wall of insane magic and looked at her. "What is it?" he asked.

Nilsa appeared unsettled. Her wings fanned and fluttered, and she seemed to look nowhere and everywhere at once. "I'm afraid to . . ." she let the words trail off and gestured helplessly. "I can't."

Garin saw the turmoil in her wide, frightened eyes. He realized she was on the verge of breaking down. He moved closer to her and drew her to him. "Tell me," he said, trying to comfort her.

Nilsa shook her head. "I cannot find the courage to . . ." She looked away, her mouth opening and shutting. "To let him in," she said. She brought her hands up and pressed her palms against her temples. "Torm, I mean. I want to, I really do, but . . ."

Garin's eyes widened. "You have not pledged fealty to Torm yet?" he asked, incredulous. "Nilsa, you must. You have no power! You cannot withstand the demons if you—"

"I know," she said, her voice breaking. "I just can't. There's a part of me that will die if I accept that Tyr has . . . has . . . Oh, Garin, I'm so scared!"

His own heart pounding, his own hands trembling, Garin firmed his grasp on his companion. He began a silent prayer.

Blessed Tyr—No. Torm, he corrected. *Blessed Torm. Grant us strength today, not just in our limbs, but in our hearts. Please guide us and grant us courage so that we may face the looming battle before us unafraid.*

Garin drew a deep breath, feeling calm wash over him. Torm's spirit infused him. It felt different from the familiar touch of Tyr, but it comforted him.

She just needs a glimpse of this to understand. Once she knows him, she'll embrace him.

"Nilsa," he said, drawing her gaze to his own. He stared deeply into her eyes. "This is real, right now. You've got to do this, or you will not survive the field today."

She nodded. "Yes," she said. "Help me."

"Torm welcomes you into the fold. It is strange and frightening, I know, but he will comfort you. Tyr wishes it. Do not be afraid. Instead, let your spirit soar, let your majestic countenance reflect Torm's might, even as your heart sings for Tyr's safety."

"I want to," she said, "but I—"

A thunderous blast erupted from the opposite side of the glade, drowning out Nilsa's final words. Fire roared into the sky. Trees and dirt sprayed everywhere. Black, churning smoke poured out of a jagged opening in the ground very near the edge of the world, blotting out the wall of nothingness beyond.

Another eruption struck to the angel's left, and then two more, almost simultaneously, to Garin's right. A cacophony of blasts reverberated through the surrounding woods as explosion after explosion tore the land apart and filled the sky with flame and ash. An entire row of the devastating blasts formed a continuous wall before the celestials.

The first of the demons rushed out of that conflagration, a motley swarm of every imaginable shape and size, all disgusting to behold. Hideous creatures of pasty white or red flesh loped on misshapen legs. Bulbous heads that seemed too fat for spindly necks jostled and bounced, while arms that looked to be too short to be useful flapped spastically. Flames licked the ground where they ran, and a foul stench preceded them. They screamed in delight at the sight of the defenders and rushed forward, waving clubs and sickles, spears and blades at their enemies. Behind them, a constant flow fed the swarm, pouring from the gashes in the ground.

Garin released Nilsa and spun to his right. "First rank, to them!" he cried, magically amplifying his voice so that the archons all down the line could hear him. "Second rank, hold!"

He turned back and found Nilsa down on her knees, gaping at the onrushing horde. She was not issuing orders to her troops. They were milling in confusion as his side of the line pressed forward.

Garin repeated his orders to the celestials under Nilsa's command, then squatted down and grabbed her face in his hands.

"Nilsa!" he shouted at her, making her look at him. "I need you, right now! Open your heart to Torm! His presence will give you strength, but you have to trust him as you always trusted Tyr."

He risked a glance up at the field of battle and saw that the demons and the archons were only thirty paces apart by then, two rows of combatants charging full tilt at one another.

Nilsa sobbed. "I'm so scared!" she cried. "I cannot abandon Tyr! He will fade away! I could not bear it!"

Garin fought back his panic with every ounce of his self-control. He pulled his gaze away from the impending melee and returned his attention to the angel weeping at his feet. "Nilsa," he said as calmly as he could, "Tyr's destiny is his own. You cannot control it. You can only follow the path set before you. Torm needs you. These soldiers need you." He drew a deep breath and added, "I need you."

Please, Nilsa, stand up and fight.

Nilsa swallowed and closed her eyes. "Very well," she said, her voice trembling.

A great shout erupted as the two moving walls, archon and demon, slammed together. Garin shot a glance up. The battle had been joined.

Garin looked down to see Nilsa, her lips trembling, her eyes squeezed shut, muttering something he could not hear.

That's it, he thought. You can do it. Torm will bless you if you only let him in.

Nilsa gasped, and Garin could almost see a new radiance burst around her. Her features smoothed, and the anguish and fear faded, leaving her body. Her mouth widened in a contented smile. She opened her eyes, and they glowed with newfound reverence.

"He told me that he was proud of me," she said. "He told me to be his example." She climbed to her feet. "I'm sorry. I'm ready now."

Relieved, Garin pointed to the reserve forces of archons that had remained back. "Take your command," he said. "Do not advance until I give you the signal."

Nilsa nodded, still smiling. "As we agreed," she said.

Garin turned and left her there. He pushed himself into the air and sped toward the mad clash ahead. Already, he could see countless bodies, more demons than archons, scattered across the field. The celestials fought with precision, using one another for protection, as they had been trained.

The demons swarmed in a mad, chaotic mess.

They dropped by the dozen, sliced and stabbed by the archons.

For every fiend slain, ten scampered out of the rift in the ground.

Blessed Torm, Garin prayed as he rushed toward a weak point in the archons' line. Give me the strength to withstand this.

He reached the gap and slammed his mace through the skull of a slavering demon. Without waiting to watch it fall, he shouted a holy word of power at the mass of demons behind it. The divine energy of the bellow pummeled the fiends like a shock wave, bowling them over four ranks deep. Archons advanced into the midst of them and attacked, slaying demons as rapidly as they could swing their weapons.

Garin turned and uttered the powerful holy word again, blasting another dozen demons backward. Archons surged into the hole and made short work of their downed foes.

Good, Garin thought, growing more confident. Quick and efficient. We must conserve our—

A shadow engulfed Garin, and he looked up just in time to be struck by the taloned feet of a demon. The blow caught him on the shoulder. It tore through his tunic and sliced into his flesh as it sent him flailing backward onto the torn, blood-soaked ground.

Garin scrambled to rise again. He took a better look at the stout creature and faltered. It had the pincers and markings of a glabrezu demon, but it was no ordinary member of its species. Larger and more powerfully built than any glabrezu Garin had ever seen, it sprouted broad wings that fanned out to either side of its back.

By the Maimed One, he thought out of habit, they're breeding them to fly. Ty—Torm save us all.

The demon rose to its full height and bellowed out a rumbling word in Abyssal that made Garin cringe and cover his ears. Archons for five paces on a side stumbled and faltered at the sound. They seemed to lose their way, their concentration, unable to resist as the lesser demons leaped upon them and rent them with their claws and weapons.

The winged glabrezu whipped one of its huge pincered limbs out and snagged a stunned archon in its grasp. The hound warrior struggled for a moment, pulling futilely at the razor-sharp claw encircling its neck. Then the powerful appendage flexed, and the archon's head separated from its body in a single snip. The hound warrior collapsed and the glabrezu smiled at Garin. It brought the pincer up and ran its long, forked tongue along the blood, savoring it.

"Let us dance, angel," the beast said, advancing with its claws extended toward him.

Garin adjusted the grip on his mace and motioned for the demon to come closer. "I have just the music for it."

❖ ❖ ❖ ❖ ❖ ❖ ❖ ❖ ❖

Vhok levitated above his troops, glaring toward the front of the column. The scorching, acrid wind buffeted him as he hovered, and the impatient shouts and growls rising from the morass of demons grated on his ears. He could see a great archway ahead in the distance, a monolithic stone structure rising from the broken plain. Fiery red lightning spider-webbed across the surface of the stone, but in the center, where the foremost demon troops passed through it, he could see a writhing darkness that flickered with pulsing blue light.

The arch stood as one among many, a cluster of half a dozen portals arranged in a circle. Demons surrounded the clump of arcane doorways, a sea of bodies stretching all across the desiccated, gravel-strewn plain of Lord Axithar's domain.

The hordes of the balor's army marched toward the arches in fat, disorderly columns that wound through the islands of jagged stone and thorny brambles. Lord Axithar's hulking black keep loomed in the distance, and Vhok could feel the balor's eyes on the proceedings.

And this army is just one of many, Vhok mused with a grin. *Mighty Orcus commands great power. The angels* will *fall this day.*

The cambion began counting the number of legions ahead of his, but each time he started, he lost track of where one ended and another began, as the demons could not stay in coherent groups. Already, dretches in his own unit pushed and shoved one another, chafing at being forced to wait their turn.

We'll never get there! Vhok fumed. *I will lose control of them if this goes on much longer.*

But the line crawled relentlessly forward, and Vhok passed the time cowing his charges with threats of painful, languishing deaths if they did not behave.

When they were second in line to pass through, he began to hear a strange whistling emanating from the arch, and he got a better look as the demons stepped into it. The darkness sucked them in, yanking them forward off their feet the moment a part of their bodies grazed against its surface.

Vhok felt a momentary worry. *I hope they go where Lord Axithar says they do,* he thought. *If not . . . well then, too late for us.*

He was just about to return to his own troops when an imp arrived with a message. "Vhissilka would speak with you," it said in a whiny voice, then it tittered as it raced away to continue its business.

What does she want now? Vhok wondered, disgusted.

The cambion unfurled his magical cloak and surged upward. He circled around and followed the column of troops back until he spotted the marilith's vanguard and angled toward it. The snake demon towered over the rest of her forces.

The cambion settled to the ground next to Vhissilka. "You summoned me?" he asked, trying to keep his tone deferential.

"Remember," the marilith said, "you have my right flank. Do not allow your troops to advance too far ahead. I do not want to pass through the gate to find myself surrounded by angry angels. Only when I give the signal may you commence with your charge."

"Of course," Vhok said. It's only the fifth time you've told me, you bitch.

"You have the item?" she asked.

Vhok suppressed a sigh and pulled a glass rod from within a pocket in his tunic. The tube, sealed at both ends, was not much longer than his index finger, and slightly fatter than his thumb. Like the arch, the inside of the rod swirled with a darkness shot through with blue flecks of light. He held the thing up for Vhissilka to see clearly, then returned it to the safety of his tunic.

"Very good," the marilith said. "Be ready. Watch for my signal."

"Of course."

"Go," Vhissilka said. "Return to your place. Rain death upon the enemy!"

Vhok gave her a casual salute and took to the air again, returning to his own unit. They were almost to the arch. The last ranks of the legion ahead of them were passing through the portal, drawn into the swirling black mists. He settled to the ground beside a lieutenant, a ram-headed demon corralling dretches with his polearm. The cambion was fairly certain it was the same one he had been crossing paths with lately.

"We will crush them," the demon said. "They are weak, puny things that love impotent gods."

Vhok snorted. "Do not underestimate them, fool," he said. "We fight on their lands today. They draw on powerful magic there, and if we are not careful, they will scatter us to the winds."

The ram demon gave Vhok a rheumy stare. "Bah!" it said. "If you fear them so much, perhaps you should hide here while the rest of us make sport with their heads."

Vhok smirked. "Don't say I didn't warn you."

It was their turn. The front row of his column of demons stood before the arch, on the verge of passing through it. The lead rank hesitated until the ram demon rushed forward and encouraged them with liberal use of his weapon. "Move it, you craven worms! Into the arch! Find the enemy! Slay them all! Go! Go!"

The demons shuffled forward and vanished through the portal. More followed.

Vhok shot into the air. He swung around and made his way back to the end of his command. His elite cavalry force waited there.

Unlike the craven lesser demons, the lanky winged beasts stood proud and tall, disdainful of the rabble around them. The fiends reminded the cambion of lithe, wiry gargoyles, though they had no skin. Their dark, purplish-black flesh and muscles glistened wetly, bound together by violet sinew. Black horns curved up and back from atop gaunt, skeletal ebony skulls in which red eyes glittered with fury. Their mouths hung agape, revealing rows of black, needlelike teeth and darting, forked tongues. Each one carried a slender, double-headed spear.

"We must taste the blood of angels!" one of them screamed.

The others clamored in agreement.

"Let us rend their flesh!" another cried.

"You will sate yourselves upon celestial meat soon enough," Vhok called out. "But first, we have another task to attend to."

The skinless creatures howled and gnashed their teeth. The cambion was not sure if it was in frustration or glee. He motioned them up, into the air.

"With me!" he shouted and flew toward the archway. As he neared its surface, he thought again of whether it would lead him to glory or oblivion.

Only one way to find out, he thought, diving through the portal.

CHAPTER
SIXTEEN

Garin dodged to his left as the glabrezu snapped a pincer
at his head. He swung his mace down hard upon the
bony outer casing of his foe's limb. The blow drove the arm
away from him, but his mace bounced off harmlessly.

Must find a way to crack this nut, Garin thought, shaking
his hand to alleviate the tingling sensation.

Archons and fiends battled around the two combatants.
Two hound warriors tried to join Garin and engage the
glabrezu, but after the demon sliced the head from one, Garin
motioned the other way.

"Just keep those other fiends off me!" he shouted.

Garin channeled divine energy into his body and opened
his mouth to drive the demon to its knees with a holy word.
The glabrezu, perhaps sensing what the angel was about to do,
kicked out with its taloned foot and struck a glancing blow
against Garin's wounded shoulder. Stabbing pain shot through
the angel and he cried out. The glabrezu followed with another
pincer attack, which Garin barely swatted away with his mace.
The demon motioned, and swarming, ricocheting bursts of

multicolored energy inundated the angel and struck him from every angle. Where the explosions touched his body, disruptive energy made Garin's muscles convulse.

Garin arched his back in pain. The glabrezu bounded forward, its pincers snapping. The deadly claws stretched toward his neck. Garin flung himself backward and rolled across the ground, heedless of the blood and flesh beneath him. He gestured at the oncoming demon, summoning a wall of magical flying blades as a barrier between the two of them.

The demon stepped into the whirling cloud of razor-sharp weaponry before it realized what was happening. The sound of steel ringing on bone echoed from the spot as a dozen wounds opened on the fiend's tough skin. It roared in pain and jumped back out of harm's way.

The distraction gave Garin enough time to regain his footing and recover his wits. Stay focused, he admonished himself. Don't let it get that close to you.

He backed up a step or two and cast a quick glance around.

The battle seethed around them, though the fighting had retreated as archons and demons alike avoided getting too close to the whirling, slashing pair. Demons by the score lay piled on the field, interspersed with the occasional archon. The hound warriors might have been the superior fighters, but the demons balanced that in terms of sheer numbers.

Garin cast a quick glance at the edge of the clearing and saw fiends still churning out of the slash in the earth. They rushed to join their allies, clambering over one another to get to enemies.

They just won't stop coming, Garin thought with growing dismay. We won't be able to hold them back.

He returned his attention to the hulking winged demon before him. The glabrezu had retreated from the whirling cloud of blades and was performing a little dance of pain as it rubbed its injuries with the smaller hands protruding from its chest. It snarled at Garin and vanished.

Not waiting to see what the demon had had in mind, Garin launched himself skyward, taking wing over the battle-field. He felt a faint touch against his wing as he shot out of reach. Just as he had suspected and feared, the glabrezu had teleported directly behind him. He glided in a tight circle, scanning the ground below. The fiend was up in the air too, coming after him.

Garin wasted no time. He channeled the power of Torm. When the glabrezu drew close enough, the angel shouted the holy word. The rippling energy of the focused blast struck the demon squarely, knocking it back. Its wings fluttered, but it quickly regained its balance.

The demon grinned. "Your words are useless against my superior power," it rumbled. The thing vanished again, and Garin was forced into freefall to evade its powerful pincers.

This thing is tricky, Garin thought, worried. How do I kill it?

He spun in place and smashed at the onrushing demon with his mace. The weapon whisked through empty space as the glabrezu vanished yet again. Garin dived away as the demon reappeared behind him.

I must out-clever it, he decided. Anticipate its tactic and counter it.

Garin swooped around and came at the glabrezu once more. That time, when the creature vanished, Garin did not dart away. Instead, he drew on his holy might to produce a powerful, blinding aura of goodness, a tiny bit of Torm's essence. The aura burst all around the angel, and he heard the glabrezu grunt in surprise and pain.

Garin spun and struck rapidly. The demon, blinded by the divine aura, did not see the strike coming in time and took the brunt of the blow on the side of its head. Garin hit it again, hard in the chest.

A deafening boom erupted from the point of contact, and the demon was driven back by preternatural energy. It flailed in the air, stunned, and plummeted.

Garin followed the fiend down, and when the demon struck the ground and sprawled there, the angel hammered it again with his mace. The blow landed on one of the thick pincer arms, and it cracked.

He drew his mace back for another strike, but the demon vanished and his weapon thunked into the mud.

Garin spun and swung, expecting to find the fiend there, but it had not reappeared nearby.

It wants no part of me, the angel thought with no small amount of relief.

He surveyed the battle for a moment while catching his breath. The archons had inflicted unbelievable casualties upon the demons, but they were so badly outnumbered that they had begun to succumb to the overwhelming numbers of the fiends. In many places, the hound warriors had been reduced to isolated pockets of defenders surrounded by a sea of demons.

The reinforcements! Garin thought with a panic. Nilsa!

Garin turned to find his companion. He spotted her halfway to him, her forces already on their way.

Garin sighed in relief and smiled at her as she reached him.

"I couldn't wait any longer," she said apologetically as she landed beside him. "If I didn't order the charge, all would have been lost."

"I was a fool to get so caught up with that glabrezu. Keep an eye out for him. He's tricky and bound to be lurking nearby."

"Look," Nilsa said, pointing toward the open wound in the ground where the demons poured forth.

Garin turned his gaze that direction and spotted a group of figures flying out of the crevice. They did not race toward the fight before them, but instead took to the air and flew off in another direction.

Garin shook his head. "We can't do anything about that," he muttered. "The solars will have to catch them."

Then he got a better look at the lead figure. It was Kaanyr Vhok.

"Oh no," he murmured. "We have to—"

Garin's words were drowned out by Nilsa's scream. He spun to find her flailing in agony beside him, the glabrezu right behind her with a baleful grin upon its face. Blood spattered the ground and dripped from the fiend's pincer.

One of Nilsa's wings, severed at the shoulder, lay on the muddy ground at her feet.

❖ ❖ ❖ ❖ ❖ ❖ ❖ ❖ ❖

"Look there," Aliisza said, pointing at the horizon.

Tauran and the others turned and peered that way. A cluster of dark shapes, visible in contrast to the gray, blowing clouds, hovered in the sky.

"What is that?" Kael asked.

"Whatever it is, it's coming this way," Pharaun said, rising to his feet.

Tauran saw that the black specks had become a host of small figures winging their way in the direction of the Lifespring.

"It's them," Eirwyn said. "I can feel it."

"I can, too," Aliisza said beside her.

Tauran shoved aside the worry he felt for his companions and said, "He's brought friends, as I suspected he might. He's probably going to try to use them to distract us while he attempts to get to the pool. That's what I'd do if I were in his position. So concentrate on keeping between him and the Lifespring. He's crafty, so be ready."

He took flight then, sensed his companions shoving aloft beside and behind him and, along with them, winged his way toward the horde of figures.

Already, he could see their fiendish features, from their foul, skinless black bodies to their baleful grins. There were perhaps three dozen of them, and each one carried a double-tipped spear in both hands.

Tauran aimed for Vhok, who flew near the front of the pack. He increased his speed in order to reach the cambion as far out from the Lifespring as possible. The angel gripped his mace, nervous energy coursing through him.

Today, we settle the score once and for all, Vhok. One of us dies today. By Torm's—and Tyr's—grace, may it be you.

Vhok spotted the group coming toward him and slowed. He motioned for his escort to continue onward, and Tauran heard him command them in Abyssal to slay the defenders. As the demons shot past the cambion, he slipped his sword free, and Tauran could see it crackle with that same malevolent energy that Vhok had used against Micus and Garin before.

Just before Tauran and the others reached the onrushing demons, the angel received a bit of inspiration. He cloaked himself with invisibility and altered his course. A pair of the underlings that had been targeting him faltered in midflight.

Tauran channeled Torm's divine power. The surge of energy washed over Vhok, and Tauran became visible.

The angel's hopes faded when Vhok only shuddered once and then straightened, laughing. It was only then that Tauran could see the faint, malevolent darkness enveloping the cambion.

"I thought you might try that, fool," Vhok said. "I came prepared this time. A little gift from Lord Axithar."

"It will not save you," Tauran said.

Vhok laughed.

The pair circled one another, hanging in midair, sizing one another up. In the distance, black, gaunt demons swarmed the small force defending the Lifespring, clashing in a violent cacophony of blades and shouts. Tauran delivered a couple of feints, which Vhok easily dodged. The cambion did the same, grinning the entire time.

Then the two were at each other, and Tauran had to swing his mace full force in order to parry the first real strikes of Vhok's blade.

"You should not have come back here," Tauran said, swiping repeatedly with his mace and driving Vhok back. "Turn back now and return from whence you came, or we will destroy you."

Vhok fanned his cloak hard to put some space between them. He howled with laughter. "Is that the best delivery you've got, after all this time? I really thought you'd learned to be a little more clever, after spending so much time with me." He made a show of wiping a tear of mirth from his eye. "You disappoint me, Tauran."

Tauran shrugged. "It had to be said. You know I had to offer you that chance. But I know you won't heed the warning, if for no other reason than it's coming from me. You'd stay inside a burning building just because I told you to get to safety."

Vhok lunged at Tauran. The angel gave ground until he realized what the cambion was trying to do. Tauran spun out of the way, narrowly avoiding getting cleaved in twain by one of Vhok's lackeys. He channeled divine power through the holy word and stunned the creature, then turned back to Vhok.

The cambion smirked. "I'm surprised Tyr let you come sniveling home to the nest, much less granted you your power again."

Tauran ignored the jibe and made a series of feints that forced Vhok to descend. The angel was on the verge of diving down after him when two more of the raw-fleshed demons interceded. They forced Tauran up again and Vhok took advantage of the distraction to turn and speed away, toward the edge of the pool.

Tuaran fought frantically to get through the interposed demons. "Eirwyn, stop him!" he screamed as he crushed the wing joint of the demon on his left. The other angel saw Tauran pointing and nodded, then sped toward Vhok. Tauran called on his divine might once more and brought down a torrent of blinding energy, engulfing not only the demon directly in front of him, but three others who had swarmed in close.

Having cleared the way, Tauran soared forward again, racing after Vhok.

The cambion reached the edge of the pool and was standing on the beach, battling Eirwyn, who blocked his path to the water. Tauran reached the shore on Vhok's opposite side and slammed his mace into the half-fiend's shoulder.

Vhok roared in pain and retreated out of both of the angels' reach. He drew up panting and holding his shoulder. "Bastard," he growled. "I should have killed you the moment you freed me from your accursed *geas*. But I've got a better idea for this time around." He fumbled something free of his tunic even as Tauran took a step toward him. Eirwyn closed in from the other side.

Both angels pressed the fight, but Vhok retrieved whatever he was seeking anyway. With his free hand, he snapped it in half, even as he continued parrying away their strokes with his weapon. Tauran sensed a great pop as something cosmic shifted, and a swirling mote of darkness burst into being between the celestials and the cambion. It grew from a point into a large hole, like a portal.

Tauran stepped back from the strange presence. A massive form exploded through the hole and shot past him. Tauran turned in time to see a great winged creature soaring out of the portal and into the open sky. It was already circling around to come back.

Micus, fused with Myshik, just as Zasian had described the abomination.

Blessings of Tyr, Tauran breathed. His heart climbed into his throat at the sight of his old friend.

Micus's bloated, disfigured face contorted with insane rage when he saw Tauran, and he leveled off his turn, coming directly toward him.

Kael felt the grace of Torm flowing through him as he struck out at one demon after another. His power and agility surged to divine heights, granting him the boon to slay anything in his way. He hardly felt the exertion as he moved one direction and then another, slicing into demons at will.

Euphoria filled him. Thank you, my lord, he thought in exhilaration, slashing a demon practically in half. A true servant could ask for nothing more than such blessings as these.

The body of the fiend tumbled away as Kael spun and hammered at another one, first shattering its blade, then taking its arm from it. The demon howled in anguish and tried to dart away, but a sudden swarm of hailstones slammed into it, pummeling it and sending it limply spiraling into the cloud bank below.

Kael turned to see his father give him a wry grin before he was forced to turn his attention to another pair of demons. They tried to flank him, using both direction and altitude to keep him confused. Kael shifted to one side as the closest of the two fiends jabbed at him with its spear. He yanked his blade down through the center of the weapon, snapping it in half. He kicked at the other, knocking its weapon completely free of the demon's grasp.

With a shout of elation, Kael whirled around, his blade whistling through the air. At the end of his rotation, both fiends bore mortal wounds and plummeted away from him.

With no more demons in the immediate vicinity, Kael sought Pharaun. He spotted the wizard surrounded by three more of the black fiends. With an urgency born of concern for his father, Kael willed his magic boots to get him close to the trio. He rushed at the nearest one while the drow twisted and dodged to avoid the creatures' attacks.

Kael took the head of the first one before the other two even realized he was there. As it fell from the sky, the knight rammed his heavy blade through a second one, which had turned to face him. Its expression went from smug glee to surprise as the sword impaled it, and it gave a plaintive cry as Kael shoved it back off the end of his weapon with his boot.

Pharaun unleashed a string of arcane missiles, very much like those Aliisza so often used. The swarm of glowing darts whistled as they homed in on the third demon, which watched them rush at it with wide-eyed fright. The tiny missiles struck the demon with a series of staccato pops and buried themselves in its bare chest, leaving smoking holes there. The demon gasped and clutched at its misshapen flesh.

Both demons plunged away into the clouds beneath them.

Kael cast a glance around, seeking more enemies to confront, but no more swooped or swarmed in the vicinity. It appeared that they had finished the wretched things off.

"You remember Ryld," Pharaun asked, "the weaponmaster I once fought alongside? Well, you handle a blade about as well as he did. I have to say, this little scrape has brought back more than a few memories. I'm downright giddy. Can you imagine if you had grown up with me in Menzoberranzan, instead of here in this detesta—Well, in this place?"

"I don't believe we would have found ourselves running in quite the same circles," Kael said, but he caught himself grinning just the same. "But thank you for the compliment."

"Oh, by the Great Spider," Pharaun muttered. "Look."

Kael turned to find what his companion had spotted. He gasped. The grotesque aberration that Zasian had described to Tauran and Kael, the fused beings of Micus and Myshik, soared through the air near the Lifespring. It made a wide turn and headed straight toward Tauran, who stood upon the beach near the water's edge, staring in horror at the thing. Eirwyn gaped beside him, her mace drooping at her side.

Vhok also stood there, one arm hanging limply at his side. Noting that the two celestials paid no attention to him, the cambion leaped over the side of the basin and flew into the mists beneath it, vanishing from sight.

"Come," Kael said. "We've got to help."

❖ ❖ ❖ ❖ ❖ ❖ ❖ ❖

Heeding Tauran's tactics, Aliisza tried to make her way toward Kaanyr. She shifted and dodged, zipping through the swarming demons, hoping to slip through their skirmish line and reach the cambion.

It was not to be.

The disgusting creatures with their bare muscles and raw sinew recognized her efforts and moved to block her. She engaged the first one, parrying a spear thrust with her own slender long sword. A second fiend swooped in behind her and she had to lunge to the side to evade a raking claw. As she maneuvered, she cast repeated glances toward Kaanyr.

Dread at seeing him again mingled with rising anger. She was not so much worried about his enmity as she was afraid of her own reaction.

She wanted to hurt him. She wanted him to feel the pain he had dealt her, which she was feeling all over again.

Here you are, she seethed, still trying to reach the Lifespring. Your bullheaded obsession with this place has cost you everything, and you're too blind to see it. She shook her head in disgust. Why couldn't you have cared about me this much? Half this much?

She saw Tauran appear next to the cambion and felt a pang of jealousy that the angel might do in her former lover before she got the chance herself.

Then a spear thrust ripped a small hole through one of her wings, and Aliisza gasped in pain. She turned her full attention to her own fight.

"That is going to cost you," she snarled at the fiend that had wounded her. The creature leered at her. She poured all her pent-up anger and anguish into the attack, assaulting the demon with a flurry of sword thrusts and cuts.

The second demon saw her doggedness as an opportunity to get inside her defenses and maneuvered around behind her. Aliisza expected the ploy, though, and she kept orbiting around her quarry as she hammered away at his defenses. The constant motion kept the second one from closing in.

Her target tried to block the strikes, but her hatred lent strength to her efforts, and each blow that rained down on the beast rang with power and drove it backward. The demon grew desperate and began to retreat from her. Thinking quickly, Aliisza feinted another strike at the fleeing demon, then turned her rage fully onto the second one, which was still attempting to get around behind her.

Suck on steel, you pathetic vermin, she thought, twisting suddenly and lunging into a somersault. The maneuver brought her blade under the pursuing creature and it dug deep into its thigh.

The demon screamed and writhed as it yanked itself backward. Aliisza rolled over and came after it, eager for the kill. The demon spun and fled. Aliisza chased it, twisting and turning through the air as she tried to keep up with its frantic maneuvers to escape her. When it suddenly flipped over and dived into a cloud bank, she wheeled around to keep up. It was only after she lost sight of the fiend within the cottony white that her innate sense of imminent danger struck her and she hesitated.

Ambush, she thought.

Her fears were well-founded. Two more demons loomed around her, one from the side and the other from behind. They attacked. Aliisza squirmed to evade the first sword strike, but she couldn't quite parry the second and the blade cut into her hip. The wound did not feel deep and she tried to ignore the pain.

Desperate times . . . she thought, bringing her hand up and channeling her magic.

A burst of blue fire shot from her fingertips. The glow surrounded her, making the fog of the clouds turn azure.

The inferno drove the demon back, screaming. Aliisza doubled over in pain.

Gods and devils, that hurts!

It was worse than she ever remembered. She folded her wings and dropped like a stone to avoid being struck by another enemy. She fell through the bottom of the cloud into open sky and continued to plunge for a few more heartbeats. The pain ate away at her, like some beast dwelling in her gut and devouring her from the inside.

She desperately wished for Zasian's healing touch. Or Tauran's. Please make it stop.

The pain finally subsided enough for Aliisza to catch her breath and regain control. She fanned her wings and glided levelly.

The three demons had followed her. The one she had wounded originally and the scorched one that had tried to surprise her both lagged behind, but the uninjured one closed in fast.

She could not fight all three of them, even in open space where she could see them clearly. She also could not escape.

I don't want it to hurt!

Do it.

Acting quickly before she could stop herself, Aliisza conjured magic again. She brought forth a hollow hemisphere of stone, cobalt in color. She positioned it in just the right place so that the inverted bowl engulfed the fiend. The stone, with the demon inside and beneath it, dropped away.

Aliisza vomited and saw blood spray from her mouth. No more, she pleaded with herself. You can't take this!

Have to. Can't let Kaanyr win.

Fighting against the excruciating pain, Aliisza quickly began a third spell. Before the other two demons could draw close to her, she completed the magic, summoning a large ball of cerulean fire that burst around them.

One of the remaining two fiends went limp and fell away, but the other survived the conflagration and came on.

Aliisza hardly noticed. She curled into a fetal position, her body shaking from the excruciating pain. She plummeted from the sky, slipping from consciousness.

CHAPTER SEVENTEEN

Garin launched himself at the hulking glabrezu and raised his mace high. He swung the blessed weapon down with all of his might, aiming at the demon's head. The fiend, seeing what was coming, brought an arm up to block the blow, but Garin's ferocity was too much. The mace crashed into the demon's limb and drove it downward. The head of the mace struck the glabrezu, though it was not enough to crush the fiend's skull.

The demon staggered down to one knee, still using its arm to protect itself. Nilsa writhed at its feet, sobbing.

"You are finished!" Garin shouted. He brought the mace back overhead for another strike. The fiend punched outward with its other pincer and slammed it into the angel's gut. Garin shot backward, the breath knocked from him. He dropped back to the ground, gasping for air.

The glabrezu reached down and slipped its pincer around Nilsa's neck. It grinned at Garin.

The angel stared at the beast as he tried to draw regain his breath. "No," he wheezed. "Don't!"

"You're pathetic," the demon snarled, "and weak. Your days of self-righteous demagoguery are over!"

No! Please grant me this, the angel prayed.

Garin channeled every bit of divine power he could find. He drew it from within, calling on Torm's link with him. He also absorbed it from the ground beneath him, the essence of the deity's will made manifest.

Raw energy surged through Garin. His body crackled, straining to hold and focus it. In a heartbeat, he was filled to overflowing. He could not contain the staggering force. With a cry of elation and agony mingled together, he unleashed a holy blast.

Blinding light erupted from the demon, surrounded it. A column of divine retribution shone upward into the heavens above. The burst was so brilliant, so dazzling, it filled Garin's sight. He flinched and brought his arm up, but he could not cover his eyes. The glory of the radiance overwhelmed him.

When the smiting faded, the glabrezu was no more. A circle of scorched ground smoked where the creature had been before. Nilsa lay sprawled there, shuddering.

Garin went limp, completely exhausted.

I am yours, blessed Torm, he thought as he collapsed to the ground.

As the angel tried to regain his strength so he could tend to Nilsa, he could hear the battle still raging all around him. He glanced to the side and saw the ground still disgorging demons. The remaining archons were much fewer in number than they had been. They struggled to hold lines, and often, the demons surrounded them completely, creating islands of the hound warriors in a sea of seething, chaotic fury.

When such an island began to collapse, the archons would

vanish, reappearing instantly in a more coherent line along the demons' flanks. In that way, they managed to stave off destruction.

But they were losing ground.

Garin got to his hands and knees and crawled to where Nilsa lay. The wounded angel shuddered as she cried. Garin reached her and pulled her to him.

"My wing," she sobbed. "It took my wing."

"Shh," Garin replied. He examined the stump of her ruined appendage and saw that it still bled freely. He could sense that Nilsa was weak from blood loss. Grimacing in effort, he channeled what little power he had left into a flow of healing energy. He directed the divine salve into her body, staunching the flow of blood. It was a trickle of his usual efficacy, but it would save her life.

I'm sorry it's not more, he thought, saddened. I am spent.

Nilsa ceased most of her writhing as the soothing powers ameliorated the worst of her pain. She sagged in Garin's arms. "My wing," she repeated in a near-whisper.

"We've got to get you off the battlefield," he said. He turned and peered one way and then another, seeking some able body to help him.

The archons were drawing back, losing the field. A few of them—perhaps a dozen—seeing the angel down, teleported to the pair. "Captain," one said, "we're being overrun. We need to pull back and summon reinforcements."

Garin nodded. "She can't move. We have to get her out of here."

"How?" the archon asked. "What do you wish of us?"

"Carry her," Garin said. "Back, to our own lines."

The archon nodded. "You two," he said, pointing to two

of the warriors, "lift her. The rest, fan out, keep the rabble away. Let's go!"

Garin grabbed the speaker by the arm. "You have to get word to the commanders. You have to let them know that we have lost this position. I won't leave her, and you can travel faster. Do you understand?"

"Yes," the archon said. He vanished.

The remaining eight archons formed a loose circle around Nilsa and her bearers. Two took point, four watched the flanks, and the remaining two brought up the rear. As a group, they made their way back, away from the edge of the world where the gashes in the ground belched up more demons. The ones already there pursued the archons, running to surround them.

"Faster," Garin said, feeling his strength beginning to return. "I'll clear a path."

He moved to the point and blasted the closest fiends with a word of power. The screaming, clamoring demons fell back from his efforts, and the archons surged into them, hacking and slicing them.

More filled the void.

"Don't stop," Garin said breathlessly. He watched as the divine force sent them scattering like leaves before a wind. "Keep moving!"

The group trotted along, step by step. An archon fell on the left side, and the group closed in. One of those of the rear guard took a wound and had to fall back into the circle. The group closed again.

Nilsa found some of her strength and ordered the archons to put her down so she could join the fight. She carried her ruined wing under one arm and walked, using her own divine power to channel aiding energy into the hound warriors. She healed them where she could.

Still more fiends came, redoubling their efforts to get at the celestials. Madness blazed in their eyes. Garin could see their hunger, their desperation.

We're not going to make it, he realized. But we will take many of them with us, he vowed.

The trotting became walking. Then each step went a little bit slower than the one before.

The group stopped making progress at all. The circle tightened, and the demons, gibbering and laughing, squeezed together, fighting to get closer.

The fighting went on. The fiends' bodies piled waist high. The archons used them as a barricade, climbing atop the makeshift wall to keep the demons from gaining the heights. Garin used his wings to hover, delivering aid where he could.

"We will hold them to the last of us," one of the archons said over his shoulder.

"Leave me," Nilsa called, from the center of the makeshift fortress. "Do not sacrifice all these good soldiers for me!"

Garin turned to look down at her. She stood in the center of the circle, her lone wing folded against her body, and gave him a reassuring smile. He knew she was right. He didn't want it to end like this for her, but the rest of the archons could be saved. "I'm sorry," he said. He nearly choked on the words. His chest felt leaden.

"Torm is with me," she said with that same soft smile. Then she turned away to deliver another blast of holy energy. "I will die content."

Garin was on the verge of giving the order when a horn

blared from nearby. He turned in place and peered in that direction.

Twin shapes skimmed low over the trees and soared past, throwing their enormous shadows across the group's last stand. The force of their passing ruffled Garin's hair. The demons, once so certain of victory, faltered and wailed.

The angel wasn't sure he had seen correctly. The twin forms looked like dragons, one silver and one gold.

But where—?

He whipped his head around and caught sight of them. They flew together, gliding low over the endless swarm of demons. They dipped their tails into the seething mass, thrashing them back and forth. Where they flew, bodies scattered. The gold one drew up at the closest of the fume-belching gashes in the ground and raked it with its fiery breath. The cascade of flames inundated the hole, destroying demons by the score.

Seeing it made Garin wanted to weep for joy. He felt hope again.

"Garin!" Nilsa called.

He looked down. She was beaming up at him, but what he noticed was the dozen or so new arrivals with her. Archons had joined their companions in the outer ring, strengthening it, and were driving the demons back from their position. Others filled the circle, surrounding Nilsa, waiting to escort her forward. He spied the warrior from before, the one he had sent for help, among them.

He looked toward the woods and saw a glorious sight. An entire legion of archons rushed from there, accompanied by angels, solars, and planetars, as well as other creatures he didn't even recognize. They ploughed into the demons, driving the fiends back with superior numbers. The doomed creatures cried out in anguish as they scrambled to retreat from the new onslaught.

There was nowhere for them to go, and they died in droves.

Garin settled to the ground next to the archon he had sent away. "Torm blesses us with your return," he said, grinning. "What is this?"

Nilsa stepped beside him and wrapped her free arm around him. Garin returned the embrace.

The archon gave him a quick smile in return. "The reinforcements you requested," he said.

"Yes, but who in the heavens are they?" Garin asked, bewildered. "Dragons?"

The archon chuckled. "Bahamut's legions," he said. "They have answered Tyr and Torm's call for help."

◆ ◆ ◆ ◆ ◆ ◆ ◆ ◆ ◆

Tauran nearly sank to the ground in despair upon seeing the abomination rushing toward him. His hand went to his breast.

By the gods, Micus. No!

His old friend's eyes, once so darkly intense and inquisitive, bulged with animalistic rage out from a blotched, puffy face. His long, forked tongue protruded from between twin fangs. Below, at his abdomen, Myshik's gaping maw filled with jagged dragon teeth opened and closed below a second set of eyes, beady and yellow.

You did not deserve this, Tauran thought. He wept.

The twisted thing landed upon the sands of the Lifespring

beach and glared. Both heads roared in unison as the creature reared, his front feet pawing the air. When he dropped to the ground again, Micus lunged at Tauran.

"Micus!" Tauran called, stumbling back.

The aberration swung Myshik's war axe. Even as it sliced through the air above Tauran's head, Micus reversed its momentum and took another step forward.

Tauran scrambled out of the way as the beast continued to chop at him, swinging the massive weapon back and forth wildly.

"Micus, it's me! It's Tauran!" he cried out in a broken voice. "Stop this! We can help you!"

The monstrosity rolled his head back and screamed. "Must kill you!" he bellowed. Flecks of spittle flew from his mouth, which curled in a hateful snarl. "Must kill all!" He took another step forward and aimed the axe again.

From behind, Eirwyn grabbed Tauran's arm. She dragged him back, out of reach, as the axe slammed into the sand and sent grains of it scattering on the winds. "He doesn't recognize you!" she yelled. "He's too far gone."

"No!" Tauran cried out, his voice low and husky. "We have to reverse this. This is my doing. He was my friend."

Tauran yanked his arm free of Eirwyn and tried to approach Micus again. Rage filled him, rage at Zasian and Cyric and Vhok. All of them had brought this about. But he raged at himself most of all.

I led him into it. I couldn't get him to understand. "He's this way because of me!" Tauran screamed. "Micus, I'm sorry!"

Kael and Pharaun landed upon the sandy shore of the golden waters, one to either side of the creature. The aberration reared back as Kael threatened him with his sword. While he was distracted with the knight, Pharaun fired a series of magical darts that screamed into his flank. The monstrosity reared and roared in pain.

"No!" Tauran screamed at them. "Don't hurt him!"

Blessed Tyr, please save him, he prayed, forgetting that it was to Torm that he had most recently sworn allegiance. If one of us must suffer this fate, let it be me, instead.

Eirwyn took her companion by the shoulders and turned him to face her. "I know," she said. "It's horrible. But however wrong it might be, it is his fate, and you cannot let Vhok beat us because of it."

Tauran scrubbed the stinging tears from his eyes with the back of his hand. Micus deserves better, Tyr. He was always your loyal servant. *I'm* the one who turned from you. *I'm* the one who betrayed you.

Heartbroken, Tauran nodded at Eirwyn. "Make it merciful," he said. Then, the muscles in his neck and shoulder cording, the grieving angel spun to face Vhok.

The cambion was missing.

"Find him!" Tauran croaked. "He can't be far. He will not abandon his precious goal now, not when he is so close." He turned and looked at Eirwyn. "Find him, so I can deliver him back to the hellish place from whence he was spawned!"

Tauran flung himself into the air. He dropped over the side, hunting for the cambion with raw fury in his heart. It should have been me, he thought over and over. I was the one who betrayed you. Not Micus. He was loyal. It should have been me.

He spotted Vhok circling beneath the mountain, heading back toward the top and the beach. Tauran raced after him, gripping his mace so hard his knuckles ached. The cambion landed on the sand well away from the raging battle between Kael and Pharaun and the abomination. The angel saw him watch for a moment, then take a tentative step toward the water.

Tauran hit the ground running, his mace drawn back.

Vhok heard his footsteps and spun away. He drew his blade.

Tauran's weapon hit the sand with a powerful thump where Vhok had been standing a blink of an eye before. "What you did," he growled, circling the half-fiend, looking for another chance to strike. "It was too base even for you!" he finished with a scream and a lunge. Vhok retreated and blocked the attack. "No one should have to suffer such a transformation. Until today, I wouldn't even have wished that upon you! You should have killed him!"

Vhok glared at the angel and waved his blade threateningly. "And you should never have tried to bind me to your service," he said. "I am not your lapdog, angel."

Tauran felt righteous anger overflow. "That has nothing— *nothing!*—to do with Micus." He launched another furious flurry of blows at his foe. With each one, he punctuated it with a word. "He . . . did . . . not . . . deserve . . . that!"

The rain of attacks drove Vhok back, then down to one knee. Letting his rage engulf him, Tauran drew back for one final pounding.

"Tauran, look out!" Eirwyn yelled, leaping in from nowhere. She collided with the other angel and knocked him out of the way as Micus swung Myshik's war axe at him from behind. Tauran went sprawling, landing in the shallow water. The blade caught Eirwyn instead, biting into her shoulder and back. Blood spurted everywhere as Eirwyn crumpled to the ground, crying out in agony.

Tears filled Tauran's eyes as he witnessed another of his friends suffer. Rising to his feet, his mace still clutched in his hands, he snarled, "You're finished."

He lunged at the cambion and swung his mace. As he did so, he channeled all the divine power he could muster into the holy weapon.

❖ ❖ ❖ ❖ ❖ ❖ ❖ ❖

Kael watched, sickened, as Eirwyn dropped to the sand.

He had tried to corral the raging beast, but Micus would not be denied. He had pushed past the knight, heedless of the half-drow's weapon, and tried to cut Tauran down. Kael felt helpless panic rise when he saw what was about to happen to his mentor, but before he could do a thing to stop it, Eirwyn had flashed into view.

Swearing oaths that would have gotten him punished as a youth, Kael leaped toward the aberration and brought his blade down hard.

The thing saw the movement and danced to the side. Kael's attack cut harmlessly into the damp sand. Micus used the moment to counterattack. He leaped into the air and soared past the half-drow, attempting to slice at him with the axe as he went by.

Kael barely managed to get his blade back into position to block the strike, but the force of Micus's blow spun the knight around and sent him sprawling face-first into the sand.

Kael scooped up a handful of the stuff and flung it from him. Rising to his feet, Kael saw Micus soaring out over the open sky, away from the Lifespring, but the abomination was already banking in a sharp circle to come back around. A few feet away from Kael, Pharaun made a few strange, complex gestures and flung a fist toward the cursed thing. A large glowing ball of crackling energy appeared in the air between Pharaun and Micus and, as the wizard gestured, it zipped forward, headed for the winged beast.

Micus dipped and dodged and managed to evade the dangerous sphere, but Pharaun did a little spinning motion with his hand and had the ball racing back toward Micus from behind. Just as the cursed creature alighted upon the sand between Kael and Pharaun, swinging his axe at them both, the sphere reached its mark and struck Micus.

The energy of the sphere dissipated, sending spidery tracks of electricity all across the thing's body.

Kael expected him to have a bigger fit than he did, imagining how much punishment such a spell would deliver. But the aberration only started in surprise and turned to see what had hit him.

"Immunities," Pharaun grumbled in disgust.

Micus, perhaps realizing where the attack had originated, turned on the drow wizard and lunged at him with the axe poised to strike.

Upon seeing his foe turn his attention away from him, Kael leaped close and sliced at the thing, cutting a deep gash in the aberration's flank and ruining one of its legs.

On the opposite side of the beast, Pharaun retreated and gestured at the ground in front of himself. A set of snaking, black tentacles wormed up out of the very rock and quickly latched onto the abomination. The tentacles curled around its legs and climbed to engulf its body. Howling in rage, Micus thrashed and kicked and fanned his four wings, trying to break free.

Impressive, Kael thought. Don't get caught up in those.

Kael used his magic boots to go aloft and avoid the black tentacles, then closed in to cut at the creature again. Trapped as he was, Micus could not evade the impending assault, but he didn't seem to care. All his bestial concentration seemed focused on breaking free of the magical appendages holding him.

Kael swung his greatsword in huge arcs that opened the beast from shoulder to tail several times. Micus screamed and howled, doubling his frenzied efforts to break free. Finally, with its body broken and bleeding, the thing crumpled to the ground, still thrashing.

Kael settled to the ground next to Pharaun. "What a pity," he said.

The wizard shrugged. "But also fascinating. Two creatures, fused in such a fashion. I'd love the chance to study—"

"That's enough," Kael growled. "He was a high-ranking member of the Court of Tyr and one of Tauran's closest friends, not an experiment. I will not hear him spoken of in that way."

Pharaun's mouth twitched in the faintest hint of a smile, but he gave a slight bow and said, "As you wish."

Kael nodded. "Release your tentacles," he said, "and I will finish him off."

Pharaun gestured, and the black, writhing appendages vanished, leaving the Micus-Myshik thing flailing feebly, its lifeblood soaking the sand and turning it crimson.

Kael approached the creature. "I'm so sorry, Micus," he

said. He hefted his sword. "I wish that . . . everything had been different between us."

He drew back the blade and sliced downward. Micus's grotesque, bloated head tumbled from his shoulders. Blood sprayed as the head bounced to one side and rolled away. The rest of the creature continued to flop and spasm.

Kael turned back to Pharaun. "Tauran will grieve this loss for a long—"

"Beware!" Pharaun said, grabbing Kael and shoving him aside.

Crackling, blinding light erupted from behind Kael and engulfed Pharaun. Kael staggered to the ground and flung his arm up across his face. Spots swam in his vision and he shouted in pain and horror.

When the afterimages of the stroke faded enough for him to see again, Kael, on his hands and knees, peered toward his father.

Pharaun lay unmoving. Smoke rose from his scorched body.

"No," Kael pleaded, scrambling to his father's side.

❖ ❖ ❖ ❖ ❖ ❖ ❖ ❖

Aliisza could barely keep aloft. Her muscles, weakened so much from her magic consuming her, struggled to work. She climbed slowly, gasping for breath with each pump of her wings, rising in a corkscrew fashion.

Just one more time, she'd tell herself. Just once more. An easy pace. You can do it.

But she didn't think she could.

The last of the demons were dead. She had slain them with

her blade and watched them fall away. She wondered where they would land. If they would land.

You could fall, too, she thought. Just let go. It would be easy. Get rid of this pain.

No! Just one more time around. An easy pace. See this through. Kaanyr needs to understand.

At last, Aliisza came through the tops of the clouds and spied the bottom of the great stone basin that held the Lifespring.

She almost sobbed in relief, but she couldn't give in even that little bit, or she'd lose her momentum.

Aliisza circled around three or four more times until she crested the edge. She pitched forward and went limp upon the rocks.

You did it. You got here.

Yes, she thought, gasping and panting. Now for the hard part.

She could hear the shouts of battle and urgency forced her up again. She sought her companions and spied them part of the way down the shore, still fighting. Kael and Pharaun opposed the thing that had once been Micus and Myshik. It had grown since she had seen it last.

She felt a momentary pang of guilt and regret, remembering how Micus thought she had betrayed him. Then she shook it off. I am not that person, she insisted. I did the best I could.

Farther along the narrow beach, Tauran and Kaanyr dueled one another.

Eirwyn lay crumpled on the sand.

Aliisza struggled onto her knees, then tried to stand. She wanted to rush forward, to join the fray, but her body was betraying her. She dropped back down.

I can't, she thought. The magic has taken everything from me. Just too much. I'm sorry.

No, the defiant part of her thought. Get up. Die trying. Don't lie here regretting. She listened to that defiant part, struggling to rise again. You must help them. Find a way, Aliisza.

She staggered upright once more. She took one tentative step, and then another. Confident she wouldn't tumble over from exhaustion, she moved forward, maddeningly slowly.

She saw Kael take Micus's head from his body and a sense of sadness, but also peace, filled her. Tauran will take it hard, she thought. But Micus's suffering is over, at least.

She was getting nearer to the pair when Pharaun jumped forward, knocking Kael to the ground. A booming crack of lightning erupted from the beast's corpse. The concussive blast stunned Aliisza and she fell to one knee, watching as Pharaun, his back arched in torment, was engulfed in the blast. He toppled.

"No! Pharaun, no!"

Aliisza forced herself to her feet a third time and stumbled down the beach.

By the time she reached him, Kael had recovered and had Pharaun's head cradled in his hands. She dropped down beside the two and saw then that the wizard's form had reverted back to its natural state. Kael held Zasian, whose broken and battered body sported several injuries. "Is he—?" she asked, her voice a near-whisper.

Kael looked at her. "It caught him squarely." His voice cracked. "I guess the 'imperfect vessel' finally had taken all the punishment it could. He was . . . interesting."

Aliisza stroked Kael's hair. "At least you finally got to meet him," she said. Then she looked down the beach. "Kael"—she tried to get to her feet one last time—"Tauran still needs us."

"I know," Kael said. He set Zasian down gently and pushed himself up. "Come." He took her hand.

The two of them trotted down the beach as fast as Aliisza could move. She could see Kaanyr and Tauran battling furiously. Beside her, Kael was already clenching his sword, and she could see the lines of his jaw working as he clenched his teeth.

She didn't want to tell him to go on ahead. She didn't want to be left behind. I want to be there when Kaanyr goes down, she insisted. But Tauran was in trouble, and Kael wanted to rush to his side.

"Go," she said. "Help him."

Kael looked at her gratefully and took two steps forward.

A black blur flashed in front of Aliisza's vision and plowed into Kael from behind and slightly to one side. The force of the impact took both it and the half-drow over the side.

Aliisza screamed and stumbled to the edge. She peered over and spotted Kael locked in a death grip with one of the demons. It had a hold of the knight's throat with its claws, and Kael was struggling to get his sword into position to stab at it. Both of them plummeted away from her.

"Kael!" she cried out. She wanted so desperately to tip herself over the side, to drop down there with him and aid him. She knew she could not.

You're the only one left, she thought. Go help Tauran.

Sucking in a deep breath, Aliisza struggled to her feet yet again. She trotted unsteadily toward the dueling foes, anger at Kaanyr driving her forward. All of this is your doing, she thought, staring right at the cambion. It all comes down to here and now. And I will make you understand!

Cambion and angel pummeled one another with blade and mace, their blows ringing in the air. Tauran, sporting a number of nicks and scratches that soaked his tunic with blood, swatted Kaanyr's blade away from his head and made an elaborate gesture. A shaft of holy light stabbed downward from the heavens and struck Kaanyr directly.

The cambion grunted and stumbled back a step.

Aliisza closed the distance. She only needed a few more steps. She fumbled her sword out of its sheath.

Kaanyr spied her coming. He gave her a little grin and turned to face Tauran once more.

Before Aliisza could reach them, Kaanyr muttered something and pointed at the angel with his sword. A sickly purple gout of flame burst from the tip and enveloped Tauran.

The angel went rigid and howled in misery.

Frantic to stop him, Aliisza rushed on. Her feet felt like blocks of stone. Her legs screamed for her to stop. She ignored her body's torments and raised her sword.

As the flames from Kaanyr's sword died, he took one lunging step toward the teetering angel and drove his blade deep into Tauran's chest.

"No!" Aliisza screamed. She staggered closer.

Kaanyr grinned at her.

"You bastard, no!" She staggered forward with her blade up. "I will gut you! I will make you understand!"

Purple energy crackled over Tauran. The angel gasped and dropped his mace. He put both hands on the hilt of the blade, and Aliisza could see him feebly working to remove the weapon. Then his arms dropped, he fell back, slid free of the sword, and flopped onto the sand of the beach.

Tauran, I'm sorry. I wasn't fast enough.

Aliisza reached Kaanyr and swung her sword down with everything she had left. He casually flicked his blade up and deflected it, knocking the weapon from her trembling hands.

All the rage, all the pent-up frustration, drained from her. She dropped to her knees. No more, she thought. I've got no more. But you *will* understand.

"You were a fool to try to stop me," he said, looming over her. "All of them." He gestured down the beach. "Fools. When I set out to claim the power of this Lifespring for my own, I vowed that nothing would stand in my way."

Aliisza snorted. It turned into a chuckle. "You're the fool," she said. "You'll never get what you want from the damned water, but even if you did, you missed the whole point."

"What are you talking about?" he growled at her, his fury plain on his face. He did not like being laughed at.

"No one cares about you, Kaanyr. No one gives a damn that you succeeded. You have no one to share your victory with."

"Ah, but knowing how my taking it from under the angels' noses infuriates you so is almost as sweet."

Aliisza shook her head. "I'll be dead, remember? When I'm gone, no one will care about that, either."

"Enough of this drivel," he said. "I should have killed you back in that stinking cave. You're as weak as a kitten, just like then, but I will not make the same mistake twice. When I was hanging from chains in a balor's palace, suffering for your betrayal, I vowed to get even."

"No one cares, Kaanyr. With your power and your glory, you will always be alone."

"Shut up!"

Kaanyr raised his sword. She knew she had no strength left to fend him off. She could not stop the blade as it came forward, thrusting into her belly. She gasped and fell back, but Kaanyr came with her, driving the blade deeper. The malevolent magic of the weapon crashed into and through her, leeching her life away.

Gods, it hurts, she thought, tears filling her eyes. She heard herself whimper once, the sound very small.

More tears streamed down Aliisza's face. She gazed up into Kaanyr's eyes, which burned with rage. With one trembling hand, she reached up and touched him on the cheek. Then she said, "Nobody cares about you, Kaanyr." She gasped for air. It was hard to breathe. I don't want to die! "But people used to care. I did. I used to love you."

Kaanyr smirked, but she could see a moment of doubt reflected in his eyes. They unfocused for a moment and he stared at nothing as he contemplated how much he had lost.

That's when she knew he understood.

Feeling a burden lift from her, Aliisza summoned the last remaining reserves of her magic. She poured them all into a final spell. She knew it would consume her utterly, but that was all right.

Nothing can keep me from dying now, she thought.

She uttered a single word, spoke it as loudly and clearly as she could. "*Mortalos*," she said. Her voice rang out clearly and without wavering.

Kaanyr heard her, and his eyes grew wide. He staggered onto his feet, letting go of the hilt of his sword. "What did you do?" he demanded. "Aliisza, what did you just—?"

The cambion staggered back a step. Two steps. He clutched

at his chest and toppled to the ground. With one horrific, gut-wrenching cry of anguish, Kaanyr Vhok died.

Aliisza sobbed and fell on her side.

Everything went black.

CHAPTER EIGHTEEN

K ael knelt over Aliisza in the shallow water. He bathed her forehead with the healing waters of the Lifespring, willing them to work their divine magic upon her.

The alu was still dying.

It had been too late for Pharaun and Tauran. They were both already dead by the time he reached them. But Aliisza still lived, and he had hoped.

Hope is a cruel thing, Kael thought bitterly. Maybe it's better to live without it.

Aliisza smiled up at him, her dark eyes beaming. "You fought well today," she said.

"Not well enough," he mumbled, cradling his mother's head in his lap. "And now the Lifespring won't heal you. I don't know what to do." He could hear the anguish in his voice.

What in the Hells is wrong with me? he thought, wiping away a tear. I've seen friends die in battle before. How can this hurt so much?

"The power of the spellplague within me is too strong,"

Aliisza said, her voice weak. "The magic consumed me in a way the Lifespring cannot undo."

"Well, it should," Kael said. "After all you've done for this place, your life shouldn't end like this." He fought to keep his voice steady. "It's not fair."

He looked out over the battlefield. His gaze moved from body to body, settling first on Pharaun, then on Tauran.

Two fathers, and I lost them both. And now my mother, too. An orphan three times over. None of this is fair.

Kael choked back a sob, not wanting to let the alu lying on his lap see him that way.

"Look," she said, pointing with one trembling finger. "The peak up there. It looks like a crystal mountain."

Kael turned to see what she was staring at. The sun had at last broken through the clouds and the blue sky was visible once more. The bright rays shone upon the peak where the mists of the waterfall burst from the side of the mountain. The whole thing sparkled from the dampness, refracting the light in a dazzling display.

Kael smiled. "It does," he agreed, turning back to look at her face.

"I wish I'd gotten to live with you," Aliisza said, her voice fainter. "You know, when you were a boy. I would have liked to have raised you."

Kael sniffed and rubbed a hand across his eyes. "I know," he said. "I missed you then too."

Aliisza opened her mouth to say something more, but she coughed, and blood came with it.

"Don't talk," Kael said. "Be still and rest."

She shook her head. "No time," she whispered. "I can't breathe."

Kael felt his throat constrict with sorrow. "I'm sorry," he said, his voice cracking.

"I want you to have this," Aliisza whispered, fumbling for something on her hand. "It was Pharaun's. Your father's."

Kael saw her slip a ring from her finger and hold it up to him.

"He would want it back," she said, smiling, "but since he can't have it, you should."

Kael took the ring from her. It was thick and silver and had a strange, spidery emblem etched into it. "Thank you," he said.

Aliisza died smiling at her son.

Kael spent a long time sitting on the edge of a rock, staring out over the golden water of the Lifespring. After a time, Eirwyn came and sat next to him. Though she seemed frail and weak, her own wounds had been healed by the divine powers of the pool.

"I'm sorry," she said. She put one hand around his shoulder, pulled him close in a hug, and gave him a gentle kiss on his forehead. "We tried as best as we could."

"Thank you," Kael said.

They sat together in silence for a time, until Eirwyn said, "The intuitive part of me senses that the worst of the battle with the demons is over. I can feel relief spreading through Celestia."

"That's good to know. Wait . . . Celestia?"

Eirwyn nodded. "Something tells me that we will no longer know this place as the House of the Triad. Torm intends to make a few changes. Regardless, shall we go find news?"

Kael sighed. "No," he said. "Do what you must, but I won't."

Eirwyn drew back and looked squarely at him. "What? Why?"

"I don't know who I am," the half-drow said. "Nothing makes any sense any more. I thought I understood my place, but it all vanished today. I lost one father I hardly knew, a mother I grew up despising, and a father who was as different from me as two people could possibly be, and yet I loved him most of all. Now I find myself grieving for all three of them."

Eirwyn smiled. "That's not so unusual," she said. "You came to see them as the people they were, rather than just the creatures they were."

"I suppose. But now I don't just see myself as the person I am, but also the creature."

"Be careful," Eirwyn cautioned. "Don't get sucked into the notion that your heritage is what makes you who you are."

"Isn't it, though? Can I ever be like you? Can I ever truly belong here, in this place?" Kael gestured around the two of them. "I don't think so."

"But you also can't be like Aliisza or Pharaun. You are a product of your forebears, true, but you are also what your heart says you are. In the end, if you are true to what you believe in, things should work out."

Kael chuckled ruefully. "Funny, that sounds a lot like something Pharaun told me."

"Well, then, he was a wise fellow. At least, for a drow wizard," she added.

Kael nodded. "In any event, I have to leave, at least for a while."

"You have to find your own path," she said, "and no one can tell you in what direction it lies. I understand that.

Perhaps better than you realize." She tilted Kael's chin until he was looking at her. "Your destiny may take you far from here, or it may bring you back. Wherever you go, draw on your experiences here to remember both your heritage and the love all of them gave you."

Kael stood. "I will," he said. "Thank you, Eirwyn." He hugged her, a long embrace that let him release much of his sorrow.

When he stepped back from her, she smiled. "My duty calls me in another direction. I hope our paths will cross again, Kael."

With that, the angel took flight.

Kael watched as her form grew small and eventually vanished on the horizon. Then he pushed himself aloft too, and started on his own way.

They engulf civilizations.
They thrive on the fallen.
They will cover all trace of your passing.

THE WILDS

THE FANGED CROWN
Jenna Helland

THE RESTLESS SHORE
James P. Davis
May 2009

THE EDGE OF CHAOS
Jak Koke
August 2009

WRATH OF THE BLUE LADY
Mel Odom
December 2009

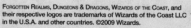

FORGOTTEN REALMS®

Award-winning Game Designer

BRUCE R. CORDELL

Abolethic Sovereignty

There are things that we were not meant to know.

Book I
Plague of Spells

Book II
City of Torment
September 2009

Book III
Key of Stars
September 2010

". . . he weaves a tale that adds depth and
breadth to the FORGOTTEN REALMS history."
—Grasping for the Wind, on *Stardeep*

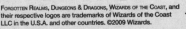

FORGOTTEN REALMS

ONE DROW · TWO SWORDS · TWENTY YEARS

A READER'S GUIDE TO

R.A. SALVATORE'S
THE LEGEND OF DRIZZT®

"There's a good reason
this saga is one of the most
popular—and beloved—
fantasy series of all time:
breakneck pacing, deeply
complex characters and
nonstop action. If you read
just one adventure fantasy saga
in your lifetime,
let it be this one."

—Paul Goat Allen,
B&N Explorations on
Streams of Silver.

Full color illustrations and maps
in a handsome keepsake edition.